The Fifth Slug

PETER

GEORGAS

ALSO BY PETER GEORGAS:

DARK BLUES

THE EMPTY CANOE

THE CURSE OF THE BIG WATER

THE EMPTY CANOE

A linotype machine casts an entire line of type on

a single lead bar, called a **slug:**

For Waseca, my hometown.

1

The phone rang.

I was ready to tell whoever it was to go to hell because I had less than ten minutes to make the first edition, and the presses wait for no man unless there's been a catastrophe. My story wasn't, at least not the subject matter. It was a review of a rather innocuous print exhibit at a downtown art gallery. I hadn't planned to write anything about it because the show was by a lesser-known group of local artists whose work was predictable and derivative. As soon as I had poked my head into the newsroom this morning Bailey shouted at me over the clacking of typewriters and teletype machines that he needed to fill nine inches in the Arts and Culture section and to get busy and do something fast.

That was twenty minutes ago. And now the phone was ringing. Damnit, I thought as I lifted the receiver, whoever you are, don't you know better than to call me just before press time?

"Kouros," I said hurriedly.

"Good morning, Bill..."

I was ready to disjoint the caller's ear with some loud and indelicate language when a warning bell binged inside my head telling me to hold off. This was not a voice belonging to my peer group. It had authority.

"...this is Samuel Brewster."

The boss. The publisher of the sheet I work for. Thank God I was more discreet than valorous.

"Mr. Brewster," I replied hastily, not bothering to ask why he wanted to talk to me, one of his lesser scribes. Time was fleeting and from the corner of the newsroom I saw Bailey eyeing me coldly. In seven minutes he would rip my copy out of the typewriter—whatever I had written, finished or not, good or bad—and my by-line would head off the piece.

"Are you in the middle of a story?" Brewster asked.

"Yes, sir, I am."

"In that case, call me when you're done."

I looked at the big Seth Thomas on the wall. "Six minutes thirty seconds."

He laughed and rang off.

I wrote furiously. There was no need to agonize over my choice of words since the exhibit was not worth it. I handed my copy to Bailey with a self-satisfied grin: I beat the deadline.

He was one of those city editors who loved the part of Walter Burns in *Front Page,* and he always gave you a performance as if he were acting the part.

"It's lousy," he said, not looking at the two yellow-second sheets filled with my brilliant prose.

"How do you know?" I asked. "You haven't read it."

"I don't intend to, Kouros. You guys in art never have anything interesting to say." He tossed my review on the horseshoe shaped copy desk he called home and yelled at his lackey, a young, raw-faced kid just out of J school who considered Bailey god.

"Mark this up," Bailey ordered, "and shoot it down to composing. Page 18, third section."

"Right, Chief!"

Jesus, he calls him Chief.

Bailey wiped his pate with the palm of his hand. His forehead was flecked with liver splotches caused by years of hard drinking, most of it on a stool at Jimmy's, a narrow dump of a bar a block down from the plant on Sixth Street. What little hair he had, a lackluster yellow, was combed straight back and hung like string down his collar. He was only forty-eight or fifty but he was tired, bone tired, and nearly worn out. Yet he wouldn't have it any other way. He would probably die of a heart attack or be immobilized by a stroke, the hazards of the profession. I have heard of only one city editor who lived to retirement.

When Bailey sent my copy through without reading it, I knew he was paying me a compliment. If he didn't think you were a good writer, he'd read every word and tear your sentences apart. He was thorough and exacting, his eager, perceptive eyes weeding out prosaic lines, imperfect syntax and bad punctuation (one of his favorite lines was, "commas come in pairs like tits"). And pray there was enough left of you to identify to your next of kin if you committed an error of fact or made an editorial presumption. Not on *his* news pages you didn't.

"Who bothered you on the phone just now?"

"Brewster."

"What did he want?"

"I don't know. I have to call back."

Samuel Brewster was the son of the founder of the Minneapolis Citizen Ledger, a silver-haired scion with a handball physique who changed the newspaper from a rather stuffy Republican posture (his father was a personal friend of Warren G. Harding) to a steadily improving Liberal-Independent point of view. Brewster was progressive-minded, anxious to keep the CL fresh and interesting with provocative writing printed in clear graphics on a convenient format.

There were critics, of course, mostly from small towns and rural areas of Minnesota, but the CL was really a metropolitan newspaper, and well received by urbanites. Most of the circulation and advertising revenue came from the Twin City area anyway, and Brewster knew that his newspaper could not be great if he tried to please everybody. And Bailey wouldn't work for him if he did try.

Brewster's secretary, Claire Quinn, answered after my second ring. "Mr. Brewster's office."

"Bill, sweetheart."

"Hi, darling."

"Boss in?"

"Waiting for your call."

"Really?" I couldn't imagine Brewster waiting for me for anything.

"Yes, and I don't have time to palaver with you."

"How about lunch?"

"I don't think you'll be here," she said cryptically.

Now what in hell did she mean by that? Before I could ask the question out loud, she became official again. "One moment, Mr. Kouros."

Then Brewster came on the line. "Bill?"

"Yes, sir," I replied.

"Can you come to my office now?"

"Right away." I replaced the receiver back on its cradle and stared at it.

Bailey was watching me. "You look worried," he said from across the aisle. The newsroom was calmer now that the first edition was put to bed; he had time to express concern for one of his troops.

"What do you suppose he wants to see me about?"

Bailey shrugged.

"I asked Claire to have lunch with me and she said she didn't think I'd be here."

"Brewster's probably going to fire you."

"Thanks," I said lamely.

"Tell me about it," Bailey said over his shoulder as I left my desk.

I took the elevator to the top floor of the plant, a series of carpeted, hushed executive suites. Brewster's office was at the end of the hall, behind a glassed-in anteroom with a phalanx of secretaries one of whom was Claire, sitting behind the desk closest to the door marked Publisher.

She was smiling as I approached, revealing slightly crooked upper teeth, which unbalanced her face in an interesting, provocative way. Claire was a tall but not-too-thin Irish beauty with a case of arresting development. She wore long, fake eyelashes that danced at you when she blinked, and her proud head was abundantly covered with shiny black hair sprinkled here and there with strands of gray.

Just because she and I were dating didn't mean I was sucking up to the boss. We merely considered ourselves good friends. We had what you might call a working relationship, not serious but not platonic either. She had married young, out of high school, and in three years got divorced with no entangling children. She would have though, have a child that is, and she confided in me one evening after a couple of martinis at Charlie's Café that she'd had an abortion. At twenty-nine she wasn't cynical about marriage, she'd marry again, I felt sure, if Mr. Right turns up at the next happy hour.

Until that happened we kept each other company. Even though we were well matched sexually there was something lacking, a spark of passion I had experienced only once before with a girl named Bev, Beverly Nordstrom. But that was a long time ago when I was still in my teens living in southern Minnesota, in a town called

Clear Lake, before I knew who I was or who I wanted to be. And when you've reached thirty-nine and still single, you don't practice a celibate's life waiting for that spark to ignite again.

"He's waiting for you," Claire said. "Go right in."

The door to Brewster's office was slightly ajar. In spite of Claire's invitation I tapped the door twice with my knuckle.

"That you, Bill?"

I stepped into a spacious corner room with windows running along both exterior walls. The morning sun was slashing sharply across the carpet. In another half hour, it would move to his desk and Brewster would, no doubt, draw the muted gray drapes. But right now the yellow light was a comforting contrast to the frost on the windows. It was January seventeenth and we were experiencing a sudden cold wave—twenty-three degrees below zero this morning when I got up at 6:45.

Brewster motioned to the sofa along an interior wall and joined me as I sat down. It was black leather, old and heavily creased, probably his father's at one time, the only visible acknowledgment to the senior Brewster's memory. The rest of the furnishings were modern: plastic, chrome and glass.

Across from me was a metal-legged conference table and grouped around it were six tubular chairs inspired by Herman Miller. An elegantly simple floor lamp with a stem of glass stood in the corner. His desk was large and spare. Everything I admired but could not afford, and on the wall an early Frank Stella striped canvas, painted before his popular protractor series you see everywhere. He overproduces.

Brewster was in his mid-fifties, yet he had the physique of someone twenty years younger. He was a large man about my height, six even, but he was beefier, broader in the shoulders and deeper in the chest. You could tell he belonged to the fitness cult, didn't smoke, didn't drink, the only puritanical holdovers of his father's influence. He was smooth-skinned and, since he did not leave for his island retreat in the Caribbean until February, his tan had to come from a sun lamp.

Every strand of his full head of silver hair was immaculately in place and carefully trimmed. His one concession to current men's fashion was a set of sideburns but other than that he was pin stripe, banker's gray and rep silk.

Brewster leaned against the corner cushion and crossed his legs. The polished black wingtip of his suspended shoe pointed at me.

"Did you read about the Schultzman murder?" he began casually, a curious way to make small talk.

"No."

"You haven't seen today's lead story?"

I didn't remind him that I was rather busy knocking out a review for the first edition.

"A farmer south of here was bludgeoned to death last night, his body found in the orchard below the house. His daughter of twelve also was beaten. She is fighting for her life in the county hospital."

I stared at him.

"Didn't Bailey fill you in?"

I shook my head, wondering why Bailey should even bother.

He folded his arms together, his biceps bulging under the sleeves of his suit jacket. "Bill, how would you like to take on an unusual assignment, one that will get you away from your Minneapolis routine for awhile?"

I thought he was changing the subject, and I envisioned a trip to New York to see the new movement called Minimalism now being featured in a big show at the Museum of Modern Art. Or, better yet, a tour of Europe's finest museums, the Louvre, the Prado, the Hermitage.

"Sure," I said, "what is it?"

"I want you to cover that murder."

I had the sensation of my body being pushed into the leather cushion beneath me. Brewster couldn't be serious.

"You want *me* to cover a *mur*der?"

"Bailey and I feel that an art critic covering a crime would give us an unusual perspective, not the standard grist of the mill you get from city hall writers. And, most important, it will provide our readers with a unique journalistic experience. You've built a good reputation the past five years reviewing art. It would be fascinating to see your byline on a series of articles about a murder. Don't you agree?"

Brewster was smooth. He was giving me his best effort, the kind of persuasion he saves for the United Fund kickoff breakfast. No wonder he was in demand as a motivational speaker. Every non-profit in town wanted him on their steering committees. And he somehow found the time to do it.

I shook my head. "It's crazy, Mr. Brewster. I only know about museums, not morgues."

He held out an arm, touching my elbow with his fingers. "That's just the point, Bill, it's because you *don't* know that makes this assignment special. Look what Capote did in Garden City, Kansas. Who could possibly have guessed that a playwright of all people would write *In Cold Blood*? Like Capote you have sensitive eyes and ears and you perceive things differently from a crime reporter. You are also a damned good writer. Expression is what I'm after, look at the town as you would a work of art and analyze it. Talk to the locals, find out what they are thinking, examine their apprehensions and suspicions, ask questions and listen to their responses. That's all I want you to do. You don't have to solve the crime."

"That's comforting," I said.

"There's something else you should know. Something I thought you already learned before coming to my office."

"What's that?"

"The town. Aren't you curious where the murder took place?"

"Of course," I said. "Where?"

"Clear Lake."

Jesus, he's talking about my hometown! I stared into Brewster's cold, gray eyes. "Mr. Brewster," I said, "all that Chamber of Commerce buildup about being a perceptive writer..." I shook my head in disbelief. "...the only reason you want me to go to Clear Lake is because I grew up there."

Brewster smiled defensively. A bit of his smoothness had rubbed off. "Bill, you misread me. I meant everything I said. Of course it helps to know the territory, but that's not why I am sending you down there."

While he was talking, my mind brought back with cyclone speed all the repressed memories of my growing up in Clear Lake. My immigrant parents, the restaurant that was more home to me than the rented duplex we lived in, the shy Greek kid and the beautiful Scandinavian girl, our futile, foolish teenage love affair, the terrible fire that killed my father... "No," I said, "it's not for me. Send Stevenson."

"Stevenson is not available."

"You can make him as available as you can me. He hangs around City Hall all day looking at crime sheets. He loves blood and gore."

"Bill," Brewster's voice was as cold as the frost along the window ledge. "I want you to cover this story, no one else. I want you to pack your bag and get down there today, right now. I want your first piece filed in time for the Blue Streak Edition."

"My god, that only gives me six hours!"

He smiled. The old confidence was back. Brewster had trapped me into responding on a professional rather than personal level.

"Well, then, we're wasting time. I don't want to use a local stringer any further."

He was through appealing. He was a publisher talking to his reporter now. The job was what was important, not personal misgivings about visiting a town I had no wish ever to see again, a place whose memories were all gray and in shadow.

No, Brewster didn't give a damn about my feelings. What he wanted was a story about a small town murder and he wanted me, a former resident of that town, to write it.

2

I said goodbye to Claire on my way out. When she replied, "Take care," I told her I'd be back on Friday. I returned to the newsroom, quiet now with reporters heading off to Jimmy's for a before-lunch bump, and found Bailey propped in his chair, his feet on top of his typewriter, reading the first edition. He had the paper spread open on his uplifted lap and, although I know he saw me coming, he didn't take notice of me until I said, "Hi."

"You're back," he replied, still perusing the columns of type.

"Only for a minute," I said. "I have to go home and pack."

"Oh?"

"As if you didn't know."

He folded the newspaper and handed it to me, the right hand corner of the front page up and out. "Read."

The article was inserted in the main slot, but the headline was no larger than the others on page one. It wasn't screamer news since Clear Lake is 80 miles from Minneapolis. Like automobile accidents, only the most spectacular are played up.

The headline read:

Father Slain,
Daughter Beaten
on Clear Lake Farm

The dateline read Special to the Citizen Ledger, which meant that the city desk had got in touch with somebody in Clear Lake for the story. That somebody was probably Maynard Sorenson, who published the Clear Lake weekly newspaper, The Independent.

"Why didn't you show this to me?" I asked, looking down on Bailey's pale scalp.

"I had to get that review out of you first. And then Brewster called, beating me to it. Besides, he's a better persuader than I am."

"You could have briefed me before I went upstairs. I thought we were friends."

"There are no friends in a newsroom", he said, his voice low and menacing.

This was one of those times you couldn't tell whether or not he was kidding, and so I replied, "Shit" so he knew I wasn't buying it.

The story was bare bones, as first newsbreaks always are. Sketchy information, little more than names and location:

Alfred Schultzman, 49, rural Clear Lake was found bludgeoned to death on his farm late Tuesday night. A daughter, Sarah, 12, was found beaten in an upstairs bedroom and was taken to the county clinic in a coma.

Her injuries were caused by blows to the head with a blunt instrument. Sarah was found by Schultzman's son, Bruno, 15, who had gone into town to visit friends. Upon his return, he found his sister lying on the floor in a pool of blood.

It was not until later, when Sheriff John Amundson arrived on the scene, that the elder Schultzman was found dead in the orchard behind the house.

According to the Sheriff, it is not known if the victim died as a result of the blows or was frozen to death in the subzero cold.

That was it, the story complete on page one. No details, no in-depth coverage. These would have to wait until I get down to Clear Lake and start filing stories.

"Do I get a photographer?"

"No."

"Still economizing, eh?"

"Just call in your delicate word pictures."

"I'll be back on Saturday to cover the new show at Walker Art Center." This was a major retrospective titled Pop Goes the Easel and I was looking forward to being there. Several of the top-rank artists were coming: Claes Oldenburg, Roy Lichtenstein, Jimmy Rosenquist and Tom Wesselman. Even Andy Warhol was rumored to make an appearance with his current girlfriend Viva. I was already burning with excitement at the prospect of writing about these super-heroes of the avant-garde.

Bailey yawned. I took this to mean that he was genuinely tired, not bored. He gets up at five. "Don't give it a second's thought. If you're not back I'll be glad to cover it for you."

"You?" I snorted.

"Sure, it doesn't matter what you write about modern art. No one understands it anyway."

"I'll be back before the art world has to suffer *that* possibility."

He smiled benignly. "I'll let you know when to come back. In the meantime keep close track of your expenses."

"I'll sleep in my car."

"You really aren't looking forward to this assignment are you?"

I shrugged. I wasn't going to admit to my personal misgivings. "It might turn out to be interesting. By the way, whose idea was this, yours or Brewster's?"

He didn't say anything.

"Brewster didn't know where I grew up."

"I did."

"You bastard."

"What if you win the Pulitzer? Then you will have to thank me." He put a fatherly hand on my shoulder. I twisted my head and looked down at it in surprise.

He quickly dropped his hand. "It's an avuncular gesture I use once in awhile to show people that I have feelings."

I wanted to say that I appreciated it but the moment was gone too quickly. I wished I hadn't reacted so nervously to his touch but it *was* unexpected, like having a grizzly lick your hand.

I slipped on my overcoat and instinctively felt for my gloves where I always put them, in the right-hand pocket. There is security in the knowledge that you haven't lost them on a bitter cold day like this one.

"See you Saturday," I said and left Bailey and his newsroom behind. When I reached the hallway leading to the elevators I turned to wave but he was busy barking an order to his lackey.

I stopped at my apartment and made a pressed ham sandwich, wolfing it down with a kosher dill and a bottle of Grain Belt. Then I threw a few clothes and my toilet articles into a canvas flight bag left over from my service days. It's the only piece of luggage I own; I never take more with me than I can stuff into this bag, even to Europe.

Though the gas tank on my Chieftain showed a little more than three-quarters full I drove down Third Avenue to Bernie and Jim's before starting my journey. A full tank offered the same kind of security against January as a pair of gloves. The Jim half of the partnership waited on me, his body encased in thermal underwear, fur cap and rubber-soled boots.

"Fill her up, Jim, and check the oil," I said through a half-inch slot I created by lowering the window.

Jim had barely got the hood up when the automatic shutoff on the gas filler stopped the flow of premium. He returned to my window. "For what you just got, I could've splashed the gas on the ground and you wouldn't have missed it."

I slipped my credit card through the slot, laughing, and waited for my bill. Just under three gallons, a dollar fourteen.

The needle jammed on full, the oil checked, the engine humming smoothly and the defroster keeping the windshield clear, I off-ramped to 35W and headed south for my home town, my first trip there in ... my god, has it been twenty years?

It can't be, I thought to myself, speeding along an open ribbon of concrete which, in a few hours, would be so packed with traffic it would remind you of refugees escaping a besieged city. Had I so effectively blocked my life in Clear Lake that I had practically forgotten I ever lived there, had not gone back to visit since my father died, had not even wanted to?

Then my memory dredged up an unwanted image of my mother in the Brooklane Nursing Home, strapped in her bed chair, staring vacantly at the walls, at the framed sampler "Beatitudes," at the glass bowl of African violets, comprehending nothing. It was a merciful escape from her body when she finally stopped breathing a little over a year ago.

My parents had settled in Clear Lake in the late nineteen-twenties after meeting and marrying in Minneapolis, at that time immigrants who scarcely knew English. I came along nine years later following two miscarriages (this news I learned from a cousin of my mother's after mom died). When the fire burned down the restaurant and killed my father, I took my mother, a shocked and forlorn widow, to Minneapolis using the insurance money as a stake in my education and an apartment for us to live in.

The metropolitan area of the Twin Cities ended at the Minnesota River, save for a cluster of recent housing developments to the south. Apple Valley, Lakeville, River Hills – artless nomenclature for repetitious ramblers on strands of winding asphalt despoiling once fertile farmland. Beyond lay gently rolling hills and flat acre upon flat acre of frozen earth. In the summer these were verdant with soybeans, alfalfa and corn. Now the ground cover was snow, freshly white in the fields but gray and greasy along the freeway.

I loved winter growing up in Clear Lake—the sledding, the skating, the frosty walks to and from school. Now, winter for me was like suffering through a long dirge. Maybe the automobile was at fault. In Minneapolis, winter is grime, salt, traffic snarls and plumes of exhaust gases blocking the cityscape. What happened to white so brilliant it bruised your eyes, to the sounds of sleigh bells and kids laughing as they swished down the slopes on their American Flyers or cracked the whip on a frozen pond?

Smiling, I realized finally that there *were* some things worth recalling about my boyhood. Yes, winter was fun, and summer wasn't so bad either, now that the floodgates of my memory had opened. There were those lazy days swimming in Clear Lake, the body of water for which my home town was named, and then biking home in time to deliver my newspapers—an afternoon route of the Citizen Ledger, no less. I was even working for the Brewster family at the tender age of twelve.

The personnel department at the newspaper had that bit of information stored in my dossier, safely hidden away, or so I thought, until an enterprising writer in promotion had what to him was a bright idea to find out how many reporters had been paper boys for CL. The information was going to be used in a campaign to attract teenagers to careers in journalism by getting them involved in paper routes.

Thankfully the campaign never got off the ground. Someone along the approval process probably thought it was a dumb idea to show what a seasoned reporter looked like as a 12-year-old paperboy with a yellow bag hanging from his shoulders. I couldn't agree more.

I reached Faribault in less than an hour, stopping for an intersection semaphore at a temporary freeway turnoff before continuing on 35W for another thirteen miles. I exited the freeway at County 14, an old, familiar stretch of pavement with special memories. This was the highway my father used for an evening's drive to Meriden's Corner, a small, wayside town with a filling station, grain elevator, and fewer than a dozen houses. The hamlet was halfway between Clear Lake and Owatonna, just the right length for a pleasant ride in the old Nash on a warm summer evening.

But now this short stretch of narrow, outdated concrete was a hostile trail, its raised rim fighting my right hand tires for control. Maybe it was trying to shake me loose, send me careening into the ditch or across the tight lane into an opposing car.

I'll get rid of you I'll get rid of you the cracks in the concrete seemed to be telling me as my Firestones thumped over repair patches of tar, like black varicose veins on a cadaver.

Perhaps I should pay attention to the highway's ominous warning echoing and reechoing in my head: turn around, go back to Minneapolis and tell Brewster to shove this assignment up someone else's ass. Of course it was foolish nonsense I tried telling myself but, as each second brought me closer to Clear Lake, an ambivalent anxiety rose in me. The highway noise was driving my pleasant childhood memories from my mind and, as they bounced away under the wheels of the car like so many hit and run victims, a new specter rose to take their place: my father's ghost embracing the bitter, frustrating, defeated years of my adolescence.

I thought I had buried those years along with my father, whose grave I have yet to visit. But now with Clear Lake just over the crest of the hill ahead, he had returned to rob me of my security again, and there he was dancing on the fields of snow, high-stepping to the *I'll get rid of you I'll get rid of you...*

Jesus, Kouros! Snap out of it! I inhaled deeply, forcing myself to relax.

Admittedly, those were hapless times for me, but expecting my old man to have compassion was like begging a hangman for mercy. He had no patience for a son who was suffering not only a teenage identity crisis (am I Greek or am I American?) but also adolescent love. I still feel the pain I endured trying to follow the dictatorial orders from the High Command: stay away from that Nordstrom girl, *afti Americanetha!* he would spit out. Despite this ridiculous edict, my love for her continued to smolder beyond my teens until a real fire ended my father's life and I left Clear Lake forever, or so I thought at the time.

I passed the crest of the low hill and before me I saw the body of water for which my hometown was named, frozen and dotted with fish houses. The shoreline merged with lake ice under a common blanket of snow and the sight jammed my stomach against my diaphragm. I was home again. For the first time in twenty years, I was home again.

I followed the bend of the highway around the south end of the lake until it straightened and became a residential street lined with stately late nineteenth and early twentieth century homes for people of means. As the street, named Elm, neared the business district, the houses became smaller, middle class and a half-century newer. I began to feel better. The reality of something is always less terrifying than the idea of it. No bogeyman lurking on Elm, just pedestrians scurrying through the cold air.

Before getting to work (my first stop would be the Independent, whose owner, Maynard Sorenson, was my mentor) I decided to drive around for a while, revisit familiar landmarks and reacquaint myself with the town. I felt I deserved a few moments to myself under the circumstances, though I could not forget that I was on assignment and I had to act like a newspaperman, not a pilgrim.

Still, I could not keep my heartbeat from quickening as I approached Main Street. My pulse seemed to expand until my entire body was vibrating. At the intersection of Main and Elm once stood my father's restaurant, the Chryseis, where my whole life had revolved, where I ate breakfast, lunch and dinner, where I worked long hours, where my parents spent the substance of their lives cooking, baking and frying for the customers of Clear Lake.

This corner store with its wood booths and marble-top soda fountain, its glass cigar case holding the scrolled cast-iron cash register, and its candy case displaying row upon row of homemade chocolates—this store is what my father named The Chryseis after the obscure daughter of Apollo's priest who, in the Iliad, was given to Agamemnon by the Greeks.

I had thought naming an eatery, whose menu featured hash on Monday made from weekend leftovers, after a graceful character in Greek mythology was not only the height of ostentation but also an egregious overreach bordering on vulgar tastelessness. But that was just the opinion of a teenager in full rebellion.

Because of this I look back on my puerile self with embarrassment. It reminded me that I never honored my father for what he really was: a fiercely proud man who missed his mother country and hung on to its old-world traditions, fair or not to his son. If Dad had lived, I wondered, would I eventually have come to terms with him and his Greekhood?

In retrospect, it was all so foolish and wasteful. He had his pride and I had mine, and our terms were so unacceptable to one another that we warred and thrashed. Meanwhile my mother suffered in pained silence. She didn't know how to handle our storms; when it got too much for her, all she could do was cross herself three times and cry out *Kirie Eleieson!*

My father insisted that I be as Greek as he, (if he could have willed it, even more so), that only Greek be spoken in the house, and that I date only Greek girls, thereby effectively eliminating the possibility of dating at all in Clear Lake since we were the only Greek family for thirty miles around.

Against this backdrop of absurdity stood Beverly Nordstrom, blonde, blue-eyed, as Scandinavian as lefse, her father a doctor and member of the community's elite. She and I, crazily, fell in love, as opposites are prone to do, I a senior in high school and she a junior.

The Chryseis rose from its ashes as I waited for the light to change: the long brick wall, the narrow glass front with the arched entrance, the neon sign diagonally suspended over the sidewalk. The semaphore turned green. Someone impatiently honked his horn behind me, and the image popped and disappeared like a soap bubble. The old Chryseis was now a shiny aluminum and glass walled one-story building, the Commerce State Bank of Clear Lake.

I stepped on the gas and turned right, down Main Street toward my home, passing the shops and stores of Clear Lake—Leuthold's Clothing, Lewer's Hardware, Didra Drugs, the Busy Bee—all wearing their turn of the century brick and stone facades.

I drove by the Clear Lake Hotel, a cubicle gray-stucco structure with three floors and a flat roof, the trim on the storm windows painted black. Its style was indistinct, you couldn't tell what period it belonged to, but it was old. In all the years I lived in Clear Lake, I had never set foot beyond the lobby. What lay upstairs on floors two and three, the kind of accommodations the hotel offered, would remain a mystery until I checked in.

On the opposite side of the street was the County Courthouse, honey-bricked, whose wide entrance was

adorned with Romanesque columns and arches, and a bell
tower with a giant clock ticking the time of day, typical of
many small-town courthouses built in the nineteenth
century. On its snow covered lawn was a Civil War
cannon resting impotently on a concrete base. Framing it
was a memorial bronze plaque honoring the men of Clear
Lake country who died in the wars America fought, either
with a foreign enemy or with itself.

I turned right at the first intersection beyond the
courthouse, drove past Trowbridge Park where I played
ball or skated depending on the season, and turned left
onto Second Street. I drove slowly passed 404 and 406, the
side-by-side duplex with the two front entrances that the
Kouroses once shared with the Hacketts. The front porch
had been winterized. Other than this, nothing appeared to
have been altered or improved. The thin-boarded siding
was still weather-beaten and in need of paint. The
basement window to the coal chute still bore dark stains
even though by now the house had to have a gas furnace.
The matching pair of cement stoops, the small plots of
frozen earth, the single sidewalk that split into a Y at the
two front doors—nothing was different, and for the first
time I was aware of the schizoid personality of the house.
It was suffering from a sickening, unrelieved duality. I
wondered who was crazy enough to live here now.

I continued up the narrow street, houses on my right,
the park on my left and turned in the circle that fronted the
old bandstand. This antiquated WPA project of concrete
and stucco looked like a Shinto shrine with its swooping
overhang and ceramic roof tiles. I don't know who
designed it, probably nobody, but it had distinction, a style
all its own.

The bandstand was a source of another fond memory,
of those hot summer nights when the Shriners band in their
splendid uniforms played concerts with more enthusiasm
than skill, as if Professor Harold Hill himself were

directing. The music wafted across the park to the softball field that became an ice rink in winter. But in summer, families spread blankets on the grass or parked their cars in the circle or sat on park benches in front of the bandstand, while those who lived in the houses bordering the park, like ours, sat on their front steps or in their porches. It seemed the whole town was there, except my mother who stayed in the kitchen to wash dishes or press clothes. But she swore she could hear the music from there.

I wouldn't know since I was at the park, being stirred by the Sousa marches. And when the concert was over, I raced to the store ahead of the crowd to help out at the Chryseis, scooping ice cream into cones and mixing malteds.

Staring at the empty bandstand, now cold and lifeless, I could not help but think of Bev again, remembering that I had no one with whom to share those wonderful nights under the stars until I met her.

I broke the spell by looking at my watch. Already two-thirty. I had better start my rounds if I expect to get a story written by six. I drove back to Main Street, and turned right at the courthouse to Third Avenue where the Independent was located.

I parked diagonally in front of the one-story, concrete-block building that housed the office and, in back, the printing plant. As I got out of my car I noticed things were different. The building facade was faced with new brick and there was a large display window with a sign painted on it:

Clear Lake Independent
Stationery and Greeting Cards
Serving All of Your Printing Needs
No Job Too Small

It looked as if Maynard Sorenson was prospering. As a young man I worked for him reporting school sports. He paid me the highest compliment by giving me a byline. He was a great teacher and from him I learned how to write a lead and meet deadlines. By the time I finished high school, I felt like a newspaperman.

As I pushed open the front door, a bell jangled over my head announcing my presence. I walked between shelves of office products: envelopes, ledgers, file folders, three-ring binders, pens, pencils, Scotch Tape. One entire wall was given over to Hallmark Cards. None of this existed when I worked for Maynard twenty years ago.

In the rear, behind a counter holding a silver-scrolled cash register, a door opened and then whispered shut by an automatic closer, and a gray-haired woman appeared, Rose, Maynard's wife.

"May I help you?" she asked, working her way to the aisle where I was standing. She had lost weight, quite thin, her prominent facial bones accentuating the hollows in her cheeks. She was wearing a cardigan sweater with bright patterns but her demeanor washed all the pleasure out of it. She seemed sad, indifferent.

I waited for her to recognize me but she wasn't looking closely enough. I was another customer.

"Rose?" I asked tentatively.

"Yes?" she replied, ennui being replaced by curiosity over the stranger's use of her first name.

"It's me, Bill Kouros."

She lifted her head and squinted through her eyeglasses, pushing the clear plastic frames against the bridge of her nose.

"My goodness, is it really you?" She brightened considerably. "Let me look at you." She gripped my elbows and leaned back, trying to see all of me in one take. "You've grown so tall and so handsome."

"Thank you," I said, flattered. I looked around. "I didn't recognize the place. You've really expanded."

She shrugged as if to suggest it was nothing really. "We keep busy," she admitted, and released her hold on me. "But *I* should talk. What about you? You're such a success in Minneapolis. Maynard follows your career with great pride."

I blushed. There was nothing else to do. "How is he?"

"Maynard? Same as ever." She motioned with her head toward the back room. "He's setting type, remaking the front page because of the murder. He's coming out Wednesday, a day early."

"Big news."

She nodded. "Big for Clear Lake. Haven't had anything like this since the fire of fifty-one." She glanced up, recalling the fire's special significance to me. "By the way, how is your mother, still living?"

I nodded. "She hasn't been well for a long time. She's in a nursing home."

"Poor soul. Give her my best, won't you?"

"Of course," I said. I didn't bother to tell Rose that my mother wouldn't remember her. There was an awkward pause. Mentioning my mother had always been a fatal blow to conversation.

Finally I asked if I could say hello to Maynard.

She threw up her hands. "Where are my manners? He wouldn't speak to me for a week if he thought I kept you waiting." She laughed defensively. "He hardly speaks to me as it is."

She turned on her heel and motioned me to follow, leading me through the door behind the counter into a small office with a roll top desk, a conference table and four filing cabinets. Every available surface was stacked with old newspapers, manila folders, stylebooks, typewriter paper—typical for a newspaper office.

We squeezed our way to another door, which opened into the print shop. I heard the clack-clack sound of the linotype machine before I saw it, standing like an enormous mechanical praying mantis with its pincer-like arm periodically swinging down to pick up matrixes that had just been molded and redistributing them back to the case above, each letter in its proper slot. The linotype machine was an ingenious invention from the 1870s that turned moveable type into slugs of lead that speeded up typesetting and making daily newspapers with big circulations possible. It was so perfectly designed it had but one improvement—the spacer, a tiny metal wedge that slipped between words to justify the right hand margin into a straight column. I never ceased to be amazed watching an operator working at his machine. I often walked down to CL's composing room after filing a story just to see it being turned into metal by one of the twenty machines clacking away. Before air conditioning it was hot work because lead ingots were melted in a firepot next to the operator's leg. The finished lead slugs were then transferred to trucks, steel tables on casters, each truck representing a page of the newspaper. Reading the type upside down and backwards, compositors made sure every line was where it should be, ready to be read the normal way on newsprint. I was in awe of these men who worked in composing, as well as the hot and heavy effort it took to put a newspaper together.

In front of the linotype machine, as if ready to be devoured by it, sat Maynard, pecking away at the keyboard with two fingers, setting type for his new front page. From the rear he appeared as he always had, lean, long-necked, his egg-shaped head bald except for a symmetrically shaped horseshoe of rust-colored hair neatly trimmed between protruding ears.

He was sitting on an ancient secretarial chair, its small backrest poking him in the spine. The wheels on the chair had disappeared long ago and when his wife tapped him on the shoulder and said, "You have company," the tubular legs scraped on the concrete floor as he pushed himself away from the machine to see who it was.

He squinted through eyeglasses identical to his wife's—their optometrist must have had a two-for-one-sale. Then he recognized me and jumped to his feet.

"For the love of Greece!" he shouted, using my father's favorite greeting. "If it isn't Billy the Kid!"

He slapped me on the shoulder and pumped my hand at the same time. Maynard was taller than I, loose and rangy, and his arm wrapped around my body like one of Laocoon's serpents. His shirtsleeves were folded up to his elbows, revealing large, hirsute forearms dappled with freckles.

"My, you sure are a sight for my tired old eyes!"

"It's good to see you, too, Maynard," I replied. I looked at his face. He had aged considerably. He was only in his late fifties but he looked older. Like Bailey the newspaper game was taking its physical toll on Maynard as well. His skin was wrinkled and leathery, typical of light-complected men when they start aging, and deep creases ran around his mouth like rivers on a topographical map.

There was something else, too, and it bothered me. A weariness of expression was dampening his smile.

He was a good man, to my mind a great man. He was the only person in Clear Lake I really wanted to see again. Maynard had been more than a mentor. He was also a surrogate father when the real one acted more like a tyrant. He and Rose and never had children, and I believe it gave him great personal satisfaction to provide the guidance and support my father never seemed to have time for.

Maynard was a regular customer of the Chryseis and I became attached to him at an early age. I often went to his home to seek his help on a theme for English. He taught me how to use the language. From him I learned to love words, respect them, to choose them carefully and sparingly in the way a painter applies his various colors to a canvas. When I was in high school he hired me, an act of generosity I will always remember because he and Rose printed the paper by themselves, and they didn't need an extra hand, especially an inexperienced one who might get in the way of publishing the paper on time.

Maynard edited my little notices, making a lesson out of each correction, which I never forgot, and, at the tender age of seventeen, I was a salaried reporter. His patience set my life's course, and it continues to bother me that I have never truly thanked him. Maybe he doesn't want any stammering sentiment from me. Maybe my byline in the Citizen Ledger is thanks enough.

"Do you realize," he asked, beaming, "that this is the very first time you have set foot in this place since you left town?"

I nodded.

"What a treat. Rose and I sure are proud of you."

Rose nodded.

Maynard let go of me and sat down again in his chair. "We've got to visit but first let me finish this column. Just a few lines left."

As I watched, he struck the keys with two fingers moving so rapidly they were almost a blur, releasing matrixes inside his clicking monster and, line-by-line, his words were molded into slugs of lead. Presently he finished, got up, transferred his column to a page form on the flatbed press and fitted the slugs into position. He locked the form by turning thumbscrews the way a violinist tunes his instrument, until the metal borders were locked tightly around the many pieces of lead that made up his front page. With a grunt Maynard shoved the locked metal onto the press bed, reminding me once again that printing a newspaper is a very heavy business. He inked the form with a roller, laid a large sheet of newsprint on it and cranked the impression cylinder over the newsprint. He reversed the cylinder and peeled off the printed sheet from one corner. He studied it with a practiced eye. The headline, set in 48-point woodblock type, the largest Maynard had, screamed news of the murder.

He handed it to Rose. "Proofread this, will you please, while I visit with Billy."

Without a word, she took the sheet to a chest-high proof desk and began reading under a shaded fluorescent light.

"Well," he said to me, wiping his hands on an ink-smudged rag, "you sure picked an interesting time to make a pilgrimage to your home town."

""I came on business."

"Oh?" He dropped the rag into a metal container. "Let's go to the office. I can keep an eye on the front door while Rose is proofing. I think we can find something for you to sit on."

We stepped into the crowded office and Maynard cleaned off a metal stool.

"Let me have your coat." He laid it on top of his roll top desk and sat down in a well-used desk chair—the varnish on the arms worn off, the wood legs scarred black by his rubber heels. He leaned back and the frame under the seat creaked.

"You still haven't oiled that chair of yours, " I said.

He laughed. "You remember."

"I remember every inch of this place. Except for the stationery store."

"Opened it last year. Remodeled the whole front. Like it?"

"Very nice."

"I figured I'd better get into something easier in my old age. Pushing type is getting tougher for me."

"You'll never retire."

He shrugged his sloping shoulders. "I suppose you're right. But I can always think I'm going to."

I decided to interrupt our casual exchange because I also had a deadline to meet. "What can you tell me about the Schulzman murder?" I asked.

He raised a curious eyebrow. "That why you're here?"

I nodded.

He stared at me, not understanding.

"Sam Brewster sent me."

"Why you? He has crime reporters."

"That's what I told him."

"And?"

"He likes the idea of an arts man covering a murder. He used Truman Capote as an example, a playwright going to Garden City, Kansas, to cover the Clutter murders. And you know Sam Brewster well enough to know he likes to keep his staff guessing."

Maynard smiled. "A good writer can write about anything. The only difference between real life and opera is that in the former it's not an act. I respect Sam very much. Do you know we went to school together?"

That was something I did not now.

"University of Minnesota School of Journalism, class of thirty-three. I came to Clear Lake because there were no jobs in the Twin Cities."

"Brewster's old man should have hired you."

"Then, eventually, Sam would have become my boss. Instead we're both publishers, the only difference between us is our circulation." Maynard smiled at his double entendre. "But I've never regretted being a small town newspaperman. You get into everything."

"That's why I stopped to see you first."

Maynard kept smiling, obviously flattered. "Probe my mind as much as you want."

"First bring me up to date."

Maynard pushed his glasses to his forehead and rubbed his eyes with the tips of his fingers, long, sensitive digits. "Alfred Schultzman was brutally beaten. I saw his body at Jacob's Funeral Home, you remember, in back of Engebretson's Furniture."

I nodded. That's where my father was carried after the fire.

"Jacob can't fix him up. It will have to be a closed coffin funeral."

"Where will it be, Christ Lutheran?"

"No. Schultzman was Catholic."

"Sacred Heart?"

Maynard nodded. "Friday afternoon."

"Is Father Trainer still alive?"

"I'll say. Near eighty now but he hasn't slowed down."

This blustery, red-faced Irish priest would come to the restaurant every Wednesday, sit at the soda fountain and order an egg-salad on whole wheat and a lemon coke, and imply to my father that he would go to hell if his son, at least, didn't go to church. But my old man did not take the bait or the guilt. The Catholic Church was not the Orthodox Church and, when I was a child, he drove me across town and dropped me off in front of a small, wood-frame Episcopal Church, St. John the Apostle, not the imposing granite edifice that Father Trainer ran as if he were the Holy Father himself. And, I have to repeat, my father dropped me off, he did not come in.

"I wonder if Father Trainer would remember me?" I asked.

"He never forgets a pretty face," Maynard said kiddingly

"Neither do I," I replied, thinking of Claire. What would the good Father think if he knew I was sleeping with one of his flock? She was one of those conflicted Catholics who made love with ash pasted on her forehead.

31

And wouldn't my old man pound on his coffin lid if he could see that?

Maynard interrupted my vengeful reverie by shifting his lean frame and crossing his legs. He exposed white socks under his faded brown work pants.

"Alfred was in pretty bad shape," he continued. "His face was battered to a pulp and the bones on his forearms and wrists were broken in half-a-dozen places. It appears he ran out the back door of the house toward the orchard, apparently trying to lure the assailants away from his daughter."

"Assailants?" I asked. "There was more than one killer?"

"I think so. Alfred was too big and strong a man to be brought down by one person. Jake guesses there were twenty or thirty blows to his head, arms and shoulders."

The all too vivid description was getting to me. Is this what Brewster sent me down here to write about? "What was the weapon?" I asked, forcing myself to maintain composure.

"Don't know. No murder weapon has been found."

"What about the little girl?"

"Sarah?" She was found unconscious in her bedroom, on the floor, lying in her own blood."

I began wishing Maynard didn't have to be so goddamn graphic. "Is she still alive?"

"She was when I called the clinic an hour ago and talked to Doctor Nordstrom."

"How is he?" I asked, feeling like changing the subject.

"Getting old like the rest of us. He stays quite active though. Still Chief of Staff. The clinic has expanded since you left, a new wing, deluxe operating room. Doc has done a remarkable job building that place up. Our little town is getting on the map because of him."

"Look what the Mayo brothers did for Rochester."

"You bet."

I wanted to ask Maynard about Bev, a natural extension of our conversation since it was he who had brought up her father, not I. But I hesitated, wanting to know, yet not wanting to know how she was, what she was doing, where she was living, whether or not she was married, how she looked after twenty years...

My ambivalence stemmed, no doubt, from the embarrassing—no, humiliating— memory of our affair. My father made certain I suffered tortured guilt over what he called "filthy screwing" but to me bordered on ecstasy.

He wouldn't have appreciated that phrase even if it had been labeled in Greek for him, but I was too young and afraid to stand up to him. Had I been older I would have run away with Bev, moral obligations be damned.

This was all an academic exercise anyway. Maynard probably didn't know a thing about Bev, so why continue lacerating myself over an old injustice?

But he did know, bless his heart. He also knew me, could see into my mind and read my thoughts as easily as words on his linotype machine. He broached the subject I was afraid to touch, doing it for me, helping me along.

"Doc's daughter still lives in town," he said.

I pretended languished interest, still unable to deal naturally with the mention of her name. "Oh, really? I didn't know."

"Haven't stayed in touch I take it?"

"No reason to," I lied. Plenty of reason to if I'd had the maturity and courage to do just that.

"How is she?" I asked, walking gingerly through the opening Maynard just made for me.

"Doing fine. I see her now and then on the street or in a store."

"Probably married by now, right?" I asked, venturing further through that opening, daring myself to see what was on the other side.

Maynard smiled. "A pretty girl like that doesn't stay single for long."

Of course, not, stupid! I hastily reminded myself

"There was a tragedy though...surprised you hadn't heard about it."

I stiffened on my stool, my spine going from convex to concave.

"Bev is fine." Maynard leaned forward, reassuring me. "It's her husband, Everett. He was killed in Vietnam. A helicopter pilot. He wasn't from around here, Marshall I think. Coached basketball at Central. Nice kid, well liked. Tall, good looking."

No doubt he was, I thought, torn between feeling badly for Bev and relieved that, as a widow, she was free.

"I'm sorry," was all I could think of to say. Bev got married and lost her husband—a lifetime of events in the same length of time it took me to remain single.

"When did her husband die?"

"Nearly three years already. Time sure flies."

"Has she...has she remarried?"

Maynard shook his head. "It's been tough for her. She has a boy, Tod. Four years old. Never met his dad."

I couldn't find any words to respond to news that was both stunning and sad.

Maynard sensed my conflict. "That's life in this country right now, mothers who are war widows."

I nodded. There was nothing further to say about Bev and the circumstances of her life, at least in this conversation. It was just as well, she was not the reason I came to see Maynard. I needed a story for the Blue Streak.

"The Schultzman girl," I said, "is she expected to live?"

Maynard looked up at the pendulum clock on the wall above his desk, an antique even when I was working for him, as though he was checking to see how much time Sarah had left. Elongated Roman numerals were stamped on the round, yellowed face, and delicate hands pointed to five minutes to three. Drawn to it, I became aware of the clock's sound, a soft, metronomed click as the pendulum swung hypnotically back and forth in its glass case.

"Doc Nordstrom told me her injuries are critical but there's been no change in her condition."

"I wonder if she would be able to identify her assailants?" I asked.

Maynard looked at me and shook his head.

Did that mean he didn't know or he didn't agree with me? "Any theories?"

"Oh, lots of talk around."

"What did you hear?"

"One theory is outsiders."

"Like hired killers?"

"Possibly."

"Isn't that unlikely?" I asked. "Aren't farm killings usually caused by isolation, somebody going crazy in the dead of winter?"

"You make a valid point, Bill. Farm life, especially in winter when there's little to do, can drive people nuts. The sun goes down at four in the afternoon and doesn't appear again until eight in the morning. But the REA changed all that."

"You mean the Rural Electrification program of the thirties?"

Maynard nodded. "It saved many a farm family from seeing ghosts behind flickering kerosene lamps."

This was interesting but it wasn't getting me anywhere. "All right, suppose Schultzman was the target of hired killers. The next question is why?"

Maynard shook his head again. "Doesn't make sense that a farmer in Southern Minnesota would be the target of mob assassins. Maybe in a big city like Minneapolis but not here."

"Unless Schultzman was involved in something other than farming. What kind of person was he?"

"He rarely came into town. I don't think there are twenty people in Clear Lake who ever heard of him until today."

"How long has he lived here?"

"A matter of months. Maybe a year, no longer."

"A newcomer with a past that finally caught up to him?" I speculated.

"Could be," Maynard said. "I heard his parents were German immigrants who settled in Wisconsin, near Rhinelander, and started the farm that Schultzman inherited. After his wife passed away, a couple of years ago, he sold the farm and moved to Clear Lake with his two children."

"Sarah and Bruno."

Maynard nodded.

'Why?"

"Why what?"

"Why did he move to Clear Lake?"

"Maybe he wanted a change of scene."

"Doesn't one farm look pretty much like any other?"

"Don't go talking like a city-slicker." Maynard said, hiding his grin.

"What's the son, Bruno, like?"

"Like any teenager. He ran errands for his old man, came into town to shop. Schultzman lived the life of a hermit in that old house." Suddenly Maynard gave a small shudder, as if recalling an unpleasant, unwanted memory.

"You've been to the farm?"

He smiled apologetically. "Driven past it."

"What's it like?"

Maynard became thoughtful. "The house was built well before the turn of the century, clapboard siding, high, narrow windows, a steeply pitched roof. Everything gray.

Reminds you of those houses in Civil War daguerreotypes. Depressing, lonely."

"I take it you are not crazy about the place," I said lightly, but I was also thinking that this was a fairly detailed as well as an emotional description of a place you've only driven by.

Maynard became pensive, staring at the floor abstractedly.

"Maynard?"

He looked up abruptly. "Huh? What?"

"Tell me, how did Schultzman find out about the farm?"

Maynard became nervous, almost agitated. I stared curiously as he shifted in the chair and drummed his fingers on the desk trop. "Notices go all over," he said finally. "Farmers have a network. Someone with a tractor or a combine for sale, the word goes out."

I decided not to press further and review instead what I'd learned so far, damned little: "Alfred Schultzman with his two children, Sarah 14 and Bruno 12, moved to Clear Lake from Rhinelander about a year ago. Last night he and his daughter were bludgeoned, Schultzman to death and Sarah nearly to death, possibly by hired killers, motive unknown, murder weapon unrecovered."

I tapped my pencil on the wire binding of my notebook. "Let's carry the assassin theory a little further. You said Schultzman was a first-generation son of German immigrants. Maybe there's something in his family background, an old world vendetta perhaps."

Maynard didn't say anything, but I didn't expect him to since I was musing out loud.

"By the way," I asked, "where is Bruno? Not at the farm."

"Oh, no—crime scene. Bruno is staying with the Lewises for the time being."

I drew a blank. "Lewises?"

"Stanley Lewis, the lawyer."

I nodded, remembering now. Stanley graduated from high school a couple of years ahead of me, and so I didn't know him very well, except by reputation as an ambitious, hard-driving social climber, and the fact that he disliked being called Stan. I heard he went on to law school, out east somewhere, and returned to join Walter Breck Associates, *the* law firm of Clear Lake, and before long married the boss's daughter, Anita Breck. I remember Anita very well because she was a cheerleader at Clear Lake High, spectacular in body as well as, I presumed, in mind and spirit.

"What is his connection with the Lewises?" I asked, puzzled.

"Stanley is Alfred Schultzman's attorney."

I whistled. "So the farmer of a small spread is represented by the town's most prominent law firm?"

"That's all I know." Maynard smiled wryly. "Maybe you should do your own investigating."

"Like a private eye?" I kidded.

"Sure. You might crack the case."

And get the Pulitzer, I thought, recalling Bailey's hilarious parting shot at me. "Ok," I said taking Maynard's bait, "suppose I snoop around like Phillip Marlowe in *The Big Sleep*, where do I start?"

Maynard interlaced his fingers behind his head and stared up at the ceiling as if thinking up a headline. "So you want me to give you some leads, is that it?"

"You told me yourself that a small-town newspaperman gets into everything."

Maynard dropped his arms and stretched. His nervousness had passed as though he had finally decided on something. "Ok, Bill, follow me."

He stood up, his long body filling the narrow space between us. He slid past me without saying anything further and opened the door to the print shop. I followed him, wondering what he was up to. He sat down at the linotype machine and began touching the keys with his expert, deft fingertips, setting several lines of type. Nearby, standing at the high desk, Rose glanced at him briefly and then returned to her proofreading.

In less than a minute, Maynard was finished. He picked up five lead slugs from the tray by his knee and rose from his small perch. He shifted the slugs from hand to hand, cooling then off; then he studied them as though deliberating over something. Finally he picked one of the lines of type and slipped it into his pocket.

"Here," he said, handing me the remaining four.

I nearly dropped them. "They're still hot!"

"You've been away from the composing room too long," he laughed. "Your hands are soft."

I juggled the slugs until they were cool enough for me to handle, and lined them up in the palm of my hand. They were the length of a newspaper column, an inch and seven-eighths. The shiny metal was already getting smudged from my fingerprints.

"Nine-point Century Roman on a ten-point slug," I said.

Maynard was delighted. "You remember!"

I smiled proudly as I examined the collection of raised letters. Each piece of metal had a single name molded backwards:

> nosdnumA
> nosneroS
> namztluhcS
> siweL

"Amundson is the sheriff, Lewis is the attorney, Schultzman is dead." I held up the slug bearing Maynard's name. "And I'm having a conversation with the newspaper editor." I raised my eyebrows. "Is this a riddle of some kind?"

"That's for you to figure out."

I shrugged. Had I miscalculated Maynard? So far he was of little help to me. "What about that fifth slug, the one you just put in your pocket?"

He laid the palm of his hand on the little bulge as though protecting it from a pickpocket. "I'm still undecided about this one. Come by tomorrow. Maybe I will change my mind and give it to you. In the meantime you have enough to keep you busy."

I didn't press him further. I waved goodbye to Rose and followed Maynard back to his office. I dropped the slugs in the pocket of my overcoat before putting it on. Those pieces of metal represented a personal gift, an expression of his love of the business. He probably spent more time sitting in front of his ungainly linotype machine than anywhere else, and it provided his means of expression as well as livelihood. The slugs were meant as a memento of our meeting. Whatever their significance, it was up to me to find out.

4

Through the lining of my overcoat, the lead slugs bumped softly on my thigh as I pushed open the oak-stained door varnished to a high gloss. The pebbled glass framed by the wood bore hand-painted letters in black and outlined in gold:

John Amundson
Sheriff
Clear Lake County

His office was located in the lower level of the courthouse. It had a southerly exposure, and the afternoon sun poured through the old, arched twin basement windows, promising more optimism than actually existed in this stone-walled, dungeon-like space. Two fluorescent light fixtures hung in tandem from the high ceiling, too high to be of much good without help from the sun.

A long counter bisected the room. On my side, the waiting room, three blonde-wood chairs with vertical slats and a matching side table holding tattered magazines stood dumbly along the wall like a furniture police lineup.

On the other side of the counter were two gray metal desks butted together, a row of filing cabinets and a locked gun rack with two sawed off shotguns, four rifles and a riot gun with a fat barrel that looked like it fired flares. Next to this was a bulletin board crammed with wanted posters and a jumbo calendar from the Mankato Limestone Company featuring the Cutie of the Month. The January Cutie was dressed like an Eskimo.

At the further desk sat a bulky figure wearing a khaki-colored uniform. A prism-shaped nameplate identified him as Deputy Donald Jensen. He was thirty or so. Behind him stood an antique bentwood coat tree, one of its looped hooks holding a hat with a khaki crown, a shiny black bill and a greasy band of air vents. His unbuttoned tunic sagged from his round, meaty shoulders as he crouched over the desk filling out a report. His blond hair trimmed in a crew-cut so close to his skull he appeared bald.

He did not look up when I entered, shut the door behind me, unbuttoned my overcoat, or cleared my throat.

Finally I said, "Excuse me," but that had no effect either.

I was obviously intruding upon some serious business, which required his full attention, like filling out the line that read "Arresting Officer."

"Sheriff Amundson in?" I asked, trying again, looking past him at the closed door to an inner office.

He lifted his head slowly as if it weighed too much, and a pained expression spread over his hostile features, turning them red.

"I'll be with you in a minute." He returned to his form.

I sighed audibly and studied the room some more. The top of the counter I was leaning on was hinged at the far end to allow access to the inner office. I was tempted to go to it, swing it up and step inside. But the sight of so much brute strength caged behind it, about 220 pounds worth, gave me pause.

I looked at my wristwatch. Nearly three-thirty. I was running out of time. I drummed the countertop with nervous fingers. The sound reached him instantly. I could feel his anger change the density of the air as the skin squeezing out of his collar purpled.

"You got nothing better to do?" he snarled, looking down, the pen in his hand poised over the form.

"Can you tell me if the Sheriff is in?" I asked calmly.

"You can do your business with me. What is it? Parking violation?"

"I'm from the Citizen Ledger in Minneapolis."

He swiveled his chair and looked up, studying me for the first time. "You a reporter?" he said with the contempt he'd reserve for an escaped convict.

I nodded.

"What are you here for?"

"I'm covering the Schultzman murder."

He smiled and leaned back. "You can interview me."

"I'd rather see the Sheriff."

He stiffened again. "I know just as much about it as the Sheriff does."

"We can talk later but I'd like to see the Sheriff first. Can't you just tell him I'm here?"

"Talk to me or you talk to nobody."

I finally lost it. "I don't talk to the help, just the head of the household."

He jumped up, his chair clattering behind him. I retreated a step or two. He was agile for his size and bulk. I was glad to have the counter separating us.

He glared at me. "You got a sassy mouth and I don't like it. I didn't invite you in, you busted in. And you can see the Sheriff when *I'm* ready, not you!"

Just then the door behind him opened and a questioning face looked out. "What's going on, Jensen?"

Jensen pointed a pudgy thumb at me. "This guy was just leaving."

I peered around man-mountain so Amundson could get a good look at me. He'd been Sheriff as long as I could remember and he might recognize the Greek kid.

"Bill Kouros," I called out. "I grew up in Clear Lake. My father owned the Chryseis."

"Nick Kouros's son?" he said, emerging from his office. "Why sure I remember you." He joined Jensen at the counter and shook my hand across it.

Bitter resentment puffed up Jensen's throat so much I thought the fastener on his readymade necktie would pop.

Amundson smiled conciliatorily like the dog owner who was trying to convince a wary person that his pet was harmless. "Come into my office and let's have a visit. I've been busy with a murder, maybe you heard about it, and I could use a break." He glanced briefly at his deputy. "Bring some coffee."

Jensen worked to suppress his seething anger as he walked over to a stained coffeepot sitting on top of the filing cabinet. His back to us, he poured coffee into mugs.

"I like mine on the sweet side," I said at his back.

I heard several splashes of sugar cubes dumped into my coffee. It was going to be sweet all right.

The Sheriff lifted the hinged countertop access and let me through. Jensen, barely under control, passed over the mugs of coffee with trembling hands.

I didn't feel safe till the Sheriff shut the office door behind us. He motioned me to a chair by his desk, the triplet to the pair outside, and sat down. His office was small but comfortable, filled with the plaques, framed photos and trophies that exemplify the mundane pleasures of small-town life: hunting, fishing, bowling.

His desk was a clutter of files and papers. Lying beside his in/out/hold tray was current reading material: *American Rifle, Outdoor Life* and the American Legion

Firing Line. He cleared a spot on his desk for my coffee. I didn't bother to taste it.

"Your deputy should read Emily Post," I said. "Why is he such a tight ass?"

Amundson rubbed his eyes. He was white-haired and weather-beaten, wrinkled and lined, a man in his sixties in public service too long but not willing to retire.

"Jensen is a poor loser," he said, "but maybe that's what makes him a good cop. He doesn't take to strangers easily, but he'll cool down as soon as he gets to know you."

I wasn't too sure about that. "Is he from Clear Lake?"

Amundson shook his head. "Waterville."

"How long has he worked for you?"

"He moved here about two years ago. I hired him shortly after that. Tell me," he said, wanting to change the subject, "what brings you to Clear Lake?"

I explained my mission as he sipped his coffee.

"I knew you worked for the newspaper up in the Cities," he said after I finished, "but I never read your stuff. Not much on culture, but now, I guess, I'll have to read what you write about us." He cleared his throat, a noisy loosening of phlegm. "As Sheriff you'll want a quote from me, I suppose."

"Yes, I can use anything you can give me." After the reception outside, I was pleased to be in the company of a friendly and open person. I removed my notebook and pencil, ready to put down some meaty stuff. Maybe I'd use his comments for the lead in my story.

The Sheriff straightened in his chair and began: "The Schultzman murder has been a heinous (he pronounced it hee-nee-us) crime perpetrated not only upon the poor victims but on all of the citizens of Clear Lake. As Sheriff of Clear Lake County I will do my utmost to bring the killer or killers to justice and allow our residents to once again sleep secure in the knowledge that they are behind bars."

I didn't bother to correct his messy syntax, or his screwed up antecedents or his split infinitive. I just sat with my pencil poised in the air.

"Is that it?"

Amundson smiled in acknowledgment.

"Uh...any news about the murder weapon?"

"Hasn't been found."

"Any idea what it was, a hammer, tire iron, crow bar?"

"I can't speculate on something that hasn't been recovered."

"I see," I said. "Sheriff, it would be nice for the readers of my paper, a number of whom live in this area, to have some facts regarding the crime. I'm not asking for anything that would compromise your investigation."

Amundson nodded paternally. Too paternally, as though he was talking to a delinquent teenager.

"What about fingerprints? Find any?"

"We're working on that."

"Tire marks? Footprints in the snow?"

"Were investigating."

I stared at Amundson as he finished the last of his coffee. The only difference between him and his lunkhead assistant was his smile, but I was not yet ready to give up. If I didn't bring home more bacon than this Bailey would hogtie me.

"Is Sarah Schultzman under guard?"

"Of course. I deputized two men who take turns outside her hospital room. Sarah might still be a target if the killers think she can identify them."

"Is she conscious yet?"

"Far as I know, she's not. I'll visit the clinic later for an update."

"Are you planning to ask for any help?"

The question was an affront. "Help? What kind of help?"

"Like the St. Paul Crime Bureau. Are you set up for autopsies, lab assistance, fingerprint checking?"

"We're not Hicksville," he said coolly. "The clinic can do autopsies. As for other technical matters, what we can't do here, we can order it."

"What about the farm?"

"What about it?"

"Can I see it?"

He laughed, a sound mixing condescension with indulgence. "Bill, there was a murder out there. It's a crime scene, not a public park."

"Have you got a deputy guarding it?"

"The house is locked up."

"What about the orchard where Schultzman was found? You can't lock that up."

"We covered the area with a fine tooth comb. Now, why would you want to see that?"

"Color," I said.

"Color?" he asked, probably thinking of Crayolas.

"How can I describe something if I've never seen it?"

"I appreciate the fact that you have a job to do, Bill, but so do I and it's not being a tour guide or an answering service for the press."

I didn't need any more of Amundson's dismissive manner. Besides I was heating up under my overcoat. I rose from my chair and looked down at the untouched mug sitting on the Sheriff's desk.

"Thanks" I said, "for the coffee."

5

The Sheriff did not follow me out but what did was the steely glint in Jensen's eyes. I closed the door carefully, not wanting to give that bastard the satisfaction of detecting my frustration. Back outside, where there was no one to hear, I released my anger with a very audible "Shit!"

To get to my car I had to climb over a hard bank of dirty snow along the curb, the accumulation of several street plowings. I sat behind the wheel, waiting for the engine to warm up and my temper to cool.

Presently, I pulled out and went around the block to the hotel. I parked diagonally in front of the entrance, cleared the trunk of my possessions and went inside.

The lobby was not much larger than a spacious living room and was filled with furniture relics of the thirties, Art Deco maroon sofas and easy chairs, curved side tables and lamps with half-moon metal struts. They reminded me of the elegant designs for Radio City Theater by Donald

Deskey who grew up in Blue Earth, Minnesota, just a few miles from here.

On the right side of the lobby a pair of French doors opened to a bar that once appeared to have been a three-season porch, and to the left another pair of doors led to a compact dining room. Both were dark and empty. It was hush-quiet, the only person around was a young woman in a cable knit sweater minding the desk.

I walked over and dropped my suitcase to the floor. "How much for a double?" I asked the girl who appeared to be in her late teens.

"Fifteen dollars, five more than a single."

"Hang the expense." I signed the register hoping Bailey would have a catatonic fit when he sees my expense sheet.

The girl looked at the register. "From Minneapolis?"

I nodded.

"Not many come from the Cities this time of year. Business?"

"In a way," I said, not wanting to go into detail. "Nostalgia trip mostly. I grew up here."

She looked at my name again.

"You were still a baby," I said. "When does the bar open?"

"Not till spring."

"Dining room?"

"The same, but we do offer a continental breakfast." She leaned forward as though letting me in on a secret. "You are our only guest right now."

"I guess I can handle that," I replied, smiling my kidding smile. "By the way, I'll be placing some long distance calls to Minneapolis."

"I guess I can handle that, too," she echoed, and pointed to the switchboard behind the desk. She handed me the key to 210, touching the palm of my hand with her fingers.

She has the loneliest job in town, I thought, as I picked up my suitcase and climbed creaky stairs to the second floor. The hallway was dark and haunting—the numbered doors on either side hiding a transient history of comings and goings.

I let myself into 210, a cubical room about as high as it was wide with nondescript hotel furnishings, wall hangings and carpeting. Worn but clean. The only window looked out on an alley and a dreary, snow encrusted lot bordered by a chain link fence. A radiator under the window hissed plenty of heat.

I put my suitcase on the bed and removed my overcoat and suit jacket and hung them in the closet. I rolled up my shirtsleeves as I did in the newsroom and sat on the bed by the nightstand. A thin telephone directory was in the drawer next to the Gideon Bible. I looked up the Clear Lake Medical Clinic. I picked up the phone and waited for a dial tone, imagining the girl plugging me into an outside line at the switchboard. I hoped she wasn't so bored that she would listen in on my calls, about the only action when you have one hotel guest.

Four rings later a voice as starched as the uniform it probably represented told me this was Clear Lake Medical, good afternoon.

"May I speak to Dr. Nordstrom?"

"I'm sorry, but he's left for the day. Is there a message?"

I thought a moment. A crime reporter doesn't leave a message; he delivers it, in person.

"No, thanks," I said and hung up.

I went back to the telephone book and looked up Nordstrom, Dr. Robert L, 301 North State St, LOcust 1560. I turned on the bed lamp before dialing; the afternoon sun was beginning to wane.

A thin, rather high-pitched voice, that of a little boy I figured, answered barely after the first ring. Instead of saying hello he wanted to know who I was. Taken by surprise, I didn't say anything. I probably had misdialed. I was ready to hang up when a woman said, "Hello?" in a slightly harried manner.

"Is this Dr. Nordstrom's residence?"

"Yes, it is."

The woman's voice was firm yet resonant. Familiar. "Is the Doctor home?"

"I'm expecting him any moment. But he won't be here long. He has a house call to make. May I ask who is calling?"

"Bill Kouros. I'm a reporter for the Citizen Ledger in Minneapolis."

There was a sudden intake of breath followed by silence, the kind of silence that carries with it expectation, like waiting for a cloud to uncover a full moon. The sound of her voice began to fuse in my mind with that of another. Except for a slightly lower modulation, the two voices were identical.

And the youngster who spoke to me so peremptorily? Maynard said there was a little boy...of course, it was Tod who picked up the phone before his mother could get to it.

I tensed, gripping the receiver till I thought the plastic would melt. "Is this Beverly?"

More seconds of silence, of recovery. "Yes..." A small laugh. "Bill? Is that really you?"

Indeed it was. As realization began to sink in that I had unexpectedly got Beverly on the phone, buried guilt bubbled up to thicken my blood, forcing my heart to pound, my breathing to labor.

According to my father, I would go to hell if I wronged this girl, if I foolishly gave into my yearning and ripped away her virginity. Under his grilling one terrible night I admitted it and he forbid me ever to talk to her again. His melodramatic reactions, his viciously heated words, pierced my teenage hide like nails on a fakir's bed, and now, those pricks of pain were stinging me again. And there was no way to know how Bev felt after so many years, how much she suffered from the fallout of my rejection. She never understood why I stopped seeing her, avoiding her in the school cafeteria, turning my back in the hallway as though she had a contagious disease. I deeply hurt her feelings, those of a gentle, loving girl, and she never knew why.

Entangling these emotions was my rational side trying to make sense of the moment. I never expected to talk to Beverly again. So why would I have given a second's consideration to the possibility that she was at her father's house? She's a widowed mother. She might be living with her dad, just visiting, helping him keep house, all kinds of reasons it wouldn't be unusual for her to answer the telephone. Perhaps she had moved back after her husband died, or had simply dropped by and, when the phone rang, answered it. Nothing complicated about that, is there?

All right, I continued, still arguing with myself, I should have known better, been more cautious, and left a message at the Clinic. But it's too late now, get on with it, talk to her, say something, even if it's utterly stupid, such as..."How are you?"

"I'm fine."

The ball was already back in my court. "I expected your father to answer. I tried the Clinic first but he'd already gone."

"Dad is hard to corral at the Clinic. It's much easier to talk to him when he's home. So you did the right thing by calling here." She was too polite to ask why I wanted to talk to him. She was waiting for me to explain.

"Are you...are you living with your dad?" I asked delicately. I didn't want her to think I knew what happened to her, what Maynard had told me.

"For awhile anyway. After Ev was killed in Vietnam I decided to move back home."

"Ev..."

"Everett, my husband. He was a helicopter pilot."

Ev and Bev. I couldn't help but wonder, even if her husband hadn't died, that such a combination of names had no future anyway.

"Believe it or not," Bev continued, "in the years since you moved away, I got married, had a son and lost my husband."

"I'm sorry for what you've been through."

"It was hard at first, but I'm better now. I have Tod..."

"We met on the phone."

She laughed, warm, rich, lyrical, forcing memories to the forefront of my mind and peeling away the years that separated us, one by one.

"Tell Tod I think he will become president some day."

"He has a mind of his own, that's for sure."

"You sound as though you haven't changed at all."

"Oh, but I have, Bill. But you sound the same."

I wished that it were so, that I could return to those innocent times when the future seemed only for us. "At least one thing about me hasn't changed. I'm still single."

"You've been busy building a career in Minneapolis. I enjoy reading your art reviews. You're getting famous."

By Clear Lake standards maybe. "I write for a regional daily, Bev, but I do appreciate the flattery."

"It's not flattery. I think you know me better than that."

I did once—know you better, I thought. If only I could again. But I was here not to rekindle a relationship, I was here to dig for facts and write a story, whose deadline was fast approaching. I had to get back to business.

"I really enjoyed talking to you after all these years, but I have a deadline to meet. I wonder if your Dad could return my call or maybe it would be better to call back."

There might have been a shade of disappointment in her voice that I was ending our conversation, at least I wanted to think so. "I'll have him return your call. What's your number?"

"I'm staying at the Clear Lake Hotel."

"You mean you're *here* in Clear Lake?" she asked. The surprise in her voice was palpable.

My God! Bev thought I was calling long distance. "Yes, I'm in town," I replied hurriedly, our conversation rescued, holding promise once again.

"All this time I thought you were calling from Minneapolis."

"I'm sorry, I should have told you right away." Bless me, I thought. For once I did something right by not doing it at all. "I'm covering the Schultzman murder and I was hoping to get some information from your dad, something I can quote, about the condition of Schultzman's daughter, Sarah."

"You're not writing about art anymore?"

'Oh, yes, I'll never give that up. My editor knew I grew up here and figured I'd have an easier time getting information."

"An art critic visiting his hometown to cover a murder," she mused. "Sounds intriguing."

I recalled my non-interview with Amundson, and Maynard holding back that fifth slug. "I just hope it doesn't backfire."

"Why do you say that?"

"People might be more comfortable talking to a stranger rather than someone they know."

"I wouldn't worry about that. People love to get their names in the paper no matter who is interviewing them."

"I hope you're right," I replied.

"Bill," she said, a slight scold in her voice, "do I detect a bit of a letdown?"

I laughed. She was right. Bev still knew me better than anyone else, knew how to prod me gently when my confidence waned.

"Not when I talk to you," I said, venturing further than I would have dared to earlier.

My response seemed to give her the notion that she, too, had more leeway. "Bill," she said, "I have a better idea than talking to Dad over the phone. Why don't you drop by for a drink, say around six? You can interview Dad then. You remember the house."

How could I forget? My mind sped furiously. I still had a story to call in. What I had planned was to lead off with a quote from Dr. Nordstrom, but that could wait until tomorrow when I file a full report.

Instead I'll do a human-interest story about the small-town constabulary, a pointed treatment of the reluctant sheriff and his impolite deputy. I may get some people mad at me but what the hell, I'll do it. I don't live here now. After I call it in, I'll drop by the Nordstrom house for that drink.

"I'd love to," I said. "See you at six."

6

A long line of mature junipers, their branches humbled by snow, separated the Nordstrom residence from the street where I parked. Even though the house was a few blocks from the hotel it was too damned cold to walk and, besides, I wanted to warm up the car since it would sit out all night.

Before leaving the hotel, I filed my story for the Blue Streak Edition, the first in a series datelined Clear Lake Minnesota, calling it in just before six o'clock, daringly close to the deadline. I didn't talk to Bailey but I'll bet he was sweating thumbtacks waiting for it. I wouldn't know how much he edited my copy until I read the paper in the morning. I wasn't particularly happy with it anyway, short on news and long on speculation. I decided on Walter Winchell's innuendo approach, referring to myself as "this reporter" who was not only snubbed but also insulted by local law enforcement, not naming names but making it obvious to anyone in Clear Lake who could read that I was referring to Sheriff Amundson and his overweight deputy.

Dr. Nordstrom's two-story house with its roughly hewn burgundy brick and colonial character was not to my liking stylistically, yet I always felt welcome within its walls, no doubt because of the people who lived in it rather than its architecture.

The house was fronted by a flagstone porch with a wide balustrade. Walking up the steps, I could not help but be reminded of those long-ago summers when Bev and I sat on the ledge of the balustrade, holding hands and listening to the band concert in the park behind the house. The music from the bandstand wafted across the grass in the warm night air and even the rousing Sousa marches could not get in the way of the affection I had for this wonderful girl.

Despite the cold I hesitated ringing the doorbell, breathing deeply to slow down a racing heart spurred by the anticipation of seeing her for the first time in twenty years, no longer a teenager but a mature woman. Had she aged? Gained weight? Looked like a hausfrau?

With more force than needed I pushed the button, angry with myself for making such gratuitous assumptions. If Bev were to look through the Cyclops peephole in the door and was able to visualize the physique of a bundled-up, shoulder-hunched man standing in the cold she could not help but notice a less than trim waistline, a bit of jowliness, and bags under the eyes—the result of going to bed late and waking up early, usually in Claire's apartment.

And why, you silly bastard, bring Claire up now that Bev would soon be pulling the door open, her small frame straining to overcome the grip of the weather-stripping around the jamb?

Absorbed by this vision the door opened and an unexpected male voice, firm and resonant, called out, "Hurry! Come in before you catch your death!"

Startled, I peered into the foyer, an overhead light of low wattage obscuring the person ushering me in. Expecting to see Beverly, my emotions plunged from their absurd height, like those of Icarus, and hit bottom. It was Dr. Nordstrom. Feeling almost cheated, I stepped inside while the good doctor shut the door behind me, the cold air and my dashed expectations locked outside.

As he took my coat and hat to hang in the closet I looked around. Floating on the flood of first impressions I saw that nothing had changed: the small bench, the mirror over it, the clay-colored floor tile, the nearly square hallway beyond, the piano by the stairway, the oriental rug covering the parquet floor, the archway leading to the living room.

It was as if I were once again a teenager picking up Bev to go on a date.

Reading my mind, Dr. Nordstrom said, "Beverly is upstairs with Tod. She'll be down shortly."

Dr. Nordstrom always had been polite to me, nothing more. I never learned and I probably never shall, if he knew of my intimate relationship with his daughter. If he did he bravely disguised the anger and bitterness any father must feel in such a situation. He used the same bedside manner with me he used on his patients and it tended to blur his true personality. I never saw him show any emotion. He was the diametric opposite of my mercurial father, another reason why I clung to Bev. Her home life was so calm, peaceful and rational I never wanted to leave it and go to mine.

Nordstrom had to be pushing seventy, but he looked a decade younger. He was a short man, five-six or so, with twinkling eyes and a full head of sand-colored hair. Maybe he was dying it to hide the inevitable gray that comes with aging, but he could not hide the liver spots mixed with freckles on his temples. He exuded the squeaky-clean image associated with doctors. After we exchanged the usual pleasantries, I detected a trace of antiseptic soap-smell as he raised his hand close to my shoulder to point me to the living room.

Everything was as it was before: the maroon sofa under the long front window, the walnut coffee table, a pair of matching easy chairs flanking an antique writing desk, above the desk a portrait of Mrs. Nordstrom who died before I knew Bev, and at the end of the room the umber-colored brick fireplace aglow with the embers of a slowly fading fire.

"Beverly will be down in a moment, Bill. Make yourself comfortable."

I sat in one of the easy chairs and folded one leg over the other. "Thank you," I said.

He sat across from me on the sofa. "I understand you are in town to cover the Schultzman murder for the Citizen Ledger. An odd assignment for an art critic."

"I'd say more than odd, Doctor, unheard of."

Nordstrom smiled. "I wonder why the paper sent you when we have a perfectly capable reporter right here in our midst."

"You mean Maynard Sorenson?"

"Yes. Why couldn't he report the story for your paper? Aren't writers who do that called stringers?"

"That's an old-fashioned term, Doctor, but it shows that you know something about newspapering. Editors once used a piece of string to measure the length of a story to determine how much to pay the writer. And you are right. The CL could just as easily have hired Maynard, and saved money, too. I get paid more than a stringer."

"In that case, why is the paper having you cover the murder instead of Maynard? He's a thorough reporter with years of experience, many more than you."

"I agree with you, but that was my editor's decision. He likes to mix things up, to make the paper more lively, more likely to attract readers."

"Still, I think Maynard will feel at least twinge a professional jealousy."

"He didn't seem upset to me."

The Doctor raised an eyebrow. "You've talked to him, then?"

"This afternoon."

"I see," Nordstrom shifted his back so that he leaned halfway into the stuffed arm of the sofa.

"No offense intended, Bill, but your presence puts Clear Lake in an unwelcome spotlight. It's not very comforting knowing an out-of-town reporter is, well I hate to say it, snooping around in our private affairs. Even though you grew up here, there are many people who don't know you and will consider you an outsider. You'll get everyone rattled."

"Do you think so?"

The doctor shrugged. "It's inevitable. We are a small town. There is a palpable sense of fear. People who never locked their doors are now doing just that. And little Sarah, brutally beaten..." he paused a moment. "Who could be savage enough to do that? We have a madman in our midst. And then to have all of this becoming headlines in a daily newspaper..." The doctor shook his head in dismay.

This is terrific stuff, I thought. I wanted to bring out my notebook and start writing but the Doctor would clam up if he saw me with pencil in hand. A reporter never gets this kind of unfettered commentary during an interview.

"I appreciate what you are saying, Dr. Nordstrom," I replied, my memory working overtime to store his comments, "but we do have a free press in this country, and the CL is not a scandal sheet."

"I am not trying to talk you out of anything, Bill. I know you have a job to do. I just wanted to make my feelings clear."

"I understand. But can't you still tell me something about Sarah's condition?"

He sighed. "I can tell you that her condition is grave, she has a fractured skull from a savage blow to the head. She is unconscious and on a ventilator."

"If she regains consciousness, is there any possibility she might be able to identify her attacker?"

"Not very likely. First of all she was attacked from behind, so identifying her attacker is probably a moot point. We also found bone fragments imbedded in her brain which may result in permanent loss of memory. She'd have to learn everything all over again."

"You mean walk, talk?"

"Yes, everything. Even who she is."

The image of a child in a vegetative state who may never again even recognize her own name gave me pause. I stared into the fireplace. The flickering flames fed by the glowing embers began to hypnotize me.

"Bill..."

I hadn't heard her coming down from the second floor, her steps were muffled by the carpeted treads. I stood up and turned to face her. She was standing in the arch, framed as an actress on a proscenium stage, waiting for her entrance line.

"It's great to see you again, Bev," I answered, somewhat flustered but truly meaning it. She was wearing a tan turtle-neck sweater that complemented her blonde hair, and trousers slightly flared at the ankles. There was nothing small-town about her fashion awareness.

And her face—a confirmation that nothing had changed in the intervening twenty years. Older, of course. After all, she was now a woman in her late thirties, but in her maturity there was still that blush of youthful vitality, as though eager to be alive and curious as to what was around the next corner.

Bev wore her hair longer than in high school, now falling playfully to her shoulders. Large twin curls dipped inwardly to meet the corners of her gray eyes, the only concession to control.

In my fantasy, those years of separation were shrunk to a few days. She was seventeen and I was eighteen again, to hell with thinning hair and baggy eyes, and I was picking her up to go to the Winter Carnival Sock Hop at Clear Lake High.

She pushed her light brown hair away from her face and smiled. I had a driving urge to go to her and give her at least a kiss on the cheek, as much as I could get away with in the presence of her dad. In fact, he did give the impression of a scorekeeper at a tennis match making sure I stayed in bounds.

It was up to Bev to set the lead and she did so by coming over to me and offering her hand in a gesture of friendly casualness. I took it, grateful for any contact, remembering that these delicate fingers pressing on my palm used to chart all of me once upon a time.

Our hands slid apart, and Bev sat down on the sofa next to her father as I returned to my chair. She had been a poised and self-assured teenager, and I could see that these early qualities were strengthened by maturity. Part if it was the result of the passing years, of course, but there was also the sobering effect of widowhood that clears away any lingering youthful fantasies.

"I was surprised when you called today," she said.

"No more than I was when I heard your voice," I replied. "And I wouldn't have heard it at all if it weren't for my assignment."

"You've always been welcome."

I looked at her questioningly, not knowing how to decipher that statement, but I did not want to pursue code breaking, at least for now.

"Has Dad been helpful?" she asked.

"Oh, yes," I said, meaning that I had plenty of quotable material from him, more than the good doctor bargained for once he sees his words in print. If I felt any guilt about publishing what he assumed was a private conversation, it was quickly offset by the code of professional conduct that journalists live by. The story is my chief reason for being here, I thought, not making up to the father of the girl I once loved. Besides, he did not say that he wanted his words off the record.

Nordstorm stood up. "How about a drink, Bill? I think we can all use one."

I nodded. "Scotch with a little water."

He left Bev and me for the kitchen and I could hear ice cubes breaking free of their tray and falling into glasses.

"How long will you be in town?" Bev asked me.

"Till Friday," I said.

"That only gives you a couple of days." She almost sounded regretful; at least that is what I wanted to believe.

"Well, I suppose I could stretch it into the weekend, but there is just so much you can write about a small-town murder." That came out sounding patronizing, and so I added, "unless something breaks, like an arrest..."

"Or another murder," Bev said.

I took that as a joke and laughed.

Dr. Nordstrom came back from the kitchen with drinks on a round aluminum tray stamped with a floral pattern. We sipped and talked for a while, mostly about "The Cities" as Clear Lakeans usually referred to Minneapolis and St. Paul. I bragged that only four other metro areas in America had newspapers with larger circulations than the Citizen Ledger: New York, Chicago, Los Angeles, and Philadelphia.

"You have come a long way, Bill," Dr. Nordstrom said, finishing his drink. He stood. "Time to go back to the office. I have some reports that need my attention, so if there is nothing else I can do for you…"

I stood as well. "I appreciate your time," I said.

He looked at his daughter. "I'll grab a bite at the hospital cafeteria. Don't wait up for me." He shook my hand and went into the kitchen. In a few moments I heard the back door leading to the garage open and close.

I looked at my watch, not quite six-thirty. "Mind if I use your phone? I'd like to talk to Maynard."

Bev led me to a telephone nook next to the archway. She withdrew the slim phone book from a shelf underneath. "Home or the newspaper?" she asked.

"Home." I figured Maynard would be there by now.

I watched her finely tapered fingernail run through the list of S's. We were standing so close together I could feel her breath. Once again I fought the same desire, long submerged, to kiss her—turn her by the shoulders, bend down and meet her lips with mine.

The desire was short-lived. She pointed to Sorenson's telephone number. "Here it is," she said, matter-of-factly.

My desire underwater once again, I dialed the number.

"Hello," a tired voice answered.

"This is Bill Kouros, Rose. May I speak to Maynard?"

"He's still at the shop. Lots to do because of the murder. Where are you, at the hotel?"

"No, I'm at Dr. Nordstrom's house."

There was a brief silence as though she was surprised I had already made contact with the Doctor. I wondered if she thought I had come to see Beverly. If so she was half right.

"Is it all right if I go see him at the shop?"

"I don't think he'll mind. The front is locked. Park in the rear, off the alley, and go to the back door. You better knock hard because the presses will be running."

"Thanks, I will."

Bev watched me hang up the phone. "You said you saw Maynard earlier today."

"I did, but there is some unfinished business I need to talk to him about." What I was referring to was finding out whose name was on that fifth slug. After today's frustrations I didn't feel like waiting till tomorrow.

I considered telling Bev about the strange way Maynard had of providing me with the names of people I should contact, molding them from his linotype machine, a tale worth telling because of its oddity, but I decided against it for two reasons: one, he probably wanted me to keep it private and two, telling Bev, no matter how interesting the story, would beg questions from her, questions I could not, or preferred not, to answer. She would in effect become my confidant, with all of the unintended consequences, perhaps even endangering her life—who knows, there was a murder wasn't there? Nevertheless, deep down, I really wanted to take her into my confidence so I could pretend once again that we were close enough to read each other's thoughts.

Maybe this was happening already because I sensed a shift in Bev's attention before noticing that she was smiling and gazing up at the staircase behind me. I turned, my eyes focusing on a cherubic face peering at me through the railing.

"And who is that?" I ask knowing but pretending not to.

Bev laughed at me and climbed the stairs and bent over, her pants hugging the smooth curve of her thighs, and picked up one small child.

"This is Tod," she said, descending the stairs with the boy on her hip.

His eyes never left mine, filled with curiosity at this stranger in his home. Who is he? What is he doing here? Is he a friend of mom's?

His head was covered with deep-brown curls and his eyes were large and widely spaced. Donald Duck was appliqued on his one-piece yellow sleep suit. He was the best looking kid I'd ever seen.

"Hi" I said

Tod clung to his mother's shoulders and continued to stare at me.

"This is Bill, the friend I was telling you about."

"How come you're not asleep?" I asked him.

"It's my fault," Bev said, nuzzling Tod on his rosy cheek with her nose. "I put him to bed earlier than he's used to because I was having company. But he was eaten by curiosity. I should have let him stay up to meet you."

"He took the bit in his mouth."

"He likes to do that. He's an independent little boy."

"Do you think he'll come to me?" I asked.

"How about it, Tod?" she said, and handed him over to me with a tiny grunt, and he accepted me without a moment's hesitation. I beamed.

Holding him made me feel closer to Bev, as though Tod was an extension of her, and he was. Her son, her own flesh and blood.

I hadn't appreciated why Bev made that little grunt when she handed him over to me. Tod was deceptively heavy. I always wondered how mothers managed to support their children so effortlessly and it came to me as I hoisted Tod higher in my arms. Nature made sure they were built for it. Their hips were like saddles while men had to make slings of their arms. My biceps were tiring fast but I still did not want to let him go. I was having the time of my life. Never before had I held a little kid in my arms. Apparently Tod liked it too because he settled his silken head against my shoulder and gripped my neck with both hands.

"Lovable kid," I murmured.

Bev's eyes glistened at the sight of a man holding her son. "He misses his father," she whispered.

"I'm sorry," I said, not knowing what else to say.

After an interval, Bev reached out and slowly unwrapped her son from my arms.

He seemed reluctant to let me go.

Impulsively, I leaned down and kissed Bev, but on the cheek.

Mission accomplished, at least partly.

7

The Pontiac was stiff from cold. The temperature was fifteen below and sinking according to the local radio station. Thank heaven there was no wind. Reluctantly, the motor came alive, overcoming the twin obstacles of a cold battery and congealed oil. I let the motor idle until the thermostat opened and the temp needle began to move. I eased the car into the street, the tires out of round from sitting in the cold, the four of them bumping in unison with each revolution.

"You'd better start in the morning," I said to the car, practicing a bit of anthropomorphism on these four thousand pounds of moving parts, moving, that is, unless they freeze together. Snowbirds we call them up here.

On the way to Maynard's, I pulled into a gas station and had the tank topped off, the poor attendant bundled up so completely I couldn't see his face. Then I doubled back to Maynard's shop, drove around to the back, as Rose had recommended, and into a narrow alley. My headlights beamed onto a shiny new Olds Toronado parked next to the loading dock. Must be Maynard's. Nice car, and front-wheel drive to boot. Not many of these around, not even in

Minneapolis let alone Clear Lake. Business must really be good to afford a car like this one. I squeezed into the tight space next to it making sure that I didn't accidentally mark the Toronado's glistening metal when I opened my door. Maynard wouldn't appreciate a scratch on his new wheels. I left my engine idling, figuring I could afford the luxury of a warm car having just filled the tank. Besides I wasn't planning to be gone any length of time—just long enough to find out whose name was on that fifth slug.

I climbed the steps to the loading platform. Lights were blazing behind a series of windows set high in the cement block wall, like a clerestory. There was a wide metal-plated door, held in place by giant black hinges. Over the door was a lone light bulb protected by a rusted · metal shade. It cast a weak glow, hardly enough for a deliveryman to work under.

I pushed the bell by the door and waited. Behind me the engine of my car idled pleasantly and, almost like a counterpoint, came the sound of the defrosters hard at work keeping the windshield clear. My feet began to get cold and the brittle air condensed my breath in long, steamy sheets.

Come on, Maynard, I thought, answer the damned door. You know how cold it is out here.

After several shivering seconds I decided that the bell must not be working and I started pounding on the metal with my fist.

Still nothing. Would Maynard have gone home and left the lights burning? If so, someone had to give him a ride because the Toronado was sitting here. Not likely. He wouldn't leave his new car behind. Maybe the battery died. On a new car? Nah. Maybe he ran across the street to the dinette for coffee. All lame scenarios but these were the best I could come up with. I was ready to walk down the alley and around the block to the front door, a dumb thing to do in 15 below weather since I was not wearing what is commonly referred to as survival gear—city clothes rather than a padded jacket, boots and fur cap with ear flaps. Get in the car and go back to the hotel my better judgment was telling me, you can come back tomorrow. But before doing the sensible thing, I tried the knob. It turned in my hand. It wasn't locked.

Good. At least something was going my way.

I pushed open the heavy door and stepped inside, slamming it quickly to cut off the cold air fighting to get in with me.

Straight ahead, blocking my view to the front of the building was the printing press, its complex machinery in silent repose. Why? It should be cranking out the special edition on Schultzman's murder.

I walked around it, puzzled, and stopped as suddenly as if I'd been brushed by a locomotive.

I could not believe what I saw. The California job case on the work table which held hundreds of small pieces of type alphabetically compartmentalized, had been tipped over and the pied type, as it is called when spilled in a disorderly unusable heap, was all over the floor, hundreds of little pieces of metal. It would take a week to get them in order again.

Above the worktable a large shelf was emptied of its file of old newspapers. Ripped open boxes and sheets of proof paper were strewn everywhere. The drawers of the proof table had been yanked open and stripped. The shop was a mess.

As I stared dumbfounded I thought I heard a noise in front, what seemed like hurried steps, and then a door closing. Maybe it was a phantom sound fed by growing panic. I opened the door to the stationery store and looked inside. The tornado had ripped through here, too. In the dark I still could see display shelves that had been emptied. I pushed past ankle-deep piles of ledgers, file folders, typing paper and envelopes to get to the front door. I peered through the window at the empty street outside.

Nothing, nobody.

I returned to the shop, shaking my head. I surveyed the scene once again and then I saw him.

Maynard was lying beside the linotype machine, his back away from me, his feet tangled in the legs of the old steno chair. One arm was flung over his turned head, covering his face from view. I bent over and tried to pull his arm down but something was stuck to the sleeve of his shirt. Gently I pulled his shoulders over and straightened him out. I stared as horror scratched my cheeks and constricted my throat.

Someone had poured molten lead from the linotype machine's pot onto his face, filling his eye sockets and his gaping mouth. The burning lead had overflowed into rivulets that had seared his skin like flowing lava. He must have brought up his arm in a final agonizing movement of self-defense, and his sleeve caught in the hardening metal.

I touched the death mask, shiny like alchemist's silver, cool and hard. Maynard, I sobbed, who did this awful thing to you?

I saw his glasses lying at his elbow and picked them up. They were smashed as though stepped on and ground into the floor. I stood up, weighted by shock. Fear suddenly gripped the back of my neck. I spun around, afraid that whoever had committed this gruesome act had not left, was still in the building, hiding somewhere, ready to pounce and claim another victim.

But everything was dead quiet.

8

I placed Maynard's glasses on his desk, as if this were a symbolic way of creating order out of chaos. I wiped my eyes dry with the back of my hand and dug through the spilled papers looking for the telephone. I found the receiver wedged between the wall and the desk. The rest of it was under a heavy scrapbook. I clicked the plunger several times, feeling for the cord with my free hand. No, it wasn't ripped from the wall. Finally I got a dial tone and made a collect call to the Citizen Ledger.

"City Desk," I told the operator, Maynard would have approved my calling in the story before notifying the authorities.

The night editor answered, Hal Stevens.

"Is there a chance to remake the front page of the home?" I asked. My breath was coming in spurts.

"Depends on what you got," he said in that indifferent tone editors assume when they think you're making an editorial decision for them. "Say, are you all right?"

"I'll let you know after I give you what I got."

"What's that?"

"A second murder in Clear Lake."

"Isn't that where Bailey sent you?"

"That's right."

Stevens' manner changed. "I'll see what I can do. If not the front page, you'll find it somewhere. I'll turn you over to rewrite."

I waited for the rewrite man to hook on.

"Carter, here," he said, "what have you got?"

I extemporized: "Thirty-six hours after Alfred Schultzman was found bludgeoned to death at his farm near Clear Lake, a second even more gruesome murder was discovered in this small Southern Minnesota town where, until now, the worst offense was running a red light.

"At the printing plant of the community's weekly newspaper, the Clear Lake Independent, owner Maynard Sorenson was found dead around 8 p.m. Wednesday."

"Hey," he interrupted, "that's only five minutes ago."

"I work fast," I said. "Here's the rest of it: The assailant, apparently knocked Sorenson to the floor and then poured molten lead on his face. The lead was from the pot of the linotype machine Sorenson used to set type."

"Wait a minute," Carter interrupted again.

"What now?" I asked, not happy to be uncoupled a second time from my train of thought. "Too grisly for you?"

"No, I'm surprised he still used a linotype machine."

I looked over at Maynard's body. "He was a small town publisher from the old school."

"Like Gutenberg?"

"This has been a tough day."

"Sorry. So who found him?"

"I did."

"Holy shit," Carter cried out. "The reporter finds the body. That's big news!"

"Just say the authorities discovered him after an anonymous tip."

"No way," he said. "Here's the second paragraph: Citizen Ledger reporter discovers the murder victim minutes after he was killed. Someone had poured hot lead from the linotype machine onto his face, the molten metal cooling into an ancient death mask. How do you like that?"

"Not very," I said but I had to admit that Carter was doing what Bailey always taught—put the story first and the welfare of the reporter second. "Just tone it down a little."

"No problem," he said, delighted to participate in the action.

"When we finish I'll call the Sheriff."

"You mean the local law doesn't know about it yet?"

"That's why I was able to call the story in so fast."

"I hope you don't get into trouble."

"Looks like I already have."

I took a few seconds to re-collect my thoughts. "Here's the wind-up: Sorenson's assailant then ransacked the office, ripping apart files, records, anything in his way, looking for something. Whether or not he found it remains a mystery, as does the identity of the killer.

"Sorenson leaves behind his wife, Rose, who operated the newspaper along with her late husband."

"Got it."

"See if you can tie this to the earlier piece I did for the Blue Streak."

"Will do."

I was ready to hang up.

"Hey, Kouros," Carter said quickly.

"What?"

"There's a killer out there somewhere. Be careful."

Either that or go home, I thought.

I dialed the operator a second time. "Sheriff's office."

There was some efficient clicking and then a woman's voice came on the line, an off-hour answering service apparently.

"Are you calling about an emergency or can this wait till regular office hours?"

"Emergency."

"Please state the nature of the emergency."

She was probably expecting something like a pregnant woman going into labor, a car accident, or a kid stuck in a pipe.

"Murder," I replied.

"What did you say?" She sounded as if she were jumping out of her skin.

"I said, murder. In case you are counting, the second one in two days."

She was not amused. "Can you identify the victim?"

"Maynard Sorenson."

"You mean Maynard Sorenson who owns the Independent?" she asked, still not able to digest the information

"I came to his office, where I am now, and found him dead."

"Who is this?"

"Bill Kouros of the Minneapolis Citizen Ledger."

"Are you sure he was murdered?"

I swallowed an urge to slam the phone in her ear. No one takes me seriously. "Maybe I should wake him up and ask him."

"Don't touch anything!" she ordered, taking me literally. "I'll send the sheriff."

"Tell him to come in the back door, it's unlocked."

I didn't realize how hot I was until I hung up the phone. I still had my overcoat on. I took it off and laid it across the desk. Minutes slipped by as I waited by Maynard's corpse like a loyal dog at his master's grave.

Death is undeniably hard to deal with in any case, but the way Maynard died was beyond comprehension. Why was he killed so brutally and what was the killer looking for? Is Maynard's death somehow connected to Schultzman?

As my thoughts sifted through my brain cells, I remembered the reason I came here in the first place. I bent over and gingerly pushed my fingers into the right hand pocket of Maynard's pants. Loose change, folded bills. No familiar flat piece of lead. I tried the other pockets as well, finding the GM keys to the Toronado. Nothing more. Maybe the killer had found the lead slug. Maybe that's what he was looking for…

Suddenly the metal door behind the printing press boomed open and slammed against the inside wall, sending a flat reverberation shuddering through the shop. The noise made me jump so high I felt like a human cannonball. I turned and saw Jensen coming at me at full gallop, his revolver drawn, his holster slapping his thigh.

"Don't you ever use a siren?" I asked him.

He skidded to a halt in front of me. "Hands against the wall!" he shouted, pointing the revolver at my head.

"Hands against the wall?" I repeated. It was so ludicrous I had to laugh.

My derision burned up his fuse and he exploded. He spun me around with his free arm and using his body as a battering ram slammed me against the wall. My cheek dragged against the gritty cement and I could feel it warming with blood.

Jensen forced his knee up my groin, a far from caressing gesture. I grunted in pain, finally realizing that I was in real danger from this psychopathic bully. I better stay quiet.

"Ok," he breathed heavily, "let's see if you're packing iron."

As I wondered what television show he got that line from, he put his gun back in its holster and began patting me down. No, not patting, pounding—he was pounding my body with the flats of his hands, as large as toilet seat covers. When he came to my waist he brought both hands down hard as if slapping two especially irritating mosquitos. I cried out this time. I couldn't help it, the pain was excruciating. It felt as if shards of steel were slicing through my kidneys and I almost lost control of my bladder. Jensen would have loved to see me wet my pants, that fucking, sadistic bastard!

I was at the point of passing out when I heard another voice shout, "Hold it Jensen, lay off!"

Thank god it was Amundson coming into the office and hollering at his deputy.

Jensen's fat knee came down but not without one final reminder that it was hurting me. Jensen stepped back. I lowered my arms, turned around and leaned my back against the wall. Sweat was running down my armpits.

"Sheriff," I said, between gasping breaths of air that made my sides throb. "He tried to kill me."

"Bullshit, Sheriff," Jensen said. "I was only using standard procedures to search the suspect."

Suspect? What the hell was he talking about?

Amundson ignored his deputy and came over to me. He gently touched my cheek with his fingers. "Going to be tough shaving for a couple of days."

"Going to be tough going to the toilet, too."

"What did he do?" Amundson asked.

"Punched me in the kidneys."

"I only patted him down, Sheriff," Jensen said, acting like a Labrador who stepped in his water bowl.

I doubled over and Amundson put his hand on my shoulder. "Are you all right?"

"I might throw up."

He pulled a wastebasket from under the desk and put it under my lowered head. "Just in case," he said.

I hung there for a while till my gorge settled and then straightened.

"Feeling better?"

"I think so."

"Get some rest. I'm sure you'll be ok in the morning. Where are you staying? At the hotel?"

"Yes."

"I'll drive you there."

"I have my car."

"I just want to make sure you get there ok."

"I'll be fine. I left the engine running. The car will be warm." I stared down at the pathetic figure lying on the floor. My mentor, my friend. "What about Maynard?"

"There is nothing more you can do here."

The Sheriff held my coat open for me, settling it carefully on my shoulders.

"By the way, did you touch anything?" he asked.

"Like what?"

"The body, anything at all."

"If I did does that make me a suspect?" I asked, thinking back to what Jensen yelled at me.

"Not necessarily, but if you moved or touched anything it would contaminate the crime scene. I'll need to get a statement from you. Stop by my office in the morning."

"Do you get the Citizen Ledger?"

"I read it with my coffee."

"Good," I said, and tested my sore chin with a smile. When I visit his office tomorrow he will already have read my article.

9

A persistent knock on the door woke me. I winced as I sat up. I could not isolate any individual pain, my body ached all over.

"What is it?"

A girl's voice came through the panel. "The morning paper, Mr. Kouros. You asked me to wake you as soon as it came. Shall I leave it by the door?"

"Please," I called out. I checked my watch on the side table. Seven thirty.

"I have a telephone message for you, too."

"Just a minute. I'll get that now." I struggled with my bathrobe, ran my fingers through my hair and went to the door. It was the same teenage kid who checked me in yesterday.

"Don't you ever go to school?"

"Work-study," she said. "I split my days between school and here." She handed me the folded morning edition of the Citizen Ledger and a small envelope with the hotel's logo printed in the corner and my name written across the front.

"That was terrible news about Mr. Sorenson." She looked at my face. "Say, what happened to your chin?"

I ran my fingertips gingerly across stubble and scab.

"Looks bad?"

"Well, it's swollen and bruised. Did you fall on the ice?"

I nodded. "What do I owe you for the paper?"

"Compliments of the management."

"Thanks," I said and closed the door. I opened the envelope. It was from Claire—Call me Sweetheart when you have the time—she was good at the double entendre.

I went to the can, lowered myself very slowly, and opened the paper with the top half on the bathtub ledge and the bottom half on my knees. The night editor did well by me. My story was above the fold with a good-sized head:

CITIZEN LEDGER REPORTER
DISCOVERS
SECOND CLEAR
LAKE MURDER

The kicker:

Editor is brutally
Killed by molten
Lead from antique
Linotype machine

And, of course, my by-line.

It was written pretty much as I had dictated it, with Carter's emphasis on the gruesome nature of Maynard's death, but that's what readers relish with their breakfast.

I was doing my job well, maybe too well, and at poor Maynard's expense. What a way to be remembered, not what you accomplished as a newspaperman but the way you died.

Well, I alibied, Maynard started me on the road to

journalism. He would be proud of his protégé writing the unvarnished truth.

This is also what I owe to Maynard's memory—the bad press I'm going to give the Sheriff's deputy in a follow-up piece about beating up a reporter. It will be a fair turnabout, Jensen gave me a pain in the side, and I'm going to be his pain in the ass.

Speaking of pain, I discovered that peeing wasn't as difficult as having a movement. Apparently you activate more muscles than the sphincter when taking a shit.

I checked my body in the mirror before showering; expecting to see bruises, but all I could detect was some redness, like a rash. Those who specialize in torture, I once read, know how to inflict pain without leaving evidence and it appeared that Jensen knew exactly what he was doing.

A soaking hot shower was heaven blessed, and I felt much better after toweling off. After shaving with great care around my chin, I got dressed. But before going downstairs for the promised continental breakfast I called the paper. No doubt Bailey was waiting to hear from me.

"What in hell are you doing, sleeping on company time?"

"What do you mean?"

"Do you know it's eight-thirty?"

"So what the hell do you want? I was up till midnight." I decided not to tell him about the pawing over I got. He's hysterical enough as it is.

Then Bailey laughed. It was so rare I asked him what the noise was.

"I do that only when I'm pleased," he told me.

"You? Pleased?" I asked, astonished.

"Sure. Wasn't that a great idea I had sending you down there?"

"What are you talking about?"

"Your story."

"Are you taking credit for that?" My astonishment hit a new high.

"Your name will be on the Pulitzer, not mine."

"I'd rather have a raise."

"We'll discuss that after you get back."

"Bailey, you have a heart of lead." Now why did I say that?

Bailey was riding high. "Speaking of the base medal, Bill, I will give you credit for discovering the body, the first person on that sickening scene. Instead of doing what the average citizen would do, calling the sheriff, you kept a cool head and called in the story first. That's what makes a great reporter. Brewster wants to do a series of promotion ads. 'Art critic turns detective.' Pictures of you at the crime scene. I'm sending down a photographer today."

How can this be happening? "Bailey, slow down a minute. If you keep this up, I'll never be able to write an art review again. Museum directors, curators, artists, you name them, will never take me seriously."

"Is that who you're worrying about, a handful of dilettantes? Do you know what the readership is on this story? Ten times what you get on that phony art crap. So here's what I want you to do. Keep the pressure on the sheriff and that deputy of his. Get an interview with Sorenson's widow. Keep a close eye on the Schultzman kid, the one in the hospital. If he wakes up, get an interview."

"I was planning to come home this weekend."

"You're not coming home till I say so."

Bailey hung up, leaving me holding a dead phone. I stared at it, feeling deserted and betrayed. It's not that I was disappointed by my story's success. I had a done a good job, as it turned out too good a job, and now I'm getting praise where I don't want it. All I cared about, all I ever cared about working at the Citizen Ledger was writing about art, struggling for the right phrase to describe an ambiguous object, figuring out what the artist meant by that shape, that line, that combination of colors, or an assemblage of found objects that becomes a wall relief, a crunched-up wad of car metal sitting on a pedestal. What makes these works of art worthy of being in a museum? That was my job, interpreting the artist's intent. Someone had to do that and I wanted to be that person, the one with the discerning eye. And now, Bailey was turning me into a crime reporter, nothing more than a mechanic with dirty clothes and dirty fingernails—but, and this was the hardest anomaly of all, with ten times more readers.

I decided to salve my ambivalent feelings by calling Claire. At least she had a sympathetic ear.

Her lyrical voice told me it was Mr. Brewster's office.

"Hi, baby," I said.

"Bill!" she shouted. "My hero!"

I jerked my ear out of danger. "Easy," I said, "Brewster will hear you all the way into his office."

"It's ok," she replied. "You're the main topic of conversation around here. And you're mine, got that? *Mine!*"

"It's nice to be appreciated," I said "but not on company time."

"I don't care. I want the whole world to know."

Including me obviously. Before I came to Clear Lake that's all I wanted to hear from her, but with Bev back in the picture, if not my life, my feelings were to put it mildly ambivalent.

"Claire," I said.

"What?" She was probably expecting me to answer her with something like "you're mine, too," but instead I said, "I won't be back this weekend."

I could sense her smile shrink like a Sears dress in the

laundromat. "But our date for the opening."

She was referring to Pop Goes the Easel, the sixties retrospective featuring Claus Oldenburg, Andy Warhol and Roy Lichtenstein, among a palette of famous Pop Artists, opening Saturday at the Walker Art Center.

As the Citizen Ledger's critic I had an invitation to an after-opening party at the home of the museum's director who lives on fashionable Mount Curve, the place to see and be seen. Now, I will miss it all and write a delayed review. But that's what Bailey wants.

But not what Claire wants. "You promised!"

"That was before Bailey and your boss, too, by the way sent me to Clear Lake."

"Can't you drive back up here, it's just for a few hours?"

"I have follow-up stories to do, interview more people, and meet deadlines for every morning edition. Plus the round trip and driving at night in subzero weather? Can't do it."

"I even bought a new outfit at the Oval Room just for the opening," she added, stubbornly hanging on.

In my mind, not revealed to anyone but myself, I imagined what a weekend would be like far from Claire and close to Bev. Relaxing, soothing, sharing. And with Maynard dead I needed to mourn, not party. Hard to admit it, but Bailey did me a favor by giving me an out.

"Well," I said, too glibly as it turned out, "The Oval Room has a return policy, doesn't it?"

"You bastard!" she snapped at me. "I'll wear that dress to the opening whether you take me to it or not!"

I replaced the receiver on its cradle, making less noise than Claire did when she hung up. Nothing else has gone right since Wednesday, so why should my call to Claire? I'd been the recipient of her quick Irish temper often enough to know she didn't mean half of what she said, that it was more hyperbole than threat, but this time I might be wrong. She said she was going to the opening even without me. Maybe she had another boyfriend up her sleeve, in a manner of speaking. Well, it will be interesting to find out just who that might be. I can't imagine her crashing the party alone, she couldn't get in without an invitation and that was safely tucked away in the top drawer of my desk. But Claire was resourceful and she worked for the publisher of the Citizen Ledger. If anyone could get in to an art opening she could—she knows how to pull strings especially if she is as pissed off as I think she is.

Mulling over my strained conversation with Claire, I went down to the lobby for breakfast and several cups of coffee. It had been an exhausting morning and it wasn't even eight yet. I walked into the dining room surprised at how nicely laid out the buffet table was, not just little boxes of cereal but also scrambled eggs, bacon and muffins. I was not alone, obviously some of the locals came here for breakfast on their way to work, and when I walked into the small dining room I received stares of curiosity which made me wonder how many of them popped in just to catch a glimpse of the big city reporter. One of the diners had the Citizen Ledger spread open on his table as he ate his breakfast. He was too engrossed to look up. If Amundson hasn't read my article by now, someone for sure will tell him about it, maybe even this man.

10

I lingered over coffee till nine, figuring Lewis's office would not open till then. I used the lobby phone to call the attorney who was taking care of Bruno Schultzman.

A female voice answered my first ring. "Lewis and Lewis."

"Mr. Lewis please,"

"Junior or senior?"

"Junior" I replied. Senior had to be the father, and he had to be old, my dad's age if he were still around. Maybe the elder Lewis had an emeritus title and showed up at the office once in awhile to keep his name on the shingle

"May I ask who's calling?"

"Bill Kouros of the Citizen Ledger."

"Oh, yes, Mr. Kouros. Mr. Lewis was expecting to hear from you."

Really, I told myself. Well, get used to it, this is a small town and the news gets around faster than you can write it.

Lewis came on quickly. "Bill, great to hear from you."

Even though he made it seem we were old pals who hadn't seen each other in a long time, Lewis and I rarely crossed paths in high school. He was the son of an old–line family and I was the son of an immigrant candy maker.

"Thanks, Al. I suppose you've read the morning paper?"

"Yes, yes, terrible news about Maynard Sorenson."

"I talked to him yesterday afternoon."

"But you found his body…"

"When I returned to see him again, last night."

"Dreadful."

"Maynard gave me the names of five persons I should talk to about the Schultzman killing, and yours was one of them."

"Is that right? I wonder why?"

"Well, maybe it's because Bruno Schultzman is staying at your house."

"Yes, yes, he is, but temporarily, until we find someone who will take care of him, a nice family to be his foster parents, and perhaps adopt him eventually."

"We?"

'Oh, when I said we, I meant my wife Anita and myself."

"She's with him now?"

"Well, no, as a matter of fact. Anita is in Mexico, with our two daughters. We have a home on Magdalena Island. Got to get away from this cold, you know." He laughed nervously. He certainly was uncomfortable talking to me. "Did you know I own a twin Beechcraft?"

I wasn't sure what a twin Beechcraft was. "Really? A twin?"

"Twin-engine."

I finally got it. The Beechcraft is a plane, a plane with two engines.

"I'm instrument rated. I can take off and land at night, even a small airport like ours without runway lights," he said proudly. "I'm flying down to Mexico at the end of the month to take a few days off and then we'll all fly back together."

"So who will be staying with Bruno?"

"Our housekeeper, Mrs. Annandale. As trustworthy as the day is long."

Can't be that trustworthy, I thought. In January daylight lasts maybe 8 hours.

"I'd like to ask a favor."

"Anything I can do."

"I'd like to talk to Bruno."

Lewis laughed. "I guess I should have said, almost anything."

"Problem?"

"Bruno has gone through hell, Bill, as you well understand. I think it would be callous of me to ask him if he wanted to talk to a reporter."

"Grief-stricken people are interviewed by reporters all the time, even live on television."

"Yes, yes, I understand. But as his legal guardian, I find it hard to put him through that. At least for now. Maybe later, after he has had a chance to heal…"

I didn't have time for Bruno to heal. "So the legal guardian is saying no?"

"I wouldn't put it so bluntly."

"I would." The son of a bitch.

"Is there anything else I can do for you?"

"As his guardian, can you answer a question or two?"

"I suppose so."

"How about later this morning, if I come by your office?"

"What time?"

An idea was blossoming in the hothouse section of my brain, an idea that needed the morning to come to full bloom. "How does eleven-thirty sound?"

"That's so close to noon, why not make it for lunch. The Cozy Corner. My treat. "

Perfect, but that was an unfamiliar name to me.

"Where's the Cozy Corner?"

"Across the street from my office. Three blocks south of your father's old restaurant. But the food there is not nearly as good."

How in hell does he know? He never set foot in my father's restaurant.

"I'll see you at noon."

11

After looking up Lewis's home address in the hotel phone book, I went to my room and paid another visit to the toilet before bundling up for a trek outside to my car, parked across the street like a frozen sentinel.

As I trudged through the lobby the teenage desk clerk waved at me. "Have a nice day," she said.

"I will if the car starts," I shot back.

The starter ground like a worn-out Waring blender but the engine finally caught. I waited until it stopped making angry whining sounds and then slid it into gear. Before heading for Lewis's house, I decided to warm up the car by driving past Maynard's office to see if anything was happening.

I came slowly around to the rear of the building. Next to Maynard's Olds was a black paneled vehicle with a sign on the rear door that read Medical Examiner Clear Lake County. Parked in the alley with the engine idling was the Sheriff's cruiser, a brown-colored Ford Fairlane with rack lights and a flashy medallion on the door.

I didn't want to linger too long and have Amundsen find me but I was fascinated to see the Toronado in daylight, its dark blue metal gleaming in the sun. I could see through the window that the car had leather chairs and a dashboard that would have challenged an astronaut. Power everything no doubt, AM-FM stereo, tape deck.

Top of the line Toronado, what no newspaperman could afford unless his name was Brewster. Maynard must have had his hand in something. I fingered the slugs of lead in my pocket. Perhaps too deeply and he got iced for it.

An odd thought passed my mind as I drove away: the car belongs to Rose now.

I cut back through town and took Elm Street south nearly to the lake and turned right on Eleventh Avenue where Clear Lake's old money resided. Halfway down the block I stopped in front of a large, two-story modified colonial of white-painted Roman brick. The mortar had been allowed to squeeze out between the bricks giving the house an undeserved rustic appearance.

Briefcase in hand I walked briskly up the sidewalk to the front door as though I were a businessman whose datebook was jammed with appointments, just in case anyone was looking out a window.

A woman of fifty or so answered my summons. She opened the storm door a crack but no more.

"Good morning Mrs. Annandale," I said cheerily, "I'm with Aetna insurance and Mr. Schultzman was a client of mine. I have some policies I need Bruno's signature on."

Bailey would have hysterics if he could hear me now.

"I never heard of any Aetna insurance salesman in Clear Lake."

"No ma'am, not salesman, agent. I drove over from Mankato. Just as cold here as it is there." I laughed as disarmingly as I knew how. "Mind if I come in?"

"Mr. Lewis told me not to let anyone in unless he said so." A white ribbon held her gray hair in place and she had bushy eyebrows that went up and down as she spoke.

"You mean he hasn't called?" I asked with feigned surprise. "I talked to him yesterday and told him I was driving to Clear Lake this morning. It must have slipped his mind." I hunched my shoulders to remind her how cold it was. "Mind if I come in and we can talk where it's warmer?"

She was staring at my sore chin.

"Oh, that," I said. "Slipped on some ice. Dumb thing to do, got out of the car last night and, zip, before I knew it I fell and my chin glanced off the rear view mirror. But it's better now." I touched it gently.

She gave me a sympathetic look. That and the fact that I knew her name gave her pause, and she relaxed enough to loosen her hold on the storm. She stepped back and I moved quickly into the house, shutting the door behind me.

My eye for style checked the decor. Tastelessly overdone. Everything looked as if it came from Ethan Allen.

"What did you say your name was?"

"Oh," I said, caught off guard. I hadn't bothered to have one ready. "Ole, Ole Olson." It was the best I could come up with on short notice.

She stared at me as if I had just stepped off the boat from Sweden.

"My friends call me Ole," I added hurriedly. "My real name is Olaf."

I think she wanted to trust me. "That's not so unusual for Minnesota."

"I guess not." I said, but she was suspicious of my dark hair and somewhat olive skin. "Where's Bruno?" I asked in the same breath, figuring my luck would run out sooner rather than later.

"In the kitchen having breakfast."

"It won't take long."

"Maybe I should call Mr. Lewis."

"Feel free. I'd like to get this matter cleared up as much as you do. I'll look in on Bruno while you call Al, how's that?"

She pointed to a hall running alongside the staircase with its elegantly turned newel post and rails. I followed the hall to the kitchen. Behind me, I heard her pick up a telephone and start dialing. I had to work fast.

The kitchen was resplendent with every convenience imaginable. It was large, and everything sparkled, the stainless steel appliances, the gray granite counter, the tiled floor. Bruno was sitting at the island under a bank of hanging lights. He was eating waffles. Syrup was dripping from his chin.

He looked up, surprised and suspicious.

"Who are you?"

"Mr. Lewis sent me to have you sign some insurance papers." I unbuttoned my overcoat and stood on the other side of the island, across from him. I placed my briefcase on the counter and opened it, playing the role as long as I could.

Bruno kept eating while he stole upward glances at me. He was heavyset, with strong hands and wrists. He had dirty blond hair and dull colorless eyes. He was wearing a loose-fitting gray pullover. His table manners were atrocious.

I studied his eyes. He blinked a lot as if the bright light was bothering him. The skin under them was puffy and pallid. There was something about his appearance that nagged me.

"I'm sorry about what happened to your father and sister."

He didn't say anything.

"I understand you found them."

"Sarah," he corrected. "She was in the house, Dad was in the orchard."

"What time was that?"

"I came home around eleven."

"Where were you?"

"In town at a movie. Then I shot some pool."

"You were alone?"

He nodded.

He didn't look like a kid who had many friends.

"Then you came back to the farm and found Sarah on the floor."

"In the upper hallway. It was late. I figured everyone was asleep. I came upstairs to go to bed and nearly tripped over her."

"What did you do then?"

"I looked for dad and he wasn't in his room, so I ran downstairs and called the hospital."

"Not the sheriff?"

He shook his head. "I just thought she was sick and passed out."

"You didn't see any blood?"

"It was mostly under her. Say, why are you asking me all these questions?"

"Well," I said, "we need to know everything when it comes to paying off insurance policies."

"I didn't know dad had insurance."

Just then the housekeeper came into the kitchen.

"Mr. Lewis was out seeing a client. But I told his secretary that you were here and she said she didn't know anyone named Olaf Olson."

"That's likely since I'm from Mankato. Everything is moving so fast, Mr. Lewis probably didn't have time to tell her I was coming." I winked slyly. "Sometimes secretaries don't know all that's going on, right, Mrs. Annandale?" Taking her into my confidence like that was probably more than she ever got from Al. He probably treated her like dirt. She became more relaxed, maybe even liking me a little.

"Do you want a cup of coffee?"

"That would be nice." I always added cream and sugar to my coffee but somewhere I heard that most Swedes like theirs black.

She poured a cup from a pot on the stove and set it down in front of me.

It tasted awful.

"I have to make the beds upstairs."

"We're almost through here. I can let myself out."

She left us alone. Just what I needed.

"How long will you be living with the Lewises?" I asked Bruno.

"Long as they'll have me I guess."

"Do you have any relatives?"

"Dad has some cousins in Europe. That's all I know of."

"I suppose the farm will be sold?"

"Dad didn't own it."

I raised my eyebrows. "He didn't?"

"He rented it."

That was a surprise. "Who owns it?"

Bruno shrugged. "I don't know."

I thought to myself, it would be interesting to find out who does.

I looked inside my briefcase and began to shuffle blank sheets of paper. "Can you beat that?" I said and smiled sheepishly. "You know what I did? I brought copies, not the originals. You can only sign originals. Wasn't that dumb of me? I'll leave them with Mr. Lewis, and he can bring them home for you to sign."

It was clear Bruno didn't give a damn one way or the other. He got off his stool and brought the pot from the stove. He refilled his cup. His hand was unsteady and he seemed unable to focus his eyes on the simple task at hand. I watched perplexed. What was wrong with him? Was he hung over? The kid's movements suggested something else, something I'd seen before, and then it hit me.

I should have guessed right away. In the art world I'd seen people act like this before, but I had to make sure.

I leaned across the counter as if to shake Bruno's hand goodbye, but my reach was sloppy and I knocked his cup over, spilling hot coffee all over his left arm.

He jumped up, cursing angrily. I moved quickly to his side of the island. "Sorry," I said, "let me help." I grabbed his wrist and shoved the wet sleeve up to his elbow.

"What the hell are you doing?" He jerked it away and pulled the loosely knitted material back down, but not before I saw needle marks in the crook of his forearm.

No doubt about it, the kid was a junkie.

12

I took Shore Line Drive bordering the ice-locked lake back into town. A few fish houses dotted the expanse of white. Why fisherman enjoyed sitting in a hut the size of an outhouse staring at a hole that kept wanting to freeze over was beyond my comprehension.

My sightseeing trip took me past Maplewood Park, a wooded campground overlooking the lake. Now barren of foliage, the tree trunks and limbs looked like macabre giant stick figures. On the opposite side of the road was a frozen-over wetland that, in the summer, teemed with varietal swamp grasses. I was disappointed to see several new houses popping up along this stretch of natural habitat. I suppose one day that all of this pristine lakeshore will be filled in in order to build bland, brick-clad homes with manicured lawns and precisely trimmed hedges.

I began to realize that the road around the lake was turning into memory lane for me as I passed the hibernating Clear Lake Golf Club, nine holes when I caddied there as a kid for twenty-five cents a round plus tips. It was now a proud eighteen holes. Ahead was the site of the King Melody Supper Club, a For Sale sign fronting the empty expanse, waiting no doubt for some new structure to take its place. Coming around the bend I saw the snow-encrusted bathhouse of Clear Lake Beach where I learned how to swim. Next to it once stood the open-air roller rink, now long gone.

Turning away from the lake, I drove up 8th Avenue Northeast, passing the county fair grounds whose gray 4H buildings were boarded up. No midway rides now, no cotton candy, no ring-the-bottle concession where my father, during the Great Depression and consumed by his fiery nature, blew a whole dollar trying to win a stuffed teddy bear for me.

My favorite memory of the county fair, notwithstanding, was being at the wheel of a Dodgem car. For a nickel I could pretend I was in a demolition derby.

Memories—alas, they have a tendency to slow down your thinking by pulling you into the shadowy world of the past.

Can't afford to reminisce any longer, I told myself. The lake now behind me, my mind jumped back to the present and the discovery that Bruno was a drug addict.

Fortunately I was able to leave the house before Mrs. Annandale came back downstairs. I felt guilty conning this kindly soul and I did not want to continue the charade. Lewis would find out what I had done soon enough and he would no doubt bawl her out for being so gullible, maybe even fire her. I hoped not. No wonder Lewis did not want me snooping around. He did not want a newspaper reporter to learn the truth about Bruno.

So what was the truth, the whole truth and nothing but the truth? Bruno was no ordinary kid, but a kid whose father was murdered just two days ago. What was the connection? And what was the connection to Maynard's murder? There was nothing random about that act of cruelty. And how did Bruno feed his habit? Where did the money come from and who was his supplier? Lots of questions, but no answers.

The Cozy Corner where Al Lewis told me to meet him was on a corner, all right, but there was not much that was cozy about it. The door was set back diagonally and a step up from the sidewalk. The entry floor was made up of century-old octagonal tiles, many of which were cracked or missing, leaving little holes of black connected by craggy lines. I had to circumnavigate a rusty pole that supported the overhang. The windows were frosted over and looked as if they hadn't been cleaned since the last ice age.

I pushed open the door. Apparently the scabby entrance didn't bother anyone else because the Cozy Corner was crowded and noisy. It didn't take long to understand why. The place had a funky ambience with familiar, even addictive, bar smells—beer suds, hot grease, cooking oil.

A mahogany bar had a congregation of drinkers, some sitting on stools, some standing and leaning in. Above the bar hung a big molded sign for Hamm's Beer, and next to it was a short-order griddle filled with spattering hamburgers. Along the opposite wall was a row of booths built like stalls, and down the center a series of round tables. Waitresses serving mugs of beer and platters of hamburgers and french fries, navigated the tight spaces without bumping, as though their moves had been choreographed by Agnes de Mille,

I stood at the front door looking around. Al Lewis was a distant memory, and I figured that if I remained where I was with an expectant look on my face, he would spot me first. It didn't occur to me that I was also attracting attention just standing there. It isn't that everybody stopped what they were doing, bartending or waiting tables, eating a hamburger or drinking a beer, but there was a kind of coming to attention, a quick glance at the stranger who just came in. No, not a stranger. They all knew who I was, the reporter from Minneapolis digging up dirt about their hometown. The stolen glances were suspicious, not hostile but far from friendly.

But the stare of one of the patrons was indeed hostile. He rose from his lone place at a booth and waved.

I walked over, skirting customers, waitresses and

tables.

"Hello, Al," I said.

I hung up my overcoat and sat across from him.

In high school I remembered Alvin Lewis as an overachiever who grabbed attention whenever he could, of medium build and height, and with unremarkable features, neither handsome nor homely—just, well, average.

He was pudgy, in the way a child is pudgy, as if he were still carrying around his baby fat. His suit was banker's gray, his tie rep silk—the uniform of the businessman, even in a small town. He was either wearing his shirt collar a size too small or his blood pressure was 150 over 90. His cheeks were flushed almost purple.

"Sorry I'm late," I said, knowing full well this was not the reason why he was upset.

"How could you," he asked in measured tones, "take advantage of an innocent woman?"

"You mean Mrs. Annandale?"

"You know damn well who I mean."

"Investigative reporters have to be resourceful."

Al looked up at the waffled ceiling in disbelief. "Ole Olson is resourceful?"

"She bought it, didn't she?"

He looked at me again, his eyes flashing. "There is a simple matter of ethics, Bill. You come back to Clear Lake after twenty years and this is how you act? What you did was deceitful, dishonest, indecent..."

"A, B, C, or all of the above?"

My unrepentant manner shocked him into silence. I didn't care. His name was on one of the slugs Maynard had given me and I wanted to find out why.

"That was pure bullshit about not wanting me to see Bruno because he was in mourning. You were afraid I'd find out he was a junkie."

"Keep your voice down."

"It wasn't up in the first place."

"Can't you understand what would happen if word got

out that you allege he was addicted to drugs? It would destroy any chance he has of recovery and it would tear Clear Lake apart."

Allege, I thought? Is that how lawyers talk? "What about the murders—his father's and Maynard's? Aren't they also tearing the town apart?"

We were interrupted by a waitress in a hurry. "Anything from the bar?"

"I'll have one of those beers that comes from the land of sky blue waters."

She was not amused as she wrote Hamm's on her pad. She looked at Al. "The usual, Mr. Lewis?"

He nodded and the waitress rushed away. I wondered what the usual was.

The interruption gave Al time to gather his thoughts. "This is a personal matter. The boy has a right to privacy."

"There have been two murders because of what you call a personal matter."

"Are you trying to make a connection between Bruno and the murders?"

"Al, you're a lawyer. You examine everything carefully, don't you? So why not examine the possibility of a connection between a son with a drug problem and a father who was so badly bludgeoned you couldn't recognize his face not to mention a newspaperman who was so covered with lead you couldn't recognize his face either?"

I stopped my growing rant, wondering why I was arguing so heatedly. Who was I trying to defend? Myself? Was I nothing more than a Hollywood gossip reporter who messes into private lives just to titillate readers? Should I give a damn about a quiet town gone mad even though I grew up here? I didn't have the time to think it through, but one thing I was sure of: how can I go on living with myself? I yearned to return to those quiet, reflective days when all I had to do was write about art – not death, cruelty and terror.

Al was staring at me; maybe he was reading my mind.

"As a lawyer, I would answer you by saying that your argument, if we can call it that, is improper, irrelevant and immaterial."

"Regardless of what you say, Al, I still think there is a common denominator in all of this."

"Mere speculation does not prove anything. You don't have to be a lawyer to appreciate that."

"Bruno's addiction is not speculation."

"How do you know?"

"The puncture marks on his arm."

"You are mistaken. Bruno had a blood sample taken a few days ago for anemia."

I smiled. "I know people who mainline hard drugs. The art world is full of them. And it doesn't take a Philadelphia lawyer to tell a junkie from a blood donor."

"You sit there like a judge, Bill. I didn't know you very well in high school but I can't believe you were like this. What's changed you?"

His question made me defensive. "I didn't ask for this assignment but now that I'm here, I have a job to do."

Al leaned forward. "I hope you are not planning to print any of this."

I didn't say anything.

His eyes pleaded with me. "Don't do it, Bill. Please don't do it."

The waitress brought our bar order. Al's usual turned out to be a double martini on the rocks. Al picked up his glass, his pudgy, meticulously manicured fingers shaking, and swallowed half of it.

He put the glass down and stared at it, not at me. "What will it take," he said in a carefully measured tone, "to ignore what you saw this morning?"

"Are you trying to buy me off?" I asked. "What was it you were just saying about ethics?"

His shoulders sagged. He knew he'd made a mistake. "All right, I admit that Bruno uses drugs, but it's an isolated case. It isn't like we have an epidemic in Clear Lake."

"But Bruno of all people. His dad was murdered two days ago. You can't dismiss the timing of that."

"What timing? He didn't start on drugs yesterday. I've known about his addiction for several months."

"Why didn't you do something about it?"

"Don't think we haven't tried."

"Who's we?"

Al leaned back as though he had revealed too much and was trying to put distance between us.

"Bruno's father, of course, as well as the Sheriff, Doctor Nordstrom..."

"So that means everybody?"

"Not everybody, Bill."

"Everybody who matters," I said.

Al finished his martini and abruptly stood up. "I have to be going." He put on a designer overcoat in gray herringbone. I didn't know Bill Blass made a size that wide.

"Aren't you going to eat?"

"I'm not hungry." He dropped a ten on the table and walked out.

"Where's Al?" the waitress asked when she returned to take our orders.

"I don't think he is feeling very well."

"Al needs to watch himself," she volunteered. "He's carrying around too much weight."

13

Lunch over quicker than expected; I decided to pay a call on Sheriff Amundson. He wanted a statement from me for the record and I wanted a statement from him for the Citizen Ledger. Keep feeding the bonfire, I told myself.

I opened the door and poked my head in, wary of that meathead deputy. Thankfully he was not at his desk. Maybe he takes long lunches.

I called out, "Sheriff?"

"I'm in here," he called back.

I stopped at the entrance to his office, not sure if his reply was an invitation to come in. The morning paper was lying open on his desk, covering his he-man magazines. He refolded it with the solemnity of someone who had just read an obituary, maybe mine. He glanced up at me with a hurt expression.

"You grew up here, Bill, and I thought we were friends." He tapped the paper. "I just read your article. I'm very disappointed. You made me sound like a horse's ass."

I looked down at the paper, remembering what Jensen had said after the mauling he gave me. I fingered my sore jaw so that it would not be lost on the Sheriff. "Aw, I didn't hurt you that much."

Amundson's eyebrows pulled together angrily.

"Deputy Jensen was doing his job."

"That's what I was doing, too, my job."

"You were standing over a dead body. What was he supposed to do, shake your hand?"

"He didn't have to beat me up." It sounded like whining.

The Sheriff looked at me as if he had just discovered a flaw in my character. "I can't do anything unless you bring charges."

"What would that get me?"

"Besides personal satisfaction you mean? A lot of paper work and an appearance in court."

The last thing I wanted to do was hang around Clear Lake longer than I had to. "Ok, Let's just drop it."

"Finally, you are making some sense. Now, can we get down to business?" He pulled a tape recorder out from under his desk, opened the case and hooked it up to a wall socket behind his chair. "Sit down," he ordered. "Talk into the mike, describe what happened last night at the printing plant, and what you saw."

I droned on for five minutes, noting everything except searching Maynard's pockets for the missing slug and my collect call to Minneapolis.

"Should I add anything about Jensen working me over?" I asked, firing one last shot across the Sheriff's bow.

He glared at me.

"Ok, then, I guess that's it."

The Sheriff rewound the tape, which made eerie sounds of my voice going backwards, and slid it into a manila envelope. He marked the front of it with my name, a number, the date, and put it away in a file drawer.

"Anything else?" he asked. He was speaking rhetorically. He really wanted me to get up and leave.

"As a matter of fact there is."

He became guarded. "What now?"

"Bruno Schultzman."

"What about him?"

"His drug addiction."

Deepening concern clouded his features. "Where did you hear that crazy piece of crap?"

"I didn't hear it, I saw it. I was at Al Lewis's house this morning."

He stared at me suspiciously. I expected him to draw his Smith and Wesson.

"You broke into Al's house?"

"No, I did not break into Al's house. His housekeeper, Mrs. Annandale, let me in."

"She wouldn't have let you in. You had to do something close to breaking and entering."

"You can argue that all you want, Sheriff, but you can't argue about the needle marks on Bruno's arm."

"You are jumping to conclusions. He probably had some blood work done."

"That's just what Al Lewis said. Sounds like you two are using the same script."

"You talked to Al?"

"Before I came here. I met him at the Cozy Corner for lunch—that is, if you can call a martini on the rocks and a Hamm's beer lunch. Al admitted to me that Bruno is on drugs."

"He probably misspoke."

"Oh, I see. His word against mine?"

"You enter a private home under what have to be false pretenses. So who do you expect me to believe, a lawyer from a prominent family or a fiction writer from an out-of-town newspaper?"

"I know what I heard. Al told me Bruno has been on drugs for a year and that you and Dr. Nordstrom have known it all along. Not only that, he tried to bribe me to keep me quiet."

"Any witnesses?" he asked, almost wearily.

"No. But I know what I heard. I'm not making any of this up."

"I'll talk to Al."

"To get your stories straight?"

He looked at me sternly. "You are beginning to irk me, Bill."

"Well, then, I might as well keep on irking you. Instead of talking to Al, why don't we drive over to his house and you can check out Bruno for yourself. And arrest him, too, because as far as I know, using illegal drugs is a crime isn't it?"

Amundson rubbed his eyes. He probably didn't get much sleep last night, and he probably won't get much tonight either. He brought his arms down and folded them on the desk.

"Being an art writer," he said, emphasizing his words with a mocking smile, "you probably don't know a whole lot about law enforcement, like establishing probable cause, obtaining search warrants, gathering evidence, interviewing witnesses, subpoenaing documents, convening grand juries. You just don't barge into someone's house like you did today, and arrest someone. If I did that I wouldn't be Sheriff very long. I've been in this job twenty-three years and I don't plan on retiring any time soon."

He leaned forward. "Everything you've done since coming to town has compromised my authority. It pains me to say this, Bill, but you are getting in my way. Do me a big favor. Stop writing about us and leave town. Right now. Go back to Minneapolis."

He had to be kidding. I certainly wasn't taking him seriously. "You want me to be on the noon stage, is that it?"

"This is not a western, Bill."

"Sure sounds like one, Sheriff. "This is make-believe stuff. I'm a free citizen in a free country. Even if I break the law you still can't kick me out of town."

"But I can arrest you."

"For what?"

"Breaking and entering for one," he said coolly. "I could probably think up a few other charges if I had to."

"Then I guess you'll have to arrest me because I'm going to stick around and keep on reporting. You can read all about it in the Citizen Ledger."

14

My charge of adrenalin carried me all the way back to the hotel, into my room and to the small side table where I sat down and opened my portable Olivetti. I rolled in some typing paper and began working on tomorrow's article. I led off with the deputy's manhandling of me, slamming him hard with words the way he slammed me with his hands. It was provocative, filled with phrases like police brutality and psychopathic behavior. As angry word after angry word came pouring out, all I could think of was how pleased Bailey will be and how pissed Jensen will be.

I wrote about the Sheriff's un-cordial invitation to leave town and Bruno's drug problem kept under wraps. I also threw in Al Lewis's attempt to bribe me, in effect trying to muzzle a member of the Fourth Estate. I left out any mention of Doctor Nordstrom's involvement because, I argued to myself, this was peripheral. Maybe not, after I ask the Doctor what he knows about Bruno's addiction. In the meantime, I had no desire to question why I went soft on Nordstrom while I was hard as nails on Amundson, Jensen and Lewis, but it probably had something to do with protecting Bev.

I reread my copy before calling it in, feeling pretty good about myself, as a writer at least. I'm doing one helluva job for the Citizen Ledger, and my efforts will confirm Bailey's decision to send me to Clear Lake. The one concern I did not allow myself to ponder was that if I did too good a job I may never get back to writing about art. But right now I was so angry I didn't give a shit either way.

After reading my prose to rewrite, the adrenalin pipeline shut down and I suddenly felt exhausted, fifteen rounds in a bout with no decision. I fell back on the bed, aware only for a second or two of how much the day's events had taken out of me before I fell into a troubled sleep.

I awoke with a start, as though a cold hand had touched my shoulder, and sat up, lost for a moment as to where, or who, I was. I turned on the bed lamp and checked my watch. Six o'clock. Then I saw my typewriter on the little table and my copy sitting on top of it. Everything came back to me in a conscious flood. I began to shiver. Was it cold in the room or was I reacting to an unsettling reaction to fear, an emotion that I had managed to subsume ever since my father died.

I *am* afraid, I admitted to myself. I had rolled into Clear Lake, the big-city reporter, full of self-righteous bravado mixed with self-righteous indignation, a volatile combination for an assignment I considered beneath my station—the lofty, heady atmosphere of the refined world of art. And I proceeded to act like an anti-Semite in a Jewish cemetery.

I had bulled my way into a private home, conned a gullible woman, intimidated a teenage kid, ignored pleas and threats, and served it all up to a quarter of a million readers.

I got up and stood by the radiator under the window,

needing to warm up. The exuding heat moved up my pants and caressed my sedentary groin. I immediately thought of Bev.

I needed to talk to her, someone I could confide in, someone I could trust to keep what I said just between us. If there were something else I would like to keep just between us I did not allow myself the pleasure to think about.

"I know this is short notice," I said, after she answered on the third ring, "but these four walls are closing in on me. How about a drink and dinner?"

She hesitated. "I'd love to, Bill, but you know how hard it is finding baby sitters at the last minute."

I had completely forgotten about Tod. "I'm sorry, I should not have called on short notice." But I needed to see her so badly. "How about your father, is he home?"

"No, Dad is working late."

The doctor was always working late.

I was ready to ring off when she said, "Why not come over like you did last night? I can heat up something, that is, if you don't mind leftovers."

"Mind?" I asked, elated. "That's all I eat back home."

Leftovers to Bev were warmed leg of lamb, asparagus and oven-browned potatoes, accompanied by, to my utmost surprise, a bottle of Kourtaki retsina.

It was obvious she was waiting for my reaction.

I lifted my glass of wine and said, "Eiseihian," a Greek toast with a combination of nuanced meanings of peace, calm, gentleness and serenity.

"This dinner can't be entirely by accident, Bev."

"I haven't forgotten your Greek roots."

"You remembered the best part."

Dining was far more rewarding than the simple pleasures of excellent food. Bev placed Tod next to me in his high chair, and we carried on a brilliant conversation between mouthfuls, some of it in his private language. He knew what he was talking about even if I didn't.

Foreboding thoughts, even of impending doom, were lifted in the presence of these charming dinner companions and, after Bev put Tod to bed, I was able to tell her about my day as she and I sipped brandy in front of the fire that I had rejuvenated with a new log.

"But when I turned in my story, I felt this unnerving sense of fear as though I did something wrong and it made me feel as if I had betrayed people who trusted me."

"Do you mind if I take the position of devil's advocate? It might help you see things in a more rational light."

"Be my guest."

"Well," she said, "your ultimate responsibility is to inform your readers. You agree with me on that, don't you?"

I nodded.

"And who are readers, after all? They are the public, and the public elects government officials, including sheriffs. Every elected official is accountable to the public and if there is any question of wrongdoing, the public has a right to know."

"What about Al Lewis? He's not a public official."

"But he is a partner in Clear Lake's largest law firm. Since he is powerful and influential he needs to be held to a high standard, too."

Bev's confidence in what I was doing made me feel better. I leaned back against the sofa cushion and stretched out, the heat of the pirouetting flames warming the soles of my shoes. "There's something else." I said. "I feel an obligation to Maynard."

Bev clasped her hands and stared down at them. "I was shocked beyond words when I saw this morning's paper. It must have been awful for you to have found his body."

I nodded. "I don't know what he was mixed up in, but

his death has to be connected to everything else going on here. If I never do anything else, I have to find out who killed him."

Bev looked at me, concern clouding her eyes. "Be careful. Maynard would never have wanted you to endanger your own life."

I touched her arm to reassure her, the first time we made physical contact. It was small but it sent an electric charge through me. "I'll be careful, don't worry."

The cloudiness disappeared and her smile was like the sun coming out. "I should tell you something about Al," she said.

I thought I knew all that I needed to about him, none of which I admired. "What?"

"I dated him after you left Clear Lake. "

"You did?" I asked in surprise. Why would she tell me this unless she wanted to clear the decks in case there might be an opportunity to start over, and she wanted me to know everything that might interfere with a renewed relationship.

"We were in the same class, remember? He was available and so was I. Maybe I was on the rebound."

"Did it last long?" I had no right to ask, no right to wonder how far it went.

"Only long enough to discover that I could never spend the rest of my life with him. Dad hoped I would because he liked to see a union between two prominent families." She gave me a teasing look. "If you knew I was dating Al, what would have been your reaction?"

"I would have had a combinations of reactions."

"Such as?"

"Well, I would be stunned, hurt, jealous."

"In that order?"

"All at the same time," I said, playing along. I still could not tell if she was having fun at my expense. If she was, I deserved it. "Seriously, though, I'd have to admit

119

that I would have felt mostly guilt."

"Guilt?" she asked. "Why?"

"Oh, boy," I replied, buying time. "I've buried my feelings for so long…" I looked into the fire, the blaze a metaphor for my reignited regrets. "I abandoned you, Bev. I walked out on you, left town without so much as an apology."

The expression on her face was impossible to read. "I never expected to see you again. Ever."

I straightened. "Are you glad that you have?"

"That's a question I can't answer, Bill, at least not now, not when we haven't seen each other in years. It's almost like being on a first date. So please don't put me on the spot with that kind of speculation."

I felt sheepish. "It's not the first time."

"No, not the first time, but that doesn't mean I've held a grudge all these years. I always believed your reasons for breaking up had nothing to do with me."

"It was my father…" I began.

She looked at me sharply, her eyes as hot as the fire. "For God's sake, Bill! I hope you've matured enough to stop blaming him for your mistakes."

"I was eighteen. What did I know?"

"I was seventeen. Was I supposed to know better?"

We became silent, each of us reliving our own versions of the past. Would we be able to reconcile them?

Bev was the first to break the silence. "After your father died, I thought you'd come back. I waited and waited. But you never came." Her eyes misted over.

"I didn't think you ever wanted to see me again. I'm sorry."

"Don't apologize. Please don't apologize."

I turned to look at her. Our faces were close. "I don't know what else I can do, Bev. Help me get rid of my guilt, help me bury it deep, where it belongs."

Tears gathered in her eyes like streams approaching

flood stage. They spilled over the dikes of her lower lids, leaving trails of moisture on her cheeks as they rolled down.

Without a word more, I closed the gap separating us and kissed the moisture on her face, tasting the salt and smelling the sweetness of her skin before kissing her on her lips.

15

The teenager at the desk, whose name I finally found out was Tina, told me the name of the Clerk of Records was Alice Timmins. Two new names to remember as I drove over to the court house the morning after my evening with Bev, an evening, as it turned out, filled with promise.

That's all—promise, as in potential, nothing guaranteed but nothing closed off either. That's the way we both decided was the way to go, slowly, delicately, carefully, if we were ever to find a common path to share with each other.

Driving to the court house I purposely skirted the Sheriff's office, not relishing an accidental confrontation with Amundson, and instead parked on the north side of the nineteenth century building, away from the sun, the compromise I had to make to avoid the Sheriff, leaving the car in the brittle shade of the redoubtable pile of Kasota limestone that housed the Records of the County of Clear Lake.

The office was on the lower level. I walked down a wide staircase of worn granite steps, its wrought iron railings finely turned with fleur-de-lis patterns. Pink granite graced the floors and walls. The arched hallway was too ornate for modern tastes but no doubt considered the latest design in its day. The courthouse was one big work of art. No one took the time to build like this anymore.

I opened a pebbled glass door with a sign that read Clerk of Records and entered what resembled a library but not for ordinary books—behind a high counter were shelves filled with tall, vertically stacked volumes with gold numbers intaglio-ed on their spines.

The clerk was standing behind the counter. She was old, probably close to retirement. A dainty silver chain connected the ear stems of her glasses so she could hang them from her neck. They were on her nose now as she perused one of those volumes. She was not much bigger than the book she was reading and I wondered how she managed to lift it.

"I wish they used better ink in those days," she grumbled, looking up at me. She slammed the book shut and a plume of dust almost shrouded her.

She appeared like the type of woman who keeps the same job for forty years, takes care of her mother, never marries, and still maintains a sense of humor. I took an instant liking to her.

"Alice Timmins?"

She smiled, nodding. "What can I do for you young man?"

"I need some information."

"You're new here, aren't you?"

"Yes and no. I grew up in Clear Lake but I moved away twenty years ago."

"Then we just missed each other. I came here from Albert Lea eighteen years ago after my mother died."

I smiled to myself. My assessment of Alice Timmins was pretty close. "My name is Bill Kouros. I'm a reporter for the Minneapolis Citizen Ledger."

She peered at me through her glasses. "So you're the one who found poor Maynard."

I nodded.

"Sad state of affairs," she muttered, "First that farmer and now Maynard. I should move back to Albert Lea. It isn't safe here anymore. Yesterday I did something I've never done before."

"What's that?"

"Locked my door. There is fear, real fear."

I tried to reassure her, not that I really thought it was true: "Sheriff Amundson will take care of you."

She stared at me as if I were a salesman who did not know the territory. "Don't quote me, but he's one of the reasons why I'm scared. For a sheriff he'd make a good dog catcher."

"Really?" I said, surprised by her candor. "Did you read my article about him?"

"Oh, I read it all right but I already had that opinion, and I'm not the only one either. The whole town thinks he's grown fat on the job. He's become a fixture, a figurehead, strutting around like he owns the place. And that deputy of his...." She moved her head back and forth in disdain. "I shouldn't be talking like this, it isn't Christian, but working here in the courthouse, in the same building as the Sheriff, well, you see and hear things and it isn't right. I found out today that he's going to have some competition from the St. Paul Crime Bureau. They're sending down an investigator, and Sheriff Amundson doesn't like anyone interfering in his business."

"I learned that the hard way."

"After reading your article, I'm not surprised. You better watch your back, young man."

Her comment sent an inadvertent chill through me.

She sensed my discomfort. "I guess I've said too much."

I was going to tell her that she was giving me information a reporter drools over when the door opened behind me. A man came in. "Got the size of plat sixteen for me yet?"

"Right here, Herb." Miss Timmins tore off the top sheet of a note pad with some figures written on it and handed it to him. Herb left, closing the door behind him. The interruption broke the privacy we were sharing, and I knew it was over as far as insider talk was concerned.

"Now," she said, her manner becoming professional, "you said you needed some information?"

"Yes," I replied. "I wonder if you can tell me who owns the farm where Alfred Schultzman lived. I understand he rented it from someone." I waited for a response and when I didn't get it I added, "I believe it is public information, isn't it?"

"Well, Mr. Kouros, public, yes, but I'd normally ask for a writ before making it available to a stranger, someone who isn't a local realtor or a tax assessor." She became thoughtful a moment. "I wonder why Sheriff Amundson hasn't been here. I'm just down the hall and a floor down. It's part of his job isn't it, checking out clues? Why should he leave it to a reporter? Serves him right if I help you."

She went to the stack of tall books and walked down the line, stopped and pulled a book out.

"Need help with that?"

"No," she grunted, "I do it all day." She dropped the book on the counter and opened it, turning musty pages, some of them yellower then others.

"Nobody looks at these too often do they?"

"Nope. Once you make an entry it might not be looked at again for a hundred years."

"How did you get into this business?"

"Process of elimination, Mr. Kouros. I wanted to be a school librarian but the Depression stopped my education. So I took a civil service exam and ended up doing this. A secure job is what women of my generation were looking for."

She stopped talking and checked a handwritten entry executed in the Palmer Method.

"Here we are."

"What have you got?"

"That's interesting," she said, and turned the volume around so I could see the line she was pointing to.

There was the legal description of the property, a series of tax stamps pasted alongside the entry, and something else.

"What does 'For one Dollar and Other Valuable Considerations' mean?" I asked.

"It means that the person who bought the property doesn't want anyone to know how much he paid for it. Not unusual, but it's a bit odd, don't you think, because of the murder. A clue, maybe?"

"Could be," I said. "And it doesn't list the owner?"

"Nope. But it lists the former owner."

"Who was that?"

"A man named Ed Fischer, with a c. He died last year. The farm was part of his estate."

"When was that?"

" June 25th."

I wrote this down on my pad.

"Wouldn't Schultzman have signed a lease from the owner? Would you have a record of that?"

"That would be between the lessee and the lessor."

"I guess I've drawn a blank."

It was clear she was also disappointed. She really did want to help me. "If you got a court order, then you'd know everything: who bought the farm, how much it sold for, taxes, mortgage, liens, everything."

"The Sheriff could do that."

"Sure," she said, "if only he'd get off his butt."

I wasn't going to wait for Amundson to do that.

16

The sun was in my eyes when I drove to the Cozy Corner for lunch, the bright light crackled into a million bits as it refracted through the pitted glass of the windshield, forcing me to lower the visor. The light was comforting, though, a portend of longer days and warmer temps or, as Percy Bysshe Shelley once put it much more elegantly, if winter comes can spring be far behind? It was the only line of iambic pentameter I could recall from a tough course on Romantic poets I took as an elective way back in my days as a student at the University of Minnesota.

Speaking of education, Tina must have gone to school when I returned to the hotel. A tall thin man had replaced her at the desk, the owner probably. He cast a wary eye at me as I walked past him to the stairway. I had the sense that I was fast becoming persona non grata in Clear Lake.

Once in my room, I sat on the bed and placed a call to the CL. Bailey was waiting for me like an angler for a fish.

"Why the hell haven't you called me?"

"I've been doing the paper's work, following up a lead. Want to hear about it?"

"Talk, it's your nickel."

"First, I need a court order."

"Court order? What for? Are you in trouble?"

"Depends on who you talk to."

That didn't seem to worry him. "So why do you need a court order?"

"I want to find out who owns the Schultzman farm. He only leased it. It might lead to something or it might not, but it will add up to a story in any case."

"I like it. So who's the municipal judge down there?"

"How should I know? I'm an art critic, remember?"

"That was the day before yesterday."

"What is that supposed to mean?"

"I'm reassigning you to investigative reporting."

"You *what*?"

"You're doing too good a job to write artsy-fartsy reviews any longer."

It was as if Bailey had punched me in the solar plexus while I was looking at the moon.

"That's what I do!" I shouted. "That's what I've always done! Art is all I know about! I'm not trained to be an investigative reporter! The only reason I'm having any luck is because I grew up here—that's why you sent me down, remember? Because, as Brewster said, I have contacts here no one else would have. If you think I can go to a town where nobody knows me and get the same results, you're crazy! You can stuff this assignment, Bailey. I've had it! I'm driving home right now!"

"Calm down, will you? Shut up and listen to me. You've created a major story all by yourself, and it's given you excitement and a sense of accomplishment you could not possibly match in an art gallery. You're on page one. When was the last time that happened? Never. Promotion has even redesigned the Sunday wrapper so that your story is featured. Ever get that from the arts page? No. You are a digger, you are persistent, you love the action. Are you going to throw this away before you finish?"

"Not only that," he continued without letting me get a

word in, "I read your Sunday piece and it's terrific. That damned Sheriff will never get reelected. And that fat-cat fat lawyer could lose his license to practice for shielding a drug addict in his house when he should have turned him in. You're doing top-notch work, Bill. You are a true professional. And your professionalism will not let you leave until that last story is written."

He had me there, and he knew it.

"I'll get your court order, ok? And keep digging, ok?"

"What about the opening at Walker?" I asked, making one last stab at saving my one true love: art.

"You mean that new show in town?"

He knew what I was talking about. "Yeah, Pop Goes the Easel. We talked about it, remember? The opening I was supposed to go to?"

"Oh, that. I've got it covered."

"The only person capable of covering an art exhibition is Tom Lawrence." Lawrence was the CL's drama critic. "I know he's going to the opening Saturday night of 'The Italian Straw Hat' at the Guthrie." The Walker Art Center and the Guthrie Theatre shared a common lobby on Vineland Place. This symbiotic relationship flowed over into news coverage and Lawrence and I would sub for one another when one of us was on vacation or was sick.

"I know about his assignment. I'm the City Editor, aren't I?"

"So who else is qualified to review the show? You hired a freelancer?"

"No, I'm doing it."

"*You*?" I tightened my grip on the receiver so hard my knuckles turned white. "You have to be kidding, Bailey! You think you are capable of writing a review of a major art show?"

"About soup cans? Who does those by the way?"

"Andy Warhol."

"And the cartoons?"

"Roy Lichtenstein."

"And those canvas French fries that hang from the ceiling?"

"They are not French fries. They are shoestring potatoes."

"Whatever. Some Swede, right?"

"Claes Oldenburg. He was born in Sweden but grew up in Chicago."

"So who needs a degree in art history to write about soup cans, cartoons and shoestring potatoes?"

"Bailey, you just don't brush off a major art movement without some idea of why it happened. What were the influences behind Pop Art? Twentieth century art isms are as reactive as they are original. Those guys reintroduced imagery after writing off the great decade of the fifty's misfits, the Abstract Expressionist gesture painters and color field painters, the most important art movement in the 20th century, by the way. Warhol, Lichtenstein and Oldenburg rejected the whole notion of non-representation and brought back the real world, but they did not return to conventional subject matter like flowers or landscapes. They chose instead common everyday references of our time like advertising, commercial art, television, billboards. Look at the giant work of Jim Rosenquist, a Minnesota sign painter by the way."

"Slow down, did you say his name is Rosenquist?"

"Yeah, why?"

"I'm jotting this down. You've given me the background you said I needed for the review. Thanks for helping me out."

I let out a long sigh of defeat. "You are a bastard,"

"Stop complimenting me, and remember why you called in the first place. You want a court order, right? I'll get our legal department on it right away. I'm sure we can find out whom a Clear Lake judge owes a favor to. And one more thing. A photographer is on his way down."

"Who?"

I could hear paper being shuffled on Bailey's desk. "Don Wright. He should be there around dinnertime."

"Tell him to eat first."

"Why?"

"There's no dinner service at the hotel."

I had to admit that Bailey was right. He knew I wouldn't walk away from an assignment. However, like the philosopher who said that revenge is better when eaten cold, I will wait for Bailey to make an ass of himself when his review of the Pop Art show is published.

So I spent the rest of the afternoon in my room working on a follow-up think piece, reviewing what I learned so far and trying to put it into a larger context, the possibility that a small town 85 miles from Minneapolis had been infested with drugs. No longer an urban issue, addiction had spread across the rural landscape finding vulnerable people like Bruno Schultzman, feeding his habit and raising the ugly head of crime. I posed the question of a connection between drugs and murder. Was Bruno's father complicit in providing the money Bruno needed to feed his habit, and was killed because he reneged payment, or was he going to expose the name of his supplier? Could that be why Maynard was murdered? He had a name imprinted on a little piece of lead that disappeared. He must have known something incriminating. Newsmen by their very nature have their ears to the ground, that's their professional habit. Whose name was on that fifth slug? And was Maynard killed for it, knowing that, if I got my hands on the name, it would go public?

Presumptions, only presumptions, but at least they provided deep background to my earlier reports.

I laid my typewritten sheets on the table next to the typewriter, stood and stretched. Darkness began laying its blanket over Clear Lake and I turned the lamp on. I went to the window and looked out at the gathering twilight, enervated not only by the day's events but also by the intense effort it takes to write, especially when you are so personally involved.

I fell into a kind of self-induced trance as though the pressure on my mind was too great and I had to let go of everything rational. I allowed my thoughts to wander like a dog off its leash and, instead of seeing the bleak landscape beyond the pane, I saw my reflection in the glass, becoming more distinct as it got darker outside. Like an out-of-body experience I saw myself as an easy target for an assassin, the hairlines of his telescopic sight crisscrossed on my heart.

I was now in full panic. Someone across the alley was drawing a bead on me! I jumped to one side, leaped across the bed to the opposite wall and hugged my back to it.

Slowly I slid my arm along the wall, reached out and pulled the window shade down, fully expecting to hear shattering glass and feel the stinging pain of a rifle bullet tearing through the bone and cartilage of my hand.

But nothing happened. Of course nothing happened. Breathing heavily, my heart pounding like a pile driver, I sagged down on the bed.

"Easy," I said out loud between gasps of breaths, "take it easy. There is nothing going on. Your imagination is working overtime, that's all."

After a dash of cold water on my face and a stern lecture at the reflection in the bathroom mirror, I went downstairs to watch the six o'clock news on the lobby television while waiting for Don Wright to show up. Tina was back at her post reading a textbook. We were the only ones around.

I was in the middle of Bud Kraehling's bleak weather forecast, during which he warned viewers to carry survival gear in their cars just in case. An involuntary shudder coursed through me as he read off the lows for the weekend.

The switchboard telephone rang and I heard Tina answering in the cheery, optimistic voice owned by teenage kids still unaware of the rude awakening that comes with adulthood.

She called to me, "Mr. Kouros, telephone for you."

I looked up, surprised. No one has called me at the hotel. Wonder who that was? Bailey again, wanting more insight into Pop Art, or Don Wright calling to tell me it was too cold and he'd drive down in the morning.

"You can take it on the lobby phone." Tina said, pointing to an alcove under the stairwell.

I hadn't even bothered to notice it before. I picked up the receiver.

"Hello?" I said casually.

"Bill, it's me, Bev."

The edge in her voice, the sense of concern and uncertainty crept through the wire. "What is it?" I asked, on full alert.

"Something strange has happened."

"What? What's the matter? Are you all right? Is it Tod?"

"Bill, please, slow down. Everyone is ok. But something strange happened. Someone tried to run down Dad."

"Your Dad?" I repeated. "Is he all right?"

"Yes, a little shaken but that's all."

Has Clear Lake gone mad? "Where did this happen?"

"He was coming home from the clinic, you know it's within walking distance, that's why he usually goes back after dinner. He was nearly home, crossing the street in front of the house when a car came around the corner and headed right for him."

"Jesus," I muttered.

"Thank heaven he was nearly across. He jumped over the snow bank just as the car came at him. The car hit the snow bank and bounced off. The snow is frozen hard from plowing and Dad thinks the car suffered some damage, maybe a dented fender. I heard the noise. I thought, oh-oh an accident, not knowing Dad was involved and I went to the window. I saw him standing on the sidewalk looking at the receding taillights."

"Could he tell anything about the car—the make, license number, anything at all?"

"All Dad remembers is that it was big and new."

"How could he tell if it was new?"

"He said it was shiny like a new car."

"How is he?"

"He had a stiff drink and went upstairs. I think he's in bed now. He's very reserved, you know, even stoical. Ever since Mom died he has kept his feelings to himself. If he was scared he didn't show it, but I'm sure he was."

"Maybe you should call the Sheriff."

"I asked dad if I should but he said not to bother, that it was probably a drunk who lost control of his car, got scared and drove away."

"If it's a hit and run, then the Sheriff should know about it."

"Maybe tomorrow, not now."

"Ok."

There was a moment of silence. Then she said, "It happened so fast, Bill, it was so unexpected. Why would anyone want to hurt my father?" By asking the question, she let go of her self-control and began sobbing.

"I should come over," I said.

"No," she said, recovering. "I'm all right. I just needed to talk to someone I can trust, someone I can..." she hesitated, "... someone I can depend on."

I felt light years better hearing her say that. "Thanks," I said, "that means a lot."

"Bill, I am so glad you're back."

"Me, too," I replied. "All these years we were apart—I never stopped thinking about you."

"I hope…" she began."

"Hope what?"

She didn't answer my question. Instead I heard her blow her nose and when she spoke again she was back in control. "I feel a lot better now, having talked to you. When you're sitting alone in your living room you tend to get all sorts of weird ideas and think the worst."

Substitute living room for hotel room and I couldn't agree with her more—except, of course, that her reaction was from an actual event while mine was from paranoia.

I rang off, saying something as mundane as "I'll keep in touch" when so much was left hanging in the balance, especially her unfinished sentence: "I hope…" I hope what?

I hope you come back into my life, I hope you are still in love with me, I hope you never leave…

17

I paced the lobby, Tina periodically looking up from her book but saying nothing. It hit me that I hadn't eaten since breakfast and part of my anxious state had to do with lack of nourishment. Ok, I'll go out, warm up the car, grab a bite at the Cozy Corner, get some gas and come back to sit down with Don and talk about what to photograph.

What indeed should he take pictures of? Al's house, behind whose windows a drug addict lurks? No, people, of course: Al himself, Mrs. Annandale, Bruno, the Sheriff, Jensen. Like being on assignment for Confidential Magazine, taking candid photos of people walking down the street, climbing out of their cars, leaving their houses-- everyone angry as hell that some photographer was stalking them. Another bad idea of Bailey's—sending a photographer. Something more to worry about.

"Tina," I said on my way upstairs, "I'm expecting a guy named Don Wright to check in tonight. He'll be lugging camera equipment. Tell him I'll be back in an hour."

The reference to camera equipment really perked up her ears. It will probably be all over town before bedtime.

I heeded Kraehling's advice to be in survival mode. I tied my scarf so I could lift it over my nose, and pulled my hat down over my forehead, turning my eyes into slits, and left for dinner.

At night The Cozy Corner, as it turned out, was indeed cozy, not too many customers and those who were there paid no heed to the person bundled up like a freezer package.

Eating a hamburger and fries gave me the down time I needed to reflect on the news that someone tried to run down Bev's father. If this were an isolated incident one could argue that this was an accident but, following two murders, this was clearly no accident. Doc Nordstrom described the car as big, new and shiny.

It was a long shot but worth warming up my own car for and so after dinner I drove over to Maynard's printing plant, turning into the alley where I first saw the Toronado Trofeo. My headlights cleared out the darkness ahead of me. The big Olds was gone, proving nothing except that the forensics people completed their investigation and released the car. It was probably sitting in Maynard's garage, driven home by one of the officers or by Rose herself.

It made me wonder how she was doing. Well, first things first. I drove over to Maynard's house, not to pay my respects to the widow but rather to sneak into her garage and take a look at that Olds she had inherited.

I parked down the street, cut the engine and took my flashlight from the glove box.

I'd been to Maynard's house so often as a kid that I could drive there with my eyes shut. He lived on a modest street, not far from the railroad tracks on the south side of town. The house had old-fashioned clapboard siding and storm windows with four panes instead of two. A shed-like addition in the twenties brought the bathroom into the house. The garage was built for a Model T and I wondered how in hell anyone could park a Toronado in there and, if you could, how in hell could you climb out of it?

The old-fashioned accordion fold doors were locked. I walked around to the side and tried the access door that had a small window. That too was locked. I looked at the familiar house behind me. Dark. Rose was either asleep already or she wasn't even home. I'd find out soon enough if the car was not in the garage. I brought my flashlight butt down on the windowpane and the glass shattered with a sound that, in this crisp air, could be heard in Nova Scotia. I waited, breathing frigid air, but nothing happened. Stillness prevailed. The houses were sealed against cold and thereby sealed against sound.

I reached through the broken pane until my gloved fingers found the knob. It turned with a series of rusty snaps. I opened the door and played a flashlight beam on the car beside me. I stared in surprise. It was a Dodge, a '55 or '56 Custom Royal Lancer, rusted, paint-faded, the front and rear axles resting on cement blocks—an old bucket stored for the winter.

I snapped off my flashlight and got out of there, puzzled at first and then it came to me. Maynard had moved. I laughed at my naïve assumption that he still lived in the same house he lived in twenty years ago.

I got back in the car and pulled into a Pure Oil station for a fill-up and a check of the telephone directory. It was nice to thaw out for a few minutes while looking up Maynard's home address. Just as I thought, he had gone upscale; his home was on Lake Shore Drive in one of those new developments I was complaining about.

A far cry from the South side.

Maynard's new house was a spread-out rambler in brick with fieldstone accents under the windows and wrought iron ornamentation along a narrow front porch. There was an attached, two-and-a-half car garage at one

141

end that made the house seem as long as a skyscraper lying on its side.

First I drove past the house to identify it as Maynard's, then parked down the road next to the original marsh, and walked back about a half a block with my flashlight in my overcoat pocket.

Again, a house with no lights but, this time, no neighbors close by either. The house was on an acre lot at least, plenty of privacy to engage in nefarious activity. Boy oh boy, I thought, if Sheriff Amundson could see me now, attempting a break-and-enter, his prophecy coming true: jail time for sure.

Then another scary thought gripped me. In a fancy neighborhood like this you'd expect a burglar alarm, wouldn't you?

Stymied, I walked back to the car to think it over. I started the engine and put my feet close to the heater. I opened the glove box to put the flashlight away, pushing the garage door opener aside to make room for it. As I stared at the opener, which came with the parking space in my apartment building, another far out, improbable scheme came to me.

What the hell, it would only cost another short walk in the cold air. I took the opener along with my flashlight and hiked back to Maynard's garage, my footsteps making grinding noises in the snow.

Sometimes a phantom radio wave opened the door in my building from a Northwest jet on its approach over South Minneapolis or, irritatingly, some kid without enough to keep him busy, driving through the neighborhood continually pressing his opener to see how many doors he could raise. There aren't that many remote control frequencies and so duplication is inevitable.

Maybe Maynard's garage door would answer my signal. As random as the idea was, it was worth a try. I pointed my Telectron and pushed the button, hoping to hear that whir of an activated electric motor and see the door begin to rise. Nothing. I pressed again. Still nothing. I got right up to the door and pressed one more time, unwilling to accept the fact that my plan was as stillborn as the frozen air around me. And why should I have expected anything else? There was one chance in a hundred it might work.

My breath coming in cold heaves, I grabbed the horizontal lift handle and gave it a frustrated jerk. Incredibly the door moved, not much, but enough to make me pull some more. The pulling was hard, apparently because I was overcoming the resistance of the mechanical system inside, but the door continued its slow upward climb. I briefly wondered why the door moved at all but, knowing next to nothing about garage door systems, I gave this no further thought as I relished my small victory of man over machine. I got the door just high enough to scrooch under and crawl inside. Then I pushed the door back down and turned on my flashlight. As I waited for a possible reaction to my illegal entry I realized the garage was heated. With this impressive layout why would it be any other way?

I used my flashlight to find the switch, and the bulb over my head came on, revealing the Trofeo parked between the far wall and an expansive collection of landscape equipment stored for winter. I clicked on my flashlight and walked over to the car, touching the hood. Warm. In the silence I heard occasional drips of crankcase oil. The car had been driven recently. I followed my light beam around the three tons of metal. Front end looked good, side panels ok. I finally reached the car's extended rear deck, it was a long walk, and then I spotted a heavy crease and a line of deep scratches on the rear fender that could be the result of hitting a frozen snow bank. The damage was severe enough to spring the trunk lid.

The car had been in an accident, all right, a hit and

run accident. I was sorrowful thinking of Rose behind the wheel intent on striking down Dr. Nordstrom.

But why? Why would she have tried to kill him? Did she suspect him of Maynard's murder? I shook my head. How could Dr. Nordstrom have had anything to do with the horrible way Maynard died?

None of this made sense.

I still did not want to believe that she was behind the wheel. What if someone had stolen the vehicle out of the parking space behind the plant and went on a joyride, almost hitting Dr. Nordstrom? Possible, but plausible? Doubtful.

I tried the driver's side door. Locked. Then I flashed my light through the upraised windows and checked the seats, instrument panel, center console, floors, rear window deck. Nothing. Spotless.

The popped trunk lid intrigued me and I pushed it up. A tiny light flashed on, illuminating the huge space. A family could live in here.

The spare tire was in a deep well at the front of the compartment. The wing nut that secured the hold-down rod was missing. and the tire was hanging loose. Why would anyone need to get to the spare on a new car? I examined the dark recesses with the flashlight looking for the nut but didn't find it. The spare must have been removed and in the process the nut fell out. So I checked the concrete floor. Nothing.

The tire was a J78-16, one of the biggest this side of an 18-wheeler, and the treads were clean. So why remove a spare if you are not going to use it?

Puzzled, I pointed my flashlight at one of the holes circling the chrome rim and leaned in for a closer look. There was a piece of cloth behind the tire, like a cleaning rag. I pulled the tire out and let it fall to the floor where it bounced a couple of times and then I leaned it against the bumper. I reached for the rag, it was heavy. Something was wrapped inside it. As I pulled it out I discovered that it was not a rag but a pair of denim coveralls. They felt greasy. I spread the coveralls open on the trunk deck and shone my light on what I uncovered, a crow bar with notched ends, one curved up like a claw. On the larger end was an encrustation as if had been dipped in paint and left to dry. I bent in for a closer look, doing my best to keep from throwing up. The dried matter was burgundy in color and what appeared to be matted hair stuck to it. I drew back in horror.

I had found the weapon that killed Alfred Schultzman.

18

I was so rattled when I got back to my car I forgot for a moment where I was, some dark road bordered on one side by a frozen marsh and on the other a frozen lake. I cranked the starter and let the car warm me, both body and soul, until my thought process returned to normal. But what is normal after all? Finding a murder weapon is normal?

At least I had the forethought not to touch the crow bar. I refolded it into the coveralls and tucked the package back into the tire well, and then replaced the tire as I had originally found it, hanging free of its hold-down rod.

Now what? I asked myself, putting my car in gear and driving around the lake at a crawl. Call the Sheriff and tell him what I found? That's what a normal reaction would be but, again, what the hell is normal?

What I really wanted to do was see Bev, talk to her about what I found, get her input and her support. That's what I needed more than anything, her support. I drove past her house and saw the living room lights on. It wasn't that late, just after ten.

I parked, walked up to the house and used the doorknocker rather than the bell, feeling somehow that this was less intrusive, and more likely that Bev would answer the door rather than her father.

I was right, for once this evening I was right.

"I decided to drop over," I said when she cracked open the door and looked at me questioningly but not reproachfully.

"You needn't have. We're ok, really. Dad is upstairs and Tod is fast asleep. I was reading." She widened the opening, implying an invitation to come in.

I took advantage of it and stepped inside.

She checked out my appearance, as huddled as a hibernating bear. "I think you could use a hot brandy," she said.

I couldn't agree more. I dropped my cold weather stuff over the stair railing and followed her into the kitchen where she boiled water.

I watched her pour the steaming liquid into two mugs laced with brandy, and then drop in cinnamon sticks.

We touched our mugs in a silent toast or as a symbol of a further connection between us, I don't know which, maybe both. We walked into the living room and sat on the sofa. The fire in the fireplace had gone out.

"Did you close the damper?" I asked, sipping my brandy. It was astonishingly good and equally therapeutic.

"Yes, I did," she said and turned toward me, one leg tucked under the other. "I feel responsible for dragging you out in this terrible weather."

"I was out anyway."

She stared at me quizzically.

"I followed up a hunch after you told me your dad described the car as new and shiny. It sounded exactly like Maynard's Toronado. So I checked out the Sorenson garage. The car was damaged all right, the left rear fender was dented."

I went on to explain how I got into the garage. But I didn't yet tell her what I found in the trunk. One unbelievable revelation at a time.

"What you did was dangerous, Bill. You can get into

148

serious trouble." She sighed. "I wish you hadn't done this. It was so foolhardy. And what does it do for anyone? It just tears the town apart even more."

"Don't you want to find out who tried to run down your father?"

"I don't know," she replied. "I just want everything to go away."

"It won't go away, Bev, not until we find out who is behind all of this."

"Are you suggesting Rose tried to run down my Dad?"

"All I'm saying is that someone driving Maynard's Toronado tried to hit your father. Whether it was Rose behind the wheel I don't know."

"Maybe it was damaged somewhere else. A dented car doesn't prove anything."

I was surprised how defensive she was. I had expected her to be more, well, supportive.

"No, it doesn't, but that's not all."

"What's not all?"

It was time to tell her about the murder weapon. "I found something in the trunk, a crow bar hidden behind the spare. It was wrapped in a pair of coveralls."

She stared at me expectantly.

"The crow bar was covered with dried blood and matted hair."

"Oh my god."

"I'm sure forensics can prove that this is the weapon that killed Alfred Schultzman. Now do you believe me?"

Bev sipped her brandy, not so much to taste it but to keep from having to answer me. Eventually she spoke up.

"I thought you were a reporter, not a detective."

"Why can't I be both?"

"It doesn't suit you, Bill, snooping around like this."

"Snooping? Is that the thanks I get?"

"You want me to thank you for finding something awful like that?"

"It is the murder weapon."

"That is information I can do without."

"Sorry. I thought you'd want to know."

"Bill, what in the world has come over you?"

I looked at her. "What do you mean?"

"You have some kind of messianic zeal that is truly baffling. You seem to be driven, as though you have a score to settle. Why are you acting like this?"

Although her words stung, I secretly liked being scolded by her. It showed that she cared. "I have an obligation to my readers."

"To do what? Solve the crime? That's not part of your job description, is it?"

"My job description is to get a good story. That's why I was sent here. And when I get the putdowns and rebuffs I've been getting, it makes me angry, just like my old man telling me…"

Bev put her mug down hard on the coffee table. "Back to your father again? Everything goes back to him, doesn't it? Someday you are going to have to learn that your father is not a ghost and he can't hurt you any more."

She was right. When Jensen came after me, when Amundson threatened me, when Lewis tried to bribe me, all I could see through my anger was my old man standing in their places.

I fell back against the sofa cushion and sighed.

Bev softened her stare. "I'm sorry for being so critical, Bill, but I just don't want to see you, any of us, get hurt."

"We won't be."

"I'm not so sure. You travel on a fast track."

"What if I slow down?"

She laughed. "You'll have to slow down an awful lot for me to catch up with you."

"Hey, we're not that different," I said, realizing that she was not talking about my covering the murders anymore; she was talking about how the intervening years had separated us. To her I was in the Big Time, working for a metropolitan daily and socializing with artists and curators while she still thought of herself as a small-town woman.

"We are different," she said.

"That's not true, Bev. Something about me hasn't changed at all."

"What is that?"

"Can't you tell? I still feel the same way about you. That hasn't changed and it never will."

She turned away from me. I rubbed her back, feeling her spinal column and her shoulder blades under the woolly fabric of her sweater.

"God, Bill," she said, her voice coming from a seemingly great distance. "How can we make up twenty years in just one night?"

"Not in one night. We'll start over, a new beginning for both of us. We'll be in the same place as if we met each other for the first time. I won't have to slow down and you won't have to catch up."

"You think that's possible?"

I took her gently by the shoulders and turned her to face me again. "I know it's possible because I still love you."

She let me kiss her.

Bev went into the kitchen to refill our mugs. I've been given another chance, I was thinking, and this time I won't blow it.

When she resettled on the sofa, she said, "I was thinking it over, and I realize I overreacted. Not wanting to hear the truth doesn't mean it will go away. If you want to talk about it now I'll listen." She sipped from her fresh brandy as though drawing strength from it.

"Thanks, Bev. I really need to share this with you. All I have to go on is what I saw. The car had a dented fender and the engine was still warm enough."

"Did you see Rose?"

"The house was dark. I left right away."

"I still can't believe she was driving the car. It could be someone else."

"I suppose so, but who?"

She shook her head. "I don't know, but if it was Rose why would she want to hurt Dad?" Bev looked sharply at me. "Do you think he could be mixed up in this?"

I couldn't answer her truthfully because that's exactly what I was thinking, was Dr. Nordstrom mixed up in this? Not criminally, but maybe he knew something and the near-accident was meant to warn him, not to hurt or kill him. Expressing this out loud would only serve to worry Bev further and possibly drive her away from me again. I was walking a tightrope, all right.

"Rose has been under so much stress who knows what crazy things have been going through her mind? We have to give her the benefit of the doubt. Maybe she was driving around, confused, distracted, and she happened to be driving down the street just when your father was crossing it."

"But what about that tool you found in the trunk, what you said was the murder weapon?"

"The crow bar."

"What if someone planted it in the trunk to incriminate Maynard, or even Rose?"

"That is a real possibility. But, as much as I respected Maynard, I still question his lifestyle—that new car, the remodeled store, the expensive house he was living in. There's not that much profit running a weekly newspaper."

"Then how did he get the money?"

"I think Bruno might be the answer to that."

"You mean drugs? Could Maynard have been involved in something like that?"

"I don't know." I leaned forward. "I spend a lot of time looking at abstract art, trying to analyze it, searching for the artist's motive, if I can use that word. Abstract art by its nature is waiting to be solved, like a crime. Art used to be pictorial—you looked at a painting and marveled at the artist's skill at reproducing nature. But pioneers like Cezanne and Picasso changed all that when they began to break down familiar objects and codified them into symbols and shapes. They essentially opened the twentieth century to a whole litany of artistic movements: Cubism, Fauvism, Futurism, Dada, Constructivism, Surrealism, Abstract Expressionism, Pop Art, and the latest development called Minimalism or Conceptualism."

"The last one doesn't sound like art at all."

"In a way it isn't, because Minimalism negates the traditional ways of making art, and leaves the artist out of the creative process altogether except providing the idea or concept and having someone else, such as a fabricator, make the art."

"I didn't mean to get you started." Bev said, smiling. "But what has this art history lesson, which I find fascinating by the way, what has any of this to do with a crow bar—about as far away as you can get from art."

I smiled back. "Not if you ask Jim Dine."

"Who's he?"

"An artist who uses items found in a hardware store, yes, even a crow bar. So everything is fair game in the art world. "

"It certainly sounds like it."

"But I keep wondering about that crow bar. It's a tool, not a murder weapon, not unless the killer never expected to use it that way in the first place. Maybe Schultzman surprised him. The crow bar was already in his hand and he brought Schultzman down with it."

"Now you sound more like a detective than an art critic."

"Modern art forces me see things analytically, and that is what I'm trying to do with that damned tool. What is a crow bar used for? Not to build something but to take something apart, right? To pry something open, like a piece of flooring, a tread on a stair, trim around a window or a door. What if the murderer was looking for something in the house and Schultzman saw him?"

"Like drugs?"

"Yes, hidden in the farm house."

"Do you think it was found?"

"No way to know unless we search the place." I slumped back "I'd give a week's pay to check that farm out."

"Let the Sheriff search the farm. He *gets* a week's pay for it."

I laughed wryly. "Sheriff Amundson would not be happy if he knew what I've done tonight."

"I wouldn't be surprised, but he probably never would have found the murder weapon."

"That's the irony, isn't it? I do a better job being Sheriff than he does."

"But he has to get a warrant and follow procedures. You, well, you just go and do it." She looked at me scoldingly. "You have to tell him what you've done."

"Not yet. I want to search that farm first."

Bev shook her head in frustration. "First you break into a garage and now you want to break into a farm house where someone was murdered. It's insane..."

"But, Bev, don't you see? Right now is the perfect time. Dead of night."

The look on her face made me realize this was not the best choice of words.

"It's the only time. If I don't do it now, it will be too late. Amundson told me the forensic work has been done and there is no one guarding the place. The only problem is finding it. I don't know where it is." I threw up my hands in frustration. "Do you know how to get there?"

"County 43, north of town. After the murder, Dad and I

drove out there. Like most people in Clear Lake we were fascinated and wanted to see the scene of the crime. There was a carnival atmosphere, so many people walking around. I'm sure we didn't make it any easier for the Sheriff."

I couldn't have cared less. "Can you draw me a map?"

"It's not the same as finding an address in town, Bill. A farmhouse is at the end of a private road, sometimes half a mile long. You can't see it from the highway. People use reference points like a tree, or a telephone pole or a fence."

"Shit," I said, frustrated.

"You really want to go there, don't you?"

"Of course I do. Think of the story I'd have."

An aura of compassion came over her. "Bill, you really are a reporter. It's in your blood. It's your passion."

I nodded. "I never thought that way until now. It's as if I have to prove myself."

"You've always been that way."

"Maybe so…"

"It's not a bad fault, to be like this, I mean. If you want to get anywhere in life you have to want it. My dad is like that. We would not have a clinic in Clear Lake without him."

She became pensive a moment. "Everett was like that, too."

I looked at her. There was so much about Bev's life I knew nothing about. "Tell me about him…where did you meet?"

"At a party. Ev moved here to work for EF Johnson after he got a degree in Electrical Engineering from the University of Wisconsin."

"Did you know that EF Johnson started out as an appliance repair shop right next to my dad's restaurant?"

"I remember. The company really grew making CB radios for the war. Ev worked in R and D and helped develop the Clear Channel LTR System. I don't know much about it except that it helped expand two-way radio technology. Ev had joined the Air National Guard in college and learned to fly helicopters. When the Vietnam war started he went on active duty. A year later he was dead, caught in a firefight rescuing some wounded infantry. I was carrying Tod when it happened."

"I'm sorry."

"I'm not the only war widow."

"You are the only one I know."

Bev looked at me. "Ev would have liked you, what you stand for, your determination, the way you challenge the status quo, looking for answers, righting wrongs."

"I think I would have liked Ev as well," I said

"You know what, Bill?"

"What?"

"I'll go to the farm with you. You can't go alone, you'd never find it."

"Really?" I said, both surprised and relieved.

"I have a vested interest now. Dad was nearly run down. I suppose I should stand up and be counted the same as everyone else."

"Are you sure?"

"Yes, I'm sure."

19

"What did you tell your father?" I asked as we drove out of town on County 43, heading for the Schultzman farm.

Bev had nearly emptied her hall closet dressing for the cold, donning a fur-lined parka, knee boots, a long nubby scarf that she wrapped twice around her neck, and a tasseled ski hat. On her hands she wore woolen-lined mittens. She carried with her an extra flashlight.

"I told him we were going to the Lake Club for a drink and maybe dance for awhile."

"What did he say?"

"He was fine with it. He says I spend too much time alone. He wants me to go out more."

"Even with me?"

She didn't answer.

"I wasn't sure how he would react when he saw me again."

"Dad wants me to be happy."

We drove the rest of the way in silence except when she gave me directions. It was pitch black, the only light coming from my hi-beams and a car so far behind me its headlights were the size of fireflies.

"Slow down," she said, "and turn right onto that road.

If the gate is closed we'll have to walk the rest of the way."

"No problem. We're dressed for it."

The gate was indeed secured by a padlock. Leaving the car on the road, we climbed over the fence that ran on either side of the gate into unknown darkness, and walked fifty yards or so on hard-packed snow dirty from tire tracks, hoof prints and manure. By the time we reached the house our eyes had adjusted to the black shadows.

Standing tall and narrow on a limestone foundation between groves of skeletal trees, the farmhouse loomed before us like something supernatural. The roof peaked at a perilous angle and below it, narrow windows and the front door looked like the eyes, nostrils and mouth of a ghost. Maynard was right when he described the scene as gloomy and benighted.

I tried the front door. Locked with a deadbolt. Nothing easy about that. The main floor windows were too high off the ground to get at without a stepladder. That left the back door. We walked around and in the shadowy distance behind the house we could just make out the round shape of a silo and next to it a barn and toolshed. Closer to us was a narrow structure that puzzled me at first and then it came to me: an outhouse.

I stepped onto a rickety stoop of rotting wood. Off to the left against the wall was a large cylinder I didn't recognize at first being a city person but then realized it was a propane tank, no doubt used for heating and cooking.

I opened the screen door covered by plastic sheeting to fend off the cold, holding it with my hip as I examined the lock on the inside door.

Bev stood by holding her flashlight. "Do you think you can open it?"

"It's a simple latch and the wood is pretty weak."

I pressed hard against the door with my hip. My breath

was coming out in great clouds of white. There was a sharp cracking noise that carried into the woods. It was eerie as though the house was protesting. Then I gave the door another push, this time with added weight, and the door popped open, nearly hurling me inside.

The wood around the latch had split. Easy enough to explain. Vandals broke in.

Bev followed me and played the beam around the interior. We were in the kitchen. It was like stepping back into the last century: Wood-burning stove, wallpaper of faded flowers, cast-iron sink, hand water pump, table covered in oilcloth, chintz curtains, wide-slatted wood floor. The only accommodation to modern times was a refrigerator, a large gas Kelvinator that hummed, the only sound other than our breathing.

I had expected it to be ice cold but it was reasonably warm. There had to be a furnace fueled by the propane tank that protected the pipes from freezing.

A doorway led into the sitting room. There we found more of the nineteenth century: mohair sofa, high-back chairs, rocker, gilt frames of ancestor paintings.

In the corner, the only concession to modern times, was an electric space heater. At least rural electrification had come to the Schultzman farm, if not indoor plumbing.

We pulled back an oval-braided rug and examined the exposed planks for nails that might have been jimmied. Except for wear, they looked as they must have looked a century ago when the first-growth wood was hammered together.

We climbed the stairs to the bedrooms. They were small and cramped. The largest was probably Schultzman's. My flashlight illuminated a handmade quilted bedspread, a brass headboard and a curved Art Nouveau dresser with a tilting mirror. A porcelain bowl with a pitcher sitting in it was on the floor next to the dresser.

On a corner shelf I spotted a small family photograph in a stamped-metal frame, the kind you buy at a 5-and-10-cent store. The Schultzman family in better days, including the Mrs. Just what I could use in a photo essay about the murder. I put it in my overcoat pocket.

Bev had wandered off as I got to my knees to look under the bed when suddenly she let out a yelp.

I jumped up and we met in the hall, a headlong rush into each other's arms.

"What is it?" I asked.

"In there," she pointed to the bedroom she had just vacated.

I looked in. On the floor by the bed was a chalk outline of a human form. Around the head was a large stain, as though someone had mashed a peck of tomatoes and then wiped up the mess with a towel.

"This is where Sarah was found," I said.

It was too much for Bev. "Let's get out of here, Bill," she said from the hallway.

"Stay there and wait for me."

I got on my knees and checked the old floor, staying clear of the bloodstain. Nothing. I followed through in the other bedroom, probably Bruno's, and returned for a last look in Alfred's room. Not a stick of flooring had been tampered with. I checked the hallway last.

Discouraged, I motioned Bev to follow me back downstairs. Halfway down the staircase one of the treads squeaked from my weight. I didn't recall that happening on my way up but then I was taking them two at a time and this was one I must have missed. I stopped and Bev bumped me from behind.

"What's the matter?"

"This step," I said, rocking on it. It squeaked rhythmically with my motion. I bent down and put my flashlight close to the wood. The step did not fit very snugly against the riser and the nails were not sitting firmly. I bent over and pulled on the board. It came up relatively easily.

"Bev," I said, flushing with excitement. "I found something."

She watched me remove a strongbox from the empty space under the tread.

"Bill, leave everything as it is and call the Sheriff. I'm scared."

"Nothing doing," I said triumphantly "We have to see what's inside." I tried the lid. It was locked. "Let's go to the kitchen and see if I can break it open."

Bev clung to me, and I could feel her arm shake with nervousness. "This is bad idea."

I put the box on the oilcloth table and checked the cupboards, finding ordinary kitchen stuff, china, glasses, storage containers. Then I looked in the cabinet under the sink and found a carpenter's leather apron and in it a screwdriver, hammer, pliers and a six-foot wooden folding ruler.

Perfect.

I hammered away on the lock using the flat tip of the slotted screwdriver until the lock fell apart. I opened the box and both of us shined our flashlights on the contents. We literally gasped. Neatly tucked into the box was money, lots of it—twenties, fifties, hundreds, each denomination neatly banded with paper strips. I fanned several packets with my thumb.

"There are thousands and thousands of dollars here."

"I've never seen so much money," Bev said,

I counted the packets of hundreds; there were ten of them and fifty bills in each packet. That alone came to fifty thousand dollars.

"This is a king's ransom."

I looked at her, her features accented by the beam of the flashlight. "Whoever killed Schultzman had to be looking for this money, not drugs."

"It makes for a stronger motive, doesn't it?"

"It sure does. People have been murdered for a lot less."

"But where did all this money come from?"

"Drug sales, probably. The farm could be part of a distribution system. Drugs are smuggled here in bulk, which is broken down into small packages and sold on the street, not here but in the Twin Cities where the market is. This farm could be where the money is handled, like a bank, an unlikely place to be part of a drug ring, but it makes sense—a small town, out of the way, unlikely to be on the radar by the Feds."

"How do you know things like that?"

"Drugs are not strangers to the art world."

"But why didn't we find any drugs?"

"Maybe Schultzman was waiting for a shipment. That's why he had so much money hidden away."

"Is that why he was killed?"

"Someone knew the money was in the house."

"Someone familiar with the operation, like a drug dealer?"

I nodded. "Schultzman would know him and welcome him into the house. Something goes terribly wrong. There's an argument, maybe he is holding back on money owed. There's a fight."

"But why was he killed with a crow bar? Wouldn't a drug dealer carry a gun?"

"I don't know. Maybe he left it in the car and grabbed whatever was at hand. It's possible the killer wasn't planning to murder Schultzman in the first place. The crow bar was available and so he used it."

"Then he didn't come to pull up boards looking for the hidden money, like an intruder would."

I smiled. "You sure ask a lot of questions. I should hire you as my assistant."

"I think you already have."

We both laughed, easing the stress we were both feeling.

"Ok, so let's assume the person was an intruder, and came already armed with a crow bar."

"But why would the killer turn up when Schultzman was home?" Bev asked. "Wouldn't lights be on? The car in the driveway?"

"I know that Bruno took the car into town. For the sake of argument, let's assume Schultzman is in the barn and Sarah is on her room lying down. No lights are on in the house."

"Wouldn't he have assumed the house was locked if no one was home? There was no sign of a break-in, until you made one, that is."

She was not making light of what I'd done.

"I know what you're thinking, Bev. But if I hadn't broken in, if we had just walked back to the car, we never would have found the money. Each new revelation gets me closer to who killed Maynard."

"Is that what's driving you?"

"I owe it to him." And to myself as well I thought.

"Well, we've gone this far…"

"Stick with me a little longer, Bev. Let's keep trying to figure out what went on here. Lets assume the door wasn't locked. Isn't that the way it is in small towns—people don't lock their doors? Even the Clerk of Court told me she never locked hers before the murders. So the intruder simply lets himself in. He goes upstairs and surprises Sarah. She screams. Panicked, he strikes her. Hearing his daughter screaming, Schultzman comes running toward the house. He and the intruder meet in the orchard. There is a fight to the death and Schultzman loses."

"But how did the killer know the money was there in the first place?"

"Word on the street. Somewhere out of town, Minneapolis maybe. People overhear things, like a conversation in a bar."

"None of this explains why the crow bar ended up in the trunk of Maynard's car."

I sighed. "But how could Rose be involved in any of this?"

"What if she did not act alone?"

"What do you mean?" I asked.

"What if she sat in the car while Maynard came in to steal the money? Remember, Schultzman had already been killed."

"Jesus," I said. "I never thought of that." But what I did think of was the fancy life style that Rose and Maynard had made for themselves.

My mind froze with this conjecture. How could Maynard possibly have killed Schultzman? He wasn't strong enough to overcome the brute strength of a farmer who was fighting for his life. No, it had to be someone else.

Bev looked around as though she were feeling a ghostly presence. "Let's get out of here, Bill. We've been here too long. I'm getting nervous.'

"Ok." I began putting the bills back in the box, being careful to stack them as though they had not been disturbed.

Bev held the flashlight. "When did you see Alice Timmins?" she asked abruptly.

I cradled the box under my arm the way a librarian carries a stack of books. The heft felt good. I could understand why people kill for money.

"Who?" I asked, distracted.

"The Clerk of Court. You said she told you she never locked her door before the murders."

"Oh, I went to see her yesterday. To find out who owns this farm."

"I thought Schultzman owned it."

"He leased it."

"He did?" Bev asked in surprise. "Who owns it then?"

"I don't know. The Citizen Ledger's lawyers are getting a court order to open the records. The one person I'd really like to talk to is the owner. Did he have any idea that his property was going to be a repository for drug money? He has some questions to answer."

Bev flashed her light on the box I was holding. "What are you going to do with the money? Take it with you?'"

"God no, I wouldn't want to be responsible for more cash than I will ever see again in my life. I'm putting it back where I found it, under the stairs."

"Maybe you should turn it over to the Sheriff."

"Then he will definitely have reason to put me in jail."

"Sooner or later, he will discover the lock to the back door is broken."

"He won't know I did it. He'd suspect me but he wouldn't be able to prove it. Let's hope the killer will be caught by that time."

"You're hoping a lot."

"What if he comes back to get it?"

"We've caught our killer."

Bev shone her flashlight full in my face. "And who is going to catch him. You?"

20

We walked back down the drive, the packed snow crunching under our feet, our frozen breaths pointing the way. We climbed over the gate and got into the car. It started grudgingly. I turned the heater on full, made a U-turn and headed back to Clear Lake. We drove in shared silence, each of us buried in thoughts no doubt similar: there was a killer out there who might make another try to find the money. But how in hell can we set a trap without telling the Sheriff so he can provide around-the-clock surveillance? And would he believe an out-of-town-out-of-control reporter? He might if Bev did the talking. Lots to think about on our drive back to Clear Lake.

Even though I couldn't see beyond my headlights I envisioned the flat acres of barren fields covered with snow on either side of the road. It seemed as if Bev and I were the only humans on a hostile planet, our car a space capsule protecting us from the deadly atmosphere.

I turned on the radio for signs of life beyond our isolated little world and found an all-night local station playing Perry Como.

It was nearing midnight.

"Do you think your father is worried about you?"

"The Club doesn't close till one. If I'm out late he will assume I'm having a good time."

"I hope so."

"About my dad not worrying about me or about my having a good time?"

"About you having a good time."

"Well, it may not be a good time I'm having, but it sure is adventurous." Bev became thoughtful. "You know, Bill, what you did tonight reminds me again that you never were a bore, one thing I always found thrilling about you, a prevailing sense of excitement. The expectation of the unexpected. Does any of this make sense?"

"I don't know if it makes sense but I'll take it as a compliment. I probably acted that way because I was trying to impress you, show off so that you'd notice me above the other guys in class. I always felt a few down with them, being the son of an immigrant. I never thought I'd have a chance with you."

"You needn't have worried," she said, almost wistfully.

I glanced over at her, hoping in my heart it wasn't too late. I drove on, my mind dwelling on the art of the possible, when the engine unexpectedly grabbed as though a spark plug misfired. I checked the dials on the dashboard, gas level fine, amps and oil pressure normal, engine not overheating. But my V8 was not responding to my pressure on the gas pedal.

"What's the matter?" Bev asked.

"Can't tell. The car was running fine and all of a sudden it began to miss."

I steered to the edge of the road where we rolled to a stop. The defroster blower continued to hum, Perry Como's sonorous baritone came out of the speakers, my headlights shone on an empty expanse of roadway, and my dash lights illuminated a very concerned look on Bev's face.

I doused the lights to save the battery and ground the starter, beating the foot feet to push raw gas into the carburetor. Nothing happened.

"We're dead," I said, an unfortunate metaphor that made Bev shudder.

"What's wrong?"

I didn't give her an answer because I didn't have one. I got out of the car with my flashlight and lifted the hood. The engine was stiffening quickly in the subzero temperature. I checked the wires to make sure they were seated properly in the spark plugs and the distributor. I pulled off the air cleaner and looked into the carburetor. I had the damned thing rebuilt in November in anticipation of a long winter. The interior was shiny, no carbon build-up.

"Bev!" I called through the windshield. "Get behind the wheel and turn the starter over."

Deep under the engine the starter whined and whined. I flicked the float valve in the carburetor. Nothing. I leaned over and sniffed the chamber. The rich, nauseating odor of raw gas was totally absent.

"That's enough!" I yelled. "Save the battery!"

I pushed the hood down and got back in the car.

"Frozen gas line," I said, privately cursing myself for neglecting to add a can of Heet when I filled the gas tank.

"Does anyone ever come down this road?" I asked.

"At this hour?" Was all she said, but it was more than enough.

Our anxious breathing quickly steamed the windows until they were white with frost.

"What are we going to do?" Bev asked, a tremor of fear shaking her voice.

"I'll go for help," I opened the door and looked up and down the dismal road for a rural mail box. Only black electric poles set against a less black background receding

169

into a hazy distance. I got back in and slammed the door.

"There's nothing out there."

"I'm better dressed than you are. I can hike into town."

"How far is that? Two, maybe three miles? You'd never make it." I stamped my feet on the floor and pressed my gloved hands to my ears. "We'd better stick together."

"We have to try something."

"I'll flick the headlights off and on. Someone might see them.

"How about the horn?"

"Good idea." I heard that sound travels better in cold weather. And sound unlike light spreads in all directions. Probably our best hope.

"What's Morse Code for SOS?" I asked as if a farmer would even know it. I leaned on the horn rim, alternating between long and short bursts.

In less than a minute the horn began to wane, getting weaker and weaker like an old phonograph player winding down. The horn gave one final plaintive plea for help. Suddenly we were enveloped in brittle silence, the only sound our heaving breaths.

"What do we do now?"

"Wait till someone finds us."

I reached across Bev's lap, opened the glove box, and pulled out a slightly used tenth of Southern Comfort.

"Thank God I broke the open bottle law."

"What is it?"

"Something to toast our health with. It's been sitting there since last winter. I almost forgot about it."

I unscrewed the cap and handed her the bottle.

She accepted it gratefully and swallowed. As I watched her, I thought about Tod fast asleep in his bed. What would he do without his mother?

Bev handed me the bottle. "Make it last," she said.

I pretended to take a sip.

"How are you holding up?" I asked, capping the bottle

and putting it on the seat between us.

"Better than you. You're not dressed very warmly."

"I know."

"You don't have earmuffs."

"I know."

"Or fur-lined gloves."

"I know."

"And only street shoes."

'I know.'

"Do you have any newspapers?" she asked as if giving up on me.

"Newspapers?"

"I heard newspapers make good insulation."

I laughed. "I should have. I work for one." I got out and opened the trunk where I had a stack of papers with my reviews which I had intended to clip and file away, one of those projects I never quite got around to doing. I also found stuffed in back two Red Owl grocery bags left over from who knows when. I now had at least the rudiments of survival gear. Eat your heart out, Bud Kraehling!

I climbed back into the front seat feeling optimistic because to feel anything less would admit defeat.

I lined the paper bags with several blue streak editions, sacrificing my elegant prose in the process, and stuffed my feet into them.

"It works, my feet are beginning to warm up."

"I told you."

I began folding several sheets of newsprint.

"What are you doing?"

"One of the first things I learned when I came to the Citizen Ledger was how to make a printer's hat out of newspapers. All pressmen wear them as a symbol of their profession."

It was difficult working with gloves and cold fingers. I doubled the amount of paper and turned the folds down so they would cover my ears. Then I pushed my own hat down to keep my makeshift protection in place.

"I must look like one of Napoleon's troops retreating from Russia."

"Better than frostbite."

We huddled together, burying our faces into each other's shoulders, occasionally separating for Southern Comfort, Bev sipping while I pretended to. I wanted to make sure she had the better chance of making it.

"How long have we been here?" Bev asked, her voice muffled against my coat.

I slid back my sleeve to look at my watch. "Nearly thirty minutes."

She reached for the Southern Comfort. "If help doesn't come soon I don't think we'll make it."

"Nonsense," I said and worked to maintain the bravado that was slipping away by the second. Each breath I took burned my lungs—how odd, I thought, the very opposite of how they should feel. Maybe if I put my mind on something else, something to keep my spirits up, and then I remembered a Frank Yerby novel in which a man and a woman dig into a haystack to keep from freezing to death. It made me feel better imagining Bev and me burrowing into a haystack like the fictional couple.

"Let's look for a haystack," I said.

She pulled away and stared at me. "A haystack?"

"We can dig into it to keep warm."

""I hate to disappoint you, but this is corn country. No hay here."

"Oh," I said.

I closed my eyes and the image of that haystack appeared in my mind coming closer and closer, so inviting, so secure, so warm, and Bev and I began tunneling into it, pulling loose hay behind us to make a cozy burrow, our bodies producing so much heat we pulled off each other's clothing, our nakedness pressing together in the right places, the tunnel we created becoming a metaphor for the tunnel of her love, and the inevitable happens, we are no longer fumbling, inexperienced teenagers but sophisticated adults taking our time, caressing one another, holding off the inevitable moment…

"Bill!"

Bev was slapping my face. "Wake up! Wake up!"

"I *am* awake," I heard myself shout but the words seemed to come not from me but from a recording of my voice.

"You were falling asleep! "You can't sleep!" She began beating my chest with her fists. Fear flashed in her eyes. "Don't leave me alone, Bill!"

I snapped back to the present—the bitter cold, the windows covered in clouded ice, our breath paths of frozen vapor—and I realized in a frightening flash how easy it is to freeze to death. If Bev hadn't noticed I was dozing off, hadn't slapped me awake, my blood would have slowed to a gummy consistency, finally congealing and shutting down my heart without my ever knowing it was happening.

"We have to talk to each other," she said, shaking my shoulders, "we have to stay awake. Talk to me. Say something, anything. Just keep talking!"

"Ok, ok. Remember my '49 Ford?"

"The one with the chartreuse color?"

"Yes."

"I hated that color. It reminded me of seaweed."

I laughed. "That's funny."

"Keep talking. Why did you buy that car?"

"Don't you remember?"

"Yes, but tell me anyway."

"So we could go out together. And it was cheap; I only paid thirty-five dollars for it. I bought it from Dick Borgenhagen, he was graduating and wanted to sell it."

"We went to drive-in movies."

"It dripped oil. My father made me get rid of it."

Memories of the fight we had over the car forced itself to the forefront of my mind.

"Bill, talk to me."

"I am talking."

"No, you stopped. You have to keep talking!"

"I was thinking of my father."

"Quit doing that! He can't hurt you anymore, not unless you let him!"

"Ok."

"Promise, you have to promise."

"I promise."

"Let's drink to that." Bev reached for the bottle of Southern Comfort and shook it. "Not much left. Here, you drink first."

I put it to my lips and pretended to swallow.

She shook the bottle again. "Didn't you have any?"

I looked down.

"You didn't drink any of this, did you? You pretended so I'd have it all."

"You have a son to go home to. I have nothing."

"You *do* have something! You have *me*!" She began to cry. "You'll die! Please don't die. After all we've been through, you can't die!"

The liqueur was having its desired effect. She was fired up. Hang in there, Bev, I said to myself, hang in there.

"Listen to me, Bill!"

"I'm listening." I said, my words coming out of an echo chamber. God, but it would be nice to take a nap, just a short one, long enough to get some rest. I'm so tired…

"I love you, Bill, I never, never loved anyone else!"

The desperation in her voice was an alarm clock dragging me from the sleep I yearned for.

"I respected Everett but I did not love him. You were always in my thoughts, in my heart. I thought about you all the time—even when, even when…"

"Even when what?" I asked, wide awake now to words

I was anticipating.

"Even when Ev made love to me, I imagined you in my arms, I felt only you, Bill, only you."

In spite of her passion, a passion making every effort to break the tenacious grip of the excruciating cold enveloping me, numbing my fingers, my feet, my face, my brain, I was still focused enough to ask myself if this was a last-ditch effort to keep me from giving up, like slapping my face, or was Bev being sincere, her words filled with truth, conviction, promise? Was the liqueur removing her inhibitions, making her say more than she really meant to say? And, if we survive, will these words be overshadowed by the relief of having escaped certain death, that they instead become part of the lore of survival, recalled but not acted upon?

"Don't you understand," Bev shouted as though reading my mind and contradicting what she saw there. "If that memory could make you a father, then you *are* Tod's father!"

Bev pulled me toward her and kissed me. We formed a cocoon of warmth against the ice-cold air.

"Will you put Tod to bed and tell him a bed time story?" She murmured against my mouth.

"First chance I get."

"I'm so glad you said that."

Bev unzipped her parka and tried to fit it around the two of us. "Squeeze against me. My body will help keep you warm."

"Your parka is not big enough. Let me try my coat. It's double breasted."

I unbuttoned it. "Here," I said, stretching out across the car seat, "Lie on top of me. I'll use my coat as a blanket."

There was enough material to draw my coat around both of us. I felt our hearts beating as we maneuvered our bodies in the narrow confines of the front seat. We were definitely not teenagers in a chartreuse 1949 Ford.

My back was leaning against the door, my knees were slightly raised as my newspaper-wrapped feet still in their insulated grocery bags pressed against the opposite door, and Bev astride me.

The pressure and the lingering smell of her body wrapped with mine worked magic but it was not a dream now, and I felt truly warm, warmer than I had ever felt before...

21

Suddenly the door on my side swung open and my head fell back, bouncing off the icy asphalt like a frozen gourd. Fortunately, the newspaper padding around my head prevented me from cracking it wide open.

The only thing that made sense to me was that I had pushed down on the handle causing the door to pop open, but then I saw an inverted pair of boots inches from my nose. I lifted my head and my eyes followed the boots up a pair of legs clad in wrinkled khaki, to heavy hips surrounded by a leather jacket, a gun holster, a protruding gut, a leering grin and, behind ogling eyes, a dirty mind.

It was Deputy Jensen who had opened the car door and he was at the top of his form while I was at the bottom of mine, laughing so hard I thought surely, from where I lay, I would smell the effects of a relaxed bladder.

"Jesus!" he cried between bursts of laughter. "Balling the Doc's daughter. He's balling the Doc's daughter!"

'You cretin, you Neanderthal, you dimwit! It's not what you think!"

"I know what I see and what I see is the Big City reporter balling the Doc's daughter!"

"Shut up you imbecile and get us out of here! Can't you see we're freezing to death?"

Jensen reached down and grabbed my coat collar and dragged us out till our bodies plopped onto the pavement, no different from the way he would handle a deer carcass during hunting season.

Bev rolled out of the confines of my coat, struggled to her feet, and pulled her jacket close to her body. Still on the ground looking up, I saw the mortification on her face. I pulled myself erect, fighting to regain my balance, clear my head and stand on my numbed feet. I wrapped my unbuttoned coat around me, feeling nothing but undiluted rage for Jensen.

"Where did you come from?"

"You didn't think I'd let you freeze to death, did you? If I'd known you were balling the Doc's daughter, though, I'd let you have a couple more minutes."

"Just shut up and get us out of here."

Still laughing, Jensen led us to his cruiser idling behind my iced-up Pontiac. He opened the rear door. Comforting heat spilled out. Bev slid across the vinyl seat and pushed herself into the corner, her back to me. As I bent to get in, Jensen put his hand on my head as if I were a common criminal. In his mind I was. Maybe in Bev's mind I was, too.

Jensen got in the front seat, which was separated from the back by a wire barrier. It was just as well. I was ready to reach across and strangle him.

"You knew where we were, didn't you?" I shouted angrily. "You didn't just come along and see us, did you? You waited awhile to make sure we were nearly dead, right?"

Jensen chuckled like a little kid having a hard time keeping a secret. "Hey, why don't you take off those newspaper rags you're wearing? You look like a hobo."

I unwrapped my feet and removed my printer's hat,

stuffing the remnants of newspapers and my old reviews under Jensen's front seat. Let him throw them away.

Bev was turned away from me, huddled in the corner as if she was trying to disappear into it. She said not a word. I knew she was crying silently into her hands, crying tears of shame, tears of mortification, tears of betrayal. She had said earlier, when we faced the very real possibility of dying, that she was strong, stronger than ever, but was she strong enough to withstand the abject humiliation of this moment? Tomorrow this will be the main topic of discussion at the Cozy Corner.

I knew without having to ask, it was over. It had barely begun, and now it was over.

Jensen pulled up in front of the Nordstrom house. Bev opened the door before the cruiser had come to a stop, and jumped out. She ran up the steps to the front door. For an embarrassing, exposed moment she fumbled for the keys in her jacket pocket. Then she unlocked the door and slammed it shut behind her. At that moment I was convinced I would never see her again.

Jensen made a U-turn and headed back to town.

"Drop me off at the hotel," I said, weary and defeated, so exhausted the only thing I looked forward to was falling into my bed.

Jensen looked at me in his rearview mirror. "No hotel for you, Mr. Reporter. You're spending the night in jail."

"What?"

"You're under arrest."

"What for? I told you we weren't doing anything!"

"Not that, Kouros. I don't arrest people for balling. I give them medals." He laughed again. "I'm arresting you for breaking into Schultzman's farm, and contaminating evidence of a crime scene."

I recalled the headlights behind us when Bev and I were driving to the farm, lights so far distant they appeared as small as fireflies.

"Were you following us?"

"Doing my duty as Deputy Sheriff."

My thawing brain began to work better. "Did you do anything to my car?"

"Just a little coffee from my thermos."

"Coffee?" I thundered. "You poured coffee into my gas tank?"

"Not all of it. I saved some for myself."

"God damn you! We could have died!"

"I was parked right behind you, nice and quiet like. You couldn't see me out of your iced-up windows."

I fumed in the back seat, feeling impotent rage.

"I got your best interests at heart, Kouros, but you keep getting yourself into trouble. Sheriff Amundson told me to keep an eye on you. While you were parked in front of the farm I put just enough coffee in your tank to keep you from going too far, that was my idea not the Sheriff's, and after you left I checked the house and seen what you did. You broke the lock on the back door. That is serious criminal misconduct. I knew you wouldn't get far with Ethyl mixed with Maxwell House, so I headed back till I found you a mile away, sitting by the side of the road, and I pulled up behind you, like I said."

"And you sat there in a warm car while we were freezing, is that it?"

"I just wanted to teach you a little lesson that crime doesn't pay."

"What would law enforcement do without you, Jensen?" I sighed.

He absorbed my barb. He could take it, he was riding high. "I don't know if you can make bail, though. Breaking into where a murder took place and contaminating it isn't like running a red light. By the way, what were you looking for?"

"I just wanted to get atmosphere for an article."

"So you didn't mess with anything?"

"What was there to mess with?"

Jensen led me down a flight of outdoor stairs adjacent to the office and through a barred door, which he unlocked with one of those keys you associate with dungeons.

We entered a dank chilly cellblock, a narrow, dimly lit hallway with four cells, two on each side. We were alone. Where are the town drunks I wondered? Then I smelled ancient urine and vomit. The drunks had been here, all right, but not this night.

Jensen motioned me to a desk and switched on a gooseneck lamp. The only other adornment on the desktop was a telephone. The deputy reached into the top drawer, moving his gut back at least a foot, and pulled out a ruled pad. "Ok, empty your pockets."

I stared at him.

"Standard operating procedure when booking a new prisoner."

I unbuttoned my overcoat and emptied my pockets, dropping what I had on the desk in a random pile. It didn't look like much.

Jensen sorted through my worldly possessions, noting each item in meticulous order. His nose was close to the pad.

Cash: three one dollar bills, one ten dollar bill, one twenty dollar bill, four dimes and three pennies.

Fountain Pen: Parker brand, gold with silver clip.

Wallet: leather.

Credit Cards: Standard Oil, Sinclair, Mobile, American Express, Dayton's, BankAmerica.

Checkbook: fake leather.

"You wearing a wristwatch?"
I pulled up my sleeve.

Watch: Bulova, with gold expansion band.

"You can keep your watch to tell the time. We run a decent jail here.'

"Oh yeah? You haven't read me my rights."

"I'm not interrogating you, so don't play smart ass. I know what I'm doing."

Jensen looked at me, pencil poised over his pad. "Anything else?"

I remembered the Schultzman family photo and instinctively put my hand against my overcoat pocket.

"What you got in there?"

I shrugged. "Nothing."

"Nothing?" He reached across with his pudgy hand and felt my pocket. "What the hell is that?"

I withdrew the framed photo I'd taken from the Schulzman house and dropped it on the desk.

Jensen shook his head as though he had seen it all. "What else won't you stoop to? " he asked.

I didn't bother to correct his painful syntax. "I was going to use the photo in a background article."

"Well, you won't be using this for any article." He took out a manila envelope from a deep drawer in the desk and slid the duly recorded pile of stuff into it along with the sheet of paper he had written on.

"Ok, now your belt."

"My belt?" I asked.

"I won't be responsible for anyone hanging himself."

"That was the first thing on my mind."

I looked into one of the cells. It was about six feet wide and ten feet long. There was a stool without a lid, a sink and a hinged bunk bed with a thin mattress raised up and hooked to the wall.

Jensen was watching me. "Take your choice. They're all the same."

THE FIFTH SLUG

I lowered the bunk bed and sat on it, staring at the wall opposite. I wondered why they called this place a cellblock. Cell for sure, but where was the block? Maybe the cement blocks that were used to build it.

I was emptied of emotion, my mind a blank. I couldn't feel, I couldn't think.

Outside my cell Jensen was readying to go when the phone on the desk jangled. He laid his jacket across the back of the desk chair and answered it, turning his back to me and cupping his hand over the receiver. He listened a moment.

I strained to hear what he was saying, picking up snatches of words.

"Red-handed," I heard him say.

"Busted the back door."

"Stole a family photo."

"He wasn't alone."

Then he said loud enough for me to hear, "The Doc's daughter," purposely just to goad me.

"If you say 'balling,'" I yelled, "I'll kill you!"

Jensen turned and looked at me, his face beet red. He covered the mouthpiece. "Shut your fucking mouth!"

Then he said into the phone: "I took her home."

I hollered so loud I had to be heard outside the walls of my prison. "*Sheriff! I want to talk to you!*"

Jensen was caught between shutting me up and talking to his boss and it rattled him. He clearly was not able to handle two emergencies at once.

He turned his back to me again, listening intently on the phone. I had the feeling the Sheriff was chewing him out. His shoulders began to sag like bags of flour in the rain.

He laid the receiver on the desk and shuffled over to my cell, unlocking it. "The Sheriff wants to talk to you," he said, dispirited.

"Why don't you change the newspapers while you're

at it?" I said condescendingly, pointing over my shoulders at the cell I had just vacated.

Jensen shook with pent-up rage.

I picked up the receiver moist with his hand sweat. "Hi, Sheriff."

"What in hell have you been up to, Bill?" He was talking like a Dutch uncle.

"What have I been up to?" I shot back. "Why don't you ask your Deputy what *he's* been up to? Did he tell you he dumped coffee in my gas tank and left Bev and me to freeze for an hour?"

Jensen was trembling.

"Now cool it, Bill," the Sheriff said. "You did break into the farm house, after all. And you took a photograph. And what were you doing there anyway with Beverly Nordstrom?"

"What did Jensen tell you?"

"Nothing, but the mere fact that she was with you, essentially aiding and abetting criminal behavior, sounds pretty bad. You really want to drag her into this mess? You not only were endangering her life, you were also compromising the reputation of one of the most respected families in Clear Lake."

I stared at the cold concrete floor. The Sheriff was right. What had I done to Bev? Not only Bev but her son and her father as well. My foolhardy actions, a desire to get the story at any cost, has cost me everything.

"Remember what I said about clearing out? Apparently you didn't get the message."

"I got it now."

"Does that mean you'll leave town like I told you?"

There was really nothing left for me to do except repeat what I did twenty years ago, get out of Bev's life and get out fast, no goodbyes, no explanations.

"Ok, Sheriff, I'll leave."

"Well, now you're making some sense. I'll tell Jensen

to let you go, providing you are…"

I interrupted him, "On the noon stage?"

"Earlier than that. I want you out of here right now."

"I would except that my car has coffee in the tank."

"Shit," the Sheriff said, remembering. This was the first time I heard him swear. "I'll have it towed to the police garage first thing in the morning. It's down a block from the courthouse on Third Avenue East. Be there at noon. Your car will be ready."

So it would be the noon stage after all.

Jensen opened the manila envelope and dumped my possessions on the desk, lifting it up high so that everything scattered, the coins making clattering sounds, some of them falling to the floor.

He stretched over the desk and looked down. "Gee, how clumsy of me."

I stared at the top of Jensen's bent-over head, his receding hairline, the freckles covering his ape-shaped dome. Trapped in the moment I could feel myself splitting into two personalities, one the civilized, intellectual urbane art critic I always took myself to be and the other, a guttural savage still in a primal stage without compassion or feeling, burning only for revenge, to get even with the man who nearly let Bev and me freeze to death, the man who humiliated the only woman I ever loved.

That primitive other self took over, washing away millennia of evolutionary progress, and I saw myself, out-of-body, grab the gooseneck lamp and yank it from its cord. The startled figure in front of me straightened up, indistinct and shadowy, the only illumination from the wan fluorescent tubes hanging from the ceiling, but light enough to target the bulging head and I brought the metal shade of the lamp across it, creasing a line of dark red along its brow. Jensen expelled air and settled slowly to the floor like a mass of packaged lard.

He looked up at me, his fluttering eyes desperately trying to focus on my face, confused, overflowing with unadulterated hatred, his right hand feeling for his hip, searching, fumbling for the gun in his holster, using instinct now, police academy training for what should be second-nature, before settling back in a kind of swoon, and he began to snore.

I bent down and pulled the gun, a revolver, from the holster in case he came to before I had a chance to get out of here. I held the gun up, toward the overhead light to see it better. It was a Smith and Wesson Model 10. It seemed heavy but then what did I know about guns? I never handled one before. I placed it out of reach on the bench in my unlocked cell. Then I picked up my belongings and left the Deputy alone on the floor to snore away the night.

22

The four blocks back to the hotel passed in a blur. My heart was racing fast enough to keep my entire body warm and the fast walk only served to heat me up even more. The only thing on my mind right now was the bed in 210 and me crashing on it, clothes and all.

The night clerk was dozing in the chair by the switchboard. I tiptoed past him and climbed the stairs near the wall, not wanting him to hear a tread squeak under my foot. Night clerks sleep lightly if at all and they are also snoopy since their lives are spent essentially alone, alone except for their unfulfilled dreams, that is, and he'd love to be the first to report seeing a victim of Jensen's Big Freeze Caper.

I came to my door and saw a Do Not Disturb sign hanging from the knob. What the hell is this? I asked myself. I don't remember hanging it on my door. Unless I forgot I did it. Anything is possible given the rattled state of my poor brain. I unlocked the door and let myself in. I was ready to switch on the bedside light when I heard a murmur. I stopped and stood still in the dark. The smell of jasmine drifted under my nostrils. Did I let myself into the wrong room? But how is that possible? I carry the key with me. Puzzled, more than that, confused, I clicked on the bed light. Someone was sleeping in my bed, all right, and it wasn't Goldilocks. It was someone with raven hair lined here and there with strands of gray.

"Jesus!" I exclaimed.

The figure under the covers stirred and yawned. "Not Jesus, darling, Claire."

Claire sat up, the sheet dropping from her body revealing her breasts. Her bing cherry nipples were at ease now. When I played with them they were as hard as the cherry pits themselves.

She raised her arms over her head and stretched, languidly, arching her superb body hoping I would notice.

I noticed but not the way she expected.

"What in hell are you doing here?"

"I caught a ride with Don."

"You drove down with Don? Where is he?"

"In the room next to us, sound asleep. By the way what time is it?" She checked the clock on the nightstand. "My god, it's nearly three."

"How did you get in here?"

"A night clerk is a night clerk is a night clerk."

I shook my head. "You have the instincts of a whore."

"I thought you'd be really happy to see me. What a one-horse town. They don't even have a bar in this hotel. At least I can keep you company." For the first time she checked me over. "You look awful. Where have you been?"

"I've been through a meat grinder if you want to know, and I am in no mood for company."

"You don't have to be surly."

"You're lucky I'm not homicidal," I said, thinking of Jensen.

Claire patted the mattress suggestively. "Get out of

those rumpled clothes and climb in with me. I'll make you feel better."

I began shedding my clothes, peeling them off layer-by-layer, and left the pile on the floor.

"I'm going to shower."

The shower was an old-fashioned claw tub with a curtain drawn around it. I stood under the stream of hot water until it ran out, wondering if my spirit would last any longer.

I dried off and wiped the mirror clean, then looked closely at my reflection. I didn't recognize myself. Most of the time the mirror was simply a convenience to comb my hair and shave. I can't remember the last time I surveyed my features. I was surprised the face I was staring at was not more youthful. There were worry lines across the forehead and on either side of the mouth.

Why should that surprise me? I'm getting old, thirty-nine. When I turned thirty-nine last March, Bailey told me I was in my fortieth year. I found that difficult to comprehend. How can I be thirty-nine but in my fortieth year?

I squinted. I'd probably need glasses pretty soon. Stubble shaded my jaw; some of the tiny hairs were gray, like those on Claire's head.

Random thoughts.

"Oh man," I said aloud and then began singing Billie Holiday's great torch song: "Not much to look at, nothing to see…"

Speaking of nothing to see, what did Claire see in me? Even more important, too late for regrets, what did Bev see in me? She needs a man who offers security, permanence, loyalty—none of these was in my portfolio of attributes.

It didn't matter anyway. For the second time in my life I saw Bev for the last time.

Does that make sense?

Sadly, it does. If the shame Bev is suffering because of Jensen doesn't end our rekindled relationship, then the brunette charmer lying naked in my bed certainly will.

And then it hit me. I needed to tell Claire about Bev. Was there any good reason not to? Bev will learn about Claire soon enough. The night clerk will take care of that. I shook my head. One more bitter irony to add to all the others I'd accumulated since arriving.

So why not level the playing field? It's all over anyway. Bev was never a threat to Claire. We had a teenage love affair as common as acne, until I came back to Clear Lake and reawakened that teen-age love.

I came out of the bathroom and sat on the bed with one leg up, facing Claire.

"You look better," she said.

"Cleaner anyway."

As tired as I was I knew this was the only time for me to talk to her, tell her what was weighing on my mind. I could not sleep on it. There wouldn't be time tomorrow.

"I have to tell you something."

"I thought you were too tired to do anything, even talk."

"This is important."

"So is sex."

"Please, Claire, listen to me. You have to know what happened tonight. All of it."

And so I began, first introducing Bev as the woman I loved and then continuing with the two of us breaking into the farmhouse, finding the money under the stairs, Bev and I nearly freezing to death, her humiliating retreat to her house, banging Jensen with the lamp, and the cold, empty walk back to the hotel.

Claire listened intently, never interrupting once, which was a new record for her.

"That's it," I said, "the whole story."

She pulled the sheet up over her body as though she was suddenly self-conscious.

"Is she prettier than I am?"

"What?"

"Prettier, as in good looking, knockout, sexy."

"Come on, Claire."

"You didn't describe her to me!"

"Well, she isn't as tall as you are, she's blonde, and she's older…"

"Older?" She smiled at that.

"A bit."

Claire dropped the sheet from her body, her confidence returning. "Come on, get in bed."

"You always have to prove yourself don't you?"

"I don't like competition."

"You don't have to worry. I told you it's over."

"Ok, then you prove it to me."

The sun awakened me in the morning, streaming through the window. I opened my eyes and looked around, my mind crowded by a jumble of unmanageable thoughts. I was lying on my side facing away from Claire, I turned over. She was gone, the sheet neatly folded over a plumped-up pillow.

What time is it? I looked at the clock. Nine fifteen. Damn, why didn't she wake me?

I got up, urinated, washed my face and found my Norelco already plugged in. She had probably shaved her legs with it. Wasn't the first time. I hurriedly dressed in a fresh shirt but the same trousers; I only brought one pair, and went downstairs.

I waved at Tina who gave me one of those what-have-*you*-been-up-to looks. I walked into the dining room, about half full of customers. At a corner table sat Claire and Don. As soon as I appeared, looks of curiosity bounced off both Claire and me from people in the room.

The night clerk had done his job, all right. He should write a gossip column.

I went to the buffet table and helped myself to coffee, orange juice and a croissant, and sat down.

Don Wright was a redhead; tall and skinny with wrists like stalks of rhubarb. Next to his chair was a black camera case. He was finishing up his coffee.

Claire was her usual combination of elegance and casual, sitting on her coat, which she had thrown over the back of the chair. The coat was a rich beige color, trimmed with pale fur, long and silky, extending well below the hem and sleeves. The suede body, with delicate embroidery in shades of violet and pale green was probably meant to suggest an ethnic peasant style. But Claire gave it voguish sophistication. She'd got it in the Grand Bazaar in Istanbul on a vacation trip, and looked sleek wearing it. She looks sleek wearing anything, wearing nothing.

Don had the morning CL folded next to his plate. "Seen your article?" he asked.

"I wrote it."

"You don't pull any punches."

Claire sat quietly nibbling on an English muffin flavored with a dab of cream cheese. She was in constant fear of gaining weight.

"Did you sleep well?" she asked with a hint of condescension in her voice.

"Like a log," I said.

"Well, that's not how I would have described you last night."

"I told you I was tired."

Don shifted in his chair and kept reading.

"And people stare at me like I was a zoo animal. That couple over there," she nodded with her head, "they pretend as though they couldn't care less, but I know they keep looking at me."

"Does that surprise you?" I said. "A night clerk is a night clerk is a..."

"Oh shut up!" she snapped.

Don looked up from the CL. "Would you rather I sit at another table?"

I smiled. "Our lives are open books, Don."

"Well, don't mind me. I don't read books anyway." He folded the newspaper out of the way. "I think I'll start out taking general shots of the town to get some ambience, you know? Show me where the Sheriff and his deputy hang out, and that house where the kid is staying. It will take extra time, a couple of days anyway, to get snaps of people. I need to learn the territory first. Sneak around, you know what I mean?"

I knew what Don meant and it bothered me.

"And what are you going to do today?" I asked Claire.

"I hadn't thought about it. Hang with you I suppose."

"I will be busy."

"All right," she said, slamming her muffin on her plate. "Just say it, I'm in your way."

I leaned over the table. "You show up without a word and expect me to drop everything and be your tour guide? There is nothing here but trouble."

"Does that include Beverly what's-her-name?"

"Jesus you can be mean."

"I just want to make sure she's not the reason why I'm in the way."

Claire opened her handbag of slouchy Italian leather, and pulled out a pack of Benson & Hedges, one of her habits I didn't particularly enjoy. She put a cigarette to her lips. "Light me."

I struck a match the hotel leaves with its ashtrays.

I was about to tell her and Don that I had a departure time at high noon when Tina poked her head into the dining room.

"Call for you, Mr. Kouros." She gave a quick disapproving glance at Claire.

For a wild moment I thought Bev was calling but only for a wild moment.

"I'll take it in my room."

It was Bailey.

"Hey, Bill, how are things going?" he said to me, uncharacteristically solicitous.

Something was wrong.

"I'm glad you didn't ask me that last night," I replied, "but I do have more fodder for the Citizen Ledger."

"That's why I'm calling. Brewster stopped by this morning."

"Stopped by?" The publisher never stops by. You go to him. Something was really wrong. "What the hell did he want?"

"He wants you to lay off."

"Lay off? Did you say *lay off*?"

"He's worried about lawsuits. That lawyer buddy of yours, Al Lewis—is that his name?—called Brewster and told him he was threatening to sue the Citizen Ledger for ten million dollars for defamation of character, libel, intimidation and false entry into his home. There's more but I can't remember it all."

I was storming. "Brewster got me into this and now he's telling me to back off? Well, it's too late for that. I found the murder weapon in the trunk of Sorenson's car, which implicates his widow, Rose. I found a hundred thousand dollars under the stairs at Schultzman's farm. And that juvenile delinquent deputy sheriff put coffee in my gas tank and I nearly froze to death on a county road before he came by to save me. Imagine that? Save me? Well I got even. I hit him with a desk lamp and as far as I know he's nursing one big headache even as we speak."

There was an intake of breath and a long pause. Finally

Bailey found his voice somewhere under his typewriter. "My God, Bill, you hit a cop?"

"Add that to character assassination, libel, intimidation and false entry."

"You are a representative of the Minneapolis Citizen Ledger. You can't go around hitting cops. You better come home before you get arrested."

I didn't bother to tell him I had already been arrested and I had already been told to go home.

"What about the murder weapon, a crow bar, by the way, with blood encrusted on it, and that stash of money?"

"Who else knows about it?"

"Nobody." I didn't intend to drag Bev into this.

The editor in Bailey took over. "This is big stuff. What a scoop that would be. You know the Pioneer Press is sending a guy down there? We've been hitting this so hard, it's getting attention. It may go national, like the Chicago Tribune, maybe even the New York Times."

"You kidding me?"

"Would I kid? Leave now and write your story when you get back. We can hold the Home Edition for it."

"What about Brewster?"

"I'll talk to him. The damage is already done, so why quash a story like this?"

"I won't have wheels till noon. My gas tank has to be cleaned out."

"Rent a car."

"In Clear Lake? I'd have to get to Mankato."

"Take Don's car and let *him* get to Mankato, wherever the hell that is. I don't care how you get back, just get back."

"Why don't I write my piece here and call it in? Then you don't have to hold the Home and we can still make the newsstands by dinner."

I could imagine Bailey drooling. "But what if that Deputy comes after you?"

"If he was coming after me he would have done it by now. He's probably home with an icepack on his head."

"Ok, but as soon as you finish calling in your stuff, get your ass home. Got that?"

"Right between my teeth." No reason to worry Bailey further that I'd already been given the same ultimatum from Sheriff Amundson.

Bailey started to hang up, then changed his mind. "Hold on, Bill, are you still there?"

"Yeah, what is it?"

"I nearly forgot. I got your information."

"What information?"

"Who owns the Schultzman farm."

So much had happened since I talked to Alice Timmins that it was no longer on my radar.

"Oh, that."

"Legal got it this morning."

"So who owns it?"

"A physician named Robert Nordstrom. He's a big honcho down there. Know him?"

I stared in shock at the wall of my room. "Yeah," I replied, "I know him."

23

When I got back to the dining room Claire was on another cigarette pointedly pouting while Don was champing at the bit. Except for them, the place was empty. Apparently the curiosity seekers had had enough and were now on the town reporting what they saw. Just like me, I thought wryly.

I sat back down, still trying to get my head around the startling news that Bev's father owned the Schultzman farm. Was he mixed up in this mess, too?

Can't think about that now, too much to do and too little time.

Claire gave me a frustrated look. "I've had breakfast, three cups of coffee, two cigarettes and I'm still sitting in this dingy hotel. What's there to do?"

Get out of my hair, I thought. I took a paper napkin and wrote directions to Maynard's newspaper plant, the Sheriffs office, Al Lewis's house, the hospital where Sarah lay. I handed the napkin to Don.

"These are for starters. Have you got a long lens?"

"An eight hundred millimeter Canon."

"So you can shoot from your car and not attract attention?"

"No problem."

"Fine. I wish we could get candids of Lewis and Amundson."

"You'll have to entice them into camera range."

"I pick up my car at noon at the police garage, behind the court house. Maybe you can get Amundson then."

"If you're standing next to a uniform, yes."

"Who knows, you might even get Jensen. He'd be the uniform with a bandage on his head."

"What happened to him?"

"Long story. I'll tell you later." I pulled from my pocket the small photo of the Schultzman family I had reclaimed from Jensen. "Can you copy this?"

He studied the graininess. "We can make something out of it in the lab. Who's who?"

"The old man is Alfred Schultzman. The boy is Bruno and the girl is Sarah."

"And the old lady is the old lady?"

"She died three years ago."

Don wrote the information on the back of the photograph. "Where did this come from?"

"I stole it."

Don looked up. "When did you add robbery to your job description?"

Claire was not happy being ignored. "Do you have an assignment for me?"

"Go with Don. Be his map reader."

"What are you going to do?"

"Write a piece for the Home Edition. After that I'm going to pay a visit to Rose Sorenson."

"The newspaperman's wife?"

I nodded. "Her husband was my close friend and mentor."

"That sounds more interesting than traipsing around

with Don."

"This is a private matter. Just go with Don. I'll pick up my car and meet you in the lobby at noon."

I went to my room and wrote as if a fury possessed me, and called it in in record time. If Bailey wanted to edit anything it was all right with me.

I walked up Main Street to Leuthold's, an old-line clothing store. The capstone on the building it occupied was dated 1898.

I bought a thick wool scarf, fur-lined mittens instead of gloves so that my fingers could warm one another, insulated overshoes with metal clips and a heavy-duty cap with pull-down earflaps, the kind hunter's wear. I hoped Bailey would cover the thirty-seven dollars and ninety-five cents as an expense, and it didn't matter that I did not look fashionable. I wasn't going to an art opening.

The biting wind left few people on the street and when I turned off Main I passed no one. As I walked on Elm toward the lake I heard a siren in the distance. Ambulance or a fire truck. Or a squad car.

Moving fast I reflected on my decision to see Rose before I left town. Of course I was duty bound to express my sorrow, but in the back of my head lurked two unanswered questions: how did the Toronado get dented and how did the crow bar get in the trunk? Maybe I will find out.

If she was home, fine, if not I had a healthy outing, walking by an empty swath of ground which in the summer was packed with campers and RVs, past the high hill of Maplewood Park, and following the edge of the road because there was no sidewalk on this stretch of housing development.

I approached the Sorenson home, less threatening by daylight. The bright sun reflected off the big picture window, stinging my eyes. I pressed the bell and waited.

Presently the door opened and Rose looked out at me, her face wan and haggard.

"Why, Bill, it's you. I thought you might have left town."

"Not until I have a chance to let you know how badly I feel."

"Come in, come in."

A waist-high planter crowded with Boston ferns separated the entry from the rest of the house. I followed Rose around it and into the living room. Her taste was provincial; lots of scrolled wood stained a medium brown and accented by silver-blue, brocade upholstery. She had the big drapes drawn, turning the interior into funeral parlor bleak.

"Let me take your things."

I removed my winters including my new overshoes, which she put in the entry closet.

"Would you like some coffee? I just made it. I have sweet rolls I can warm up."

"I had breakfast, Rose, but coffee sounds great."

She escorted me to the dining room, an L off the living room, where I sat at a shellacked oak table

"I didn't see a car. Someone drop you off?"

"No, I walked. My car wouldn't start."

"Sorry to hear that. Not good in this weather."

"We're long overdue for a January thaw," I said.

Winter is a burden everyone commiserates over. We all suffer equally because of it. Rich and poor. Blessed and unblessed. Rose and Bill. Bev and Claire...

"The car will be fixed by noon. Then I'll drive back to Minneapolis."

"I'm sorry to see you go," she said from the kitchen.

I wasn't sure she meant that.

Rose carried in a small silver service and set it on the table. She poured steaming coffee and sat down across from me.

I stirred in cream and sugar, having to forego it at Al Lewis's house what seems like a lifetime ago.

"Rose, I'd like to write an obituary for Maynard in the Citizen Ledger. I know they'll print it even though he wasn't from the Twin City area. Is there a photo I can use? I promise to mail it back."

"I know Maynard would be truly flattered."

"He was a special man." Rose went into a bedroom and returned with a framed photograph. She handed it to me.

"It's about two years old but it's the best I have. We seldom made the effort to remember ourselves with pictures."

Rose put her fingers to her mouth. They were quivering

"I'm sorry."

"You found him."

I nodded. "I should have seen you sooner. Things have been hectic."

"You've been writing a lot of articles."

"You've read them?"

She nodded.

"Do you approve?"

"I wish you could ask Maynard that."

"I hope he would. I think he would."

She didn't say anything.

"What are you plans? Will you continue publishing the Independent?"

"Can't do that without Maynard. I have a sister in Pasadena. I'll sell this one and buy a little house or a condo out there, nothing fancy."

She looked at her furnishings as though she was embarrassed to have them.

"At least you won't have cold weather to suffer through."

She looked at me almost guiltily. "Among other things."

I stared at her over my raised cup. "Like what?"

"Let's not rake through the coals again. I want them to burn to ashes. That's what I did with Maynard."

"You had him cremated?"

She nodded.

"You're not having a funeral?"

"How could I?" Her eyes began to water. "Maynard had no face. I couldn't bury a man without a face."

"I'm sorry. I know how hard this is for you, but there are hundreds of Maynard's friends, me included, who would have wanted to say goodbye to him."

"It's too late. Maynard is gone. I scattered his ashes last night. I walked onto the lake and let them blow away in the wind."

"Well, what's done is done I guess."

"You were very close to Maynard, weren't you?"

"Yes, you know that, Rose. He was a father to me."

"You're disappointed."

"It would have been nice to include a funeral notice in the obituary. But I understand your feelings."

Rose wiped her tears with a napkin. "You were like a son to him, a son he wished for. I was never able to give him one."

This was news to me. "I didn't think he wanted a family. His work was his life."

"That was the paradox of our marriage. I couldn't bear him a child and so his child became the newspaper."

"How did you feel about that?"

"How do you suppose I felt? I was jealous. Can you imagine? Jealous of a linotype machine, a printing press, a proofreader's desk? I hated every day I had to work there."

"Rose…"

"It's true, Bill." She blew her nose and wadded the napkin. "Why am I telling you this? It's not what you came to hear."

"If it will make you feel better."

"I forgot my manners. Let me warm your coffee." She leaned over and poured. Steam rose from the silver spout as the dark liquid swirled around the inside of my Wedgewood cup.

"You know what it's like," she began again, "turning out a newspaper every week. Never any time off. Twenty-eight years without a vacation. I got so sick and tired printing the same social notices and laying out the same grocery ads."

"But you did all right, more than all right. Look at this house, the new car, the remodeled office."

"Having money didn't make me happy. It only intensified my sense of loss, a life wasted and for what? Nice things?"

I leaned toward her. "Where did it come from, Rose? Where did you get the money to afford all of this?" I made a sweeping gesture with my arm.

"Maynard was the one to answer that question."

"Maynard is dead." I said, challenging her.

"You have to dig, I know. You are a reporter. It's your nature to dig until you get your story. What Maynard was proud of you for doing."

She sighed as though girding up for an inevitable fight. "It's not a crime, is it, to want nice things. Maynard made some investments, they paid off handsomely."

"He was in the stock market?"

"I don't know where it came from. Maynard never confided in me and I never asked."

Two people married but leading separate lives, I thought. "How can I find out?"

"Well, there's Al."

"Al Lewis?"

Rose nodded. "He is Maynard's executor."

Everything seems to go back to Al.

"Rose, I have to tell you something. I came by your house night before last."

I expected her to act surprised, resentful, even angry but all she said was, "I know."

"You know?"

"I haven't been able to sleep. I sit in the dark and stare out the window. I saw you drive by, park down the road and walk back to the garage. I saw you get into the garage. "

"Why didn't you say something? Why didn't you stop me?"

"You are a very determined young man. You would have found what you wanted whether I tried to stop you or not."

"What I found was a big dent."

"And you are wondering how that happened."

I nodded.

"I went for a drive. The Sheriff released the car and brought it over. I never wanted to get behind the wheel of that big fancy car. I missed the old Chevy but I needed to get out for a while. I couldn't stand to be alone in the house another minute. So I went into town, drove past the office, I don't know why, curiosity maybe. I was thinking of parking and daring myself to go inside to see where Maynard died. I lost my nerve and decided to go back home. I was distraught, and I wasn't used to driving such a big car. I came around the corner a little too fast and hit a patch of ice. And skidded sideways into a light pole."

"I want to believe you, Rose, I really do, but the night you went for a drive, Dr. Nordstrom was nearly struck down by a hit and run driver."

"You're not suggesting it was me?" she asked, but it was feigned, unconvincing.

"The doctor described the car close enough to convince me it was the Toronado that nearly hit him."

She broke down suddenly, dammed up emotion finally spilling over the levee of her make-believe. She crossed her forearms on the table and lowered her head into the limited confines they provided. Her back swayed with her sobs.

I got up and came around to her side of the table and held her shoulders. "Rose," I kept saying, "Rose."

Presently the sobbing diminished and she raised her head. She wiped her eyes with the back of her hand.

"I guess it was too much to keep to myself. I'm not very strong. Probably never was."

I sat down next to her. "Did you really try to hit Doctor Nordstrom?"

It took her awhile but she finally nodded.

"Why? Why did you do it?"

"Does it matter? He wasn't hurt."

"Of course it matters. Because you missed him doesn't absolve you of responsibility. You didn't stop, you just kept driving."

"Maybe it was wrong of me, but at the time I felt perfectly justified."

"Why?"

"Just a minute."

She got up and went into the kitchen. I heard a cupboard door open and close. She returned with a sugar bowl. Puzzled, I watched as she set it on the table and poked around inside it with her fingers. She pulled out a narrow piece of metal, wiped away grains of sugar trapped in the tiny crevices and handed it to me.

"Recognize it?"

A slug of lead. I turned it face up and stared at the raised letters, reading them backwards the way a proofreader is trained to do:

mortsdroN

"Jesus," I said, "the fifth slug."

So this completed the list of names that Maynard had set on his linotype machine. The one he slipped into his pocket. Doctor Nordstrom, who also happens to own the Schultzman farm. God Almighty, I was thinking, Bev's father is involved in this mess I had walked into. Is that why Maynard didn't hand it over – he didn't want to incriminate Nordstrom because he knew how I felt about Bev?

Even worse, did he have anything to do with Maynard's death? Did he kill Maynard and take the slug because his name was on it?

I stared at Rose. I could not believe what I was thinking. "My God, do you think Dr. Nordstrom killed Maynard?"

She didn't say anything. It was too painful for her. She sat like a deaf mute waiting for my fingers to do the talking.

I continued: "How could he do anything so evil? Its unthinkable."

Rose came out of her self-induced trance. "I was in the other room when Maynard set those slugs for you, and I saw him put one of them in his pocket. I was curious but I didn't say anything. At the time I figured it was between him and you, and he would tell me later. But he died first."

"Did Maynard hide this in the sugar bowl?"

"No. I put it there."

"Then where did you find it?"

"In Maynard's pocket."

"You!"

"Maynard always drove me home to start dinner and he'd go back to close up the shop. It grew late and so I called, but there was no answer. I got worried. He had high blood pressure and he was working overtime on the Schultzman murder. I was concerned he might have passed out. So I bundled up and walked to the office. I found him, there on the floor. At first I thought he was unconscious but then I saw the lead covering his face…" She stopped talking, the memory beginning to work on her again. Tears fell from her eyes.

"When I came in the back way," I said, "I thought I

heard someone in front. Was that you?"

"Yes, I heard the back door open and I got frightened. I didn't know it was you. I was so shocked I couldn't think straight. I walked home in a daze and put the slug in the sugar bowl to hide it. And then I spent the night and the next day brooding over it. All I could think of was that Dr. Nordstrom was somehow mixed up in this. I had to talk to him, that's all. I had no intention of hurting him. I just wanted to find out if he knew anything about Maynard getting killed in such an awful way. The Sheriff released the car that afternoon. After dinner I decided to drive over to the Clinic. I knew the Doctor always worked late and so I parked across the street, waiting for him. He came out and started walking home. I was going to drive up to him, roll down the window and ask him to climb in so we could talk. I followed him, driving slowly, and when he crossed the street to his house, I could only see that awful image of Maynard with the lead mask, and I pressed on the gas. It all happened so fast, it was a blur. He jumped over the snow bank. I skidded sideways and I could feel the back of the car bouncing off a light post."

Rose looked up at me. "And that's it."

That wasn't it.

I sat back down. "I have something else I need to ask you about. I found out who owns the Schultzman farm."

"He did, didn't he?" she asked.

I shook my head. I pushed the line of type across the table and pointed to it. "The man whose name is on that slug owns the farm, Dr. Nordstrom. It's not public knowledge. I had to get a court order to find out."

"It's pretty common for wealthy people to buy farm property as an investment."

"Granted, but of all the available land how come he bought the farm Schultzman leased? It has to be more than coincidence that Dr. Nordstrom's name keeps popping up."

I hesitated a moment because the worst was yet to come.

"There's more."

She shook her head in deep weariness. "How can there possibly be more?"

"What about the crow bar?"

"What crow bar?"

"You can't tell me you don't know about it. It's the weapon that killed Alfred Schultzman. It's in the trunk of your car!"

She looked at me as if I had just landed from Mars.

"I found it in the wheel-well wrapped in a pair of coveralls. It was coated with blood."

She remained as if benumbed. Her hands began to shake and she hid them under the table.

"If you don't know about the crow bar, then there is only one answer."

"What?"

"Maynard put it there."

"Why would he have done that?"

"Because he used it to kill Schultzman."

She was aghast. "Why would he do a thing like that?"

"To pay for all the nice things he has acquired."

"How can you say that?" she screamed. She jumped from her chair as if to lash out at me. "How can you be so cruel? Maynard was a good man!"

"Then how did the crow bar end up in the trunk of his car?"

"I don't believe you. You are imagining things."

"Come with me. I'll show you." I walked into her kitchen. She remained in her chair.

"Please Rose, we have to clear this up one way or the other."

Reluctantly, she got up and followed me to the garage. Cold air mixed with fuel smell met us. The Toronado was sitting as I left it, the skin dented, the trunk ajar. I pushed up the lid, dragged the spare out of the trunk and let it fall to the floor. I bent forward and peered into the wheel-well looking for the coveralls and their blood-encrusted contents I had discovered night before last.

The wheel well was empty. In disbelief, I reached into it and pawed around with my hand. Nothing.

"The crow bar is gone, " I said, dumbfounded.

"I told you, you are imagining things," Rose replied, relief calming her voice.

"But it was there! I saw it!"

Now it was my turn to be rattled.

24

Doubting my own credibility, I left Rose's house and plodded my way back to town, thinking hard. Could Rose have been right, was I imagining things? I'd been through hell and back, to quote Audie Murphy, or more likely in my case to hell and not yet back if I was making stuff up in a desperate effort to justify my gratuitous behavior that is ruining lives, including my own.

Didn't I take the spare out of its well and discover the crow bar wrapped in stained coveralls?

Didn't I?

Yes, yes, I thought, having a dialogue with myself. You saw it. You were not imagining it. You unwrapped the coveralls, found the crow bar, and then you rewrapped the bar in the coveralls and put them back in the well, replaced the spare and lowered the trunk lid.

You see yourself doing it. You didn't make it up. It happened.

So where does that leave me? I asked myself.

Out in the cold where you happen to be right now.

So who could have removed the crow bar? Only one person knew you were snooping around, who saw you go into the garage.

Rose.

She removed the crow bar to protect Maynard.

I looked at my watch. Forty-five minutes till I had to pick up my car at the police garage and head back to Minneapolis. One good thing occurred to me however: I'll be back in time to attend the opening of the Pop Art show at the Walker. Won't Bailey be tickled about that.

No more Exclusives with my byline. Let the Citizen Ledger's competitor, the St. Paul Pioneer Press take over.

As I walked up Elm, I came to the street where Al Lewis lived and spotted his house from the corner. I hesitated, the cold air climbing my pant legs. The reporter in me ached to do a follow-up interview with Bruno— given everything I had learned since we first met—and spin him like one of those coin sorters so that all the correct answers fall into their proper question slots.

But I'd never be able to con my way into that house again, not without Al Lewis's permission and there was no chance of getting that. I began walking again, thinking about that big-shot lawyer, and a change of plan took root in my unsettled state of mind.

I had plenty of time before picking up the car. Finish with a flourish, I bragged to myself. If I can't do Bruno, then I'll get a final interview with his guardian, the town's most prominent attorney who seems to have his fingers in everything, not only as Bruno's guardian but also as Maynard's executor, a cozy relationship, cozier than the Cozy Corner. Here's a farewell finger to the town where I grew up.

I'll never come back, so why should I care?

Reaching Main Street, instead of turning right to the police garage, I turned left and walked the three blocks to Al's office, a three-story building of recent vintage featuring a cream-colored brick facade. The pink granite lintel over the entrance had an inscription chiseled into it: Lewis Building, the pretentious proprietor of mediocre architecture.

Entering the lobby I took a deep breath, doing my best to leave my anger and frustration at the door. The inside was worse than the outside. Above my head was a dropped ceiling of acoustical tile, accented by upwardly directed sconces that resembled the white bellies of bloated fish. The floor was highly polished terrazzo with sparkly things imbedded in it.

The main floor was given over to small retail: a coffee shop, a Hallmark shop, a combination barber and beauty shop. Helps pay the overhead and get a nice tax write-off, no doubt.

The elevator was at the back wall. I pushed the button and the doors separated as though the elevator had been waiting for me. I pressed three and felt myself being lifted to the sound of Muzak.

The doors parted and I stepped into a spacious office lobby, the melody lingering on as I crossed the carpet. Straight ahead, under a jumbo, hand-tinted portrait of Albert Lewis the Elder, sat a receptionist behind a mahogany counter. She was chewing gum and reading Cosmopolitan. So much for first impressions.

"Al Lewis, please," I said, interrupting her concentration on advice to the lovelorn.

She looked up. "Junior or…"

"Junior," I interrupted. Not that silly game again.

She pushed a button on her Centrex. "Name, please?"

"Kouros."

"Do you have an appointment?"

"No."

"I'll see if Mr. Lewis is available." She spoke into the receiver. "Mr. Kouros to see you, Mr. Lewis."

She disconnected. "He'll be right out,"

And he was. Al came down the hallway in a gallop; his round figure waddling like spilled Jell-O.

"Bill, Bill," he said with a voice befitting a keynote

213

speaker, "I was just thinking about you."

"I hope the thoughts were pleasant."

He scratched a quick note on the receptionist's message pad, handed it to her, and then said, "How could they be anything but?"

Al led the way into his office and dismissed his secretary, a tall, white-haired woman who had been taking dictation on a steno pad.

"Close the door behind you, Marilyn," he said at her back.

Al's office was overflow barrister: shelves of law books lined the walls, stacks of file folders were piled on his desk and, on a conference table, legal-size yellow pads were filled with notes.

"Sit down." He indicated the chair just vacated by his secretary. "What brings you to see me today?" he asked, sitting behind his desk. He was too small for it. As he leaned back in his button-tufted executive chair his feet left the floor.

"I was visiting Rose Sorenson."

"Just now?"

"Yes."

"That's where you've been."

"Have you been trying to reach me?"

"Ah…yes, in a way. But that can wait for now. Tell me, how is Rose? I haven't seen her since this awful business began."

"Mourning."

He bent his head down as if I had intoned a prayer. "The poor woman." He looked up at me. "This is a terrible time. I ordered a very large floral arrangement. It will be delivered this afternoon."

"She'll be pleased. She told me that you are Maynard's executor."

Al's face shed its obsequious mask for a split second, reveling impatience, even anger. "I should remind Rose that my professional relationship with her late husband is strictly confidential."

I shrugged. "She didn't tell me anything she wouldn't tell an old friend. She also said she plans to sell the house and move to California to be close to her sister."

Al sighed, deciding now to be sympathetic. "I suppose that is all to the good. It would be difficult for her to remain in Clear Lake."

"At least she won't have to worry about her next meal. I would say Maynard left her a bundle."

Al stiffened. "I wouldn't say."

"Why not? It shows everywhere, the new house, the new car, the remodeled office. He wasn't a wealthy man when I knew him."

"He made wise investments."

"That's what Rose said. Did you advise him?"

Al changed the direction of his chair. "Bill, what is it you came to see me about?"

"Bruno."

He reached for a silver letter opener from an orange marmalade crock on his desk. He held it point-to-heel on the tips of his forefingers.

"Why do you want to talk to me about Bruno?"

"I think he can solve a riddle."

"Really? What riddle?"

"I think he knows who killed Maynard."

Al suddenly dropped the opener between his knees. He disappeared from view as he bent down, fumbling for it. His voice came up from the depths.

"Bruno is under treatment. He is not able to solve anything."

"Treatment?" I asked. "So Bruno *is* on drugs."

"You already determined that," Al said, grunting as he straightened up. He returned the opener to the crock and leaned back in his chair.

"But you denied it at first. And then you tried to

bribe me to keep it quiet."

Al gripped the arms of his chair, barely enduring me. "What would you have done in my shoes? Keeping it quiet and keeping it out of the paper are quite different. About a quarter of a million people different."

"You saw the Citizen Ledger?"

"Delightful reading. Filled with suspense. And because of you I haven't had a moment's rest. I had to get Bruno out of the house just to get some sleep."

"Phone been ringing off the hook?"

"To coin a phrase."

"I didn't coin that one. So where is he?"

"At the Clinic. In the isolation ward."

"Incommunicado, huh? So who's taking care of him? Dr. Nordstrom?"

"Why should that make any difference to you?"

"Because Nordstrom's name has been popping up in the most unusual places."

"Such as?" Al asked casually, wanting to know more but not wanting to appear that he did.

"For example, I found out that he owns the Schultzman farm."

"That's not unusual. He probably owns other farms, as well."

"If that's not unusual, how about this?" I parried, more to get his reaction than to inform him, "Rose tried to run him down night before last in the Toronado."

Al came to attention as though he had touched a live wire, but he quickly came back under control.

"Bill," he said patronizingly, "why don't you go to the lake? You'll have better luck with your fish story."

I smiled. Al was turning into a humorist, a goddamn stand-up comedian sitting down.

"Maybe you'll believe these." I reached into my coat pocket and brought out the slugs of lead, including the fifth one that Rose had given me. I handed them over.

Al examined them. I waited patiently as he read the reverse type one slug at a time before putting it on his desk and then looking at the next one.

"Those were set on Maynard's linotype machine the night he was killed."

He gathered them up and handed them back to me.

I pocketed them but kept my eyes on Al.

"Five names," I said. "Sheriff Amundson, Maynard Sorenson, Alfred Schultzman, Robert Nordstrom and you. Two are dead and they can't talk, so that leaves the Sheriff, the doctor and the lawyer."

"And the Indian Chief?" Lewis said, mocking me.

I ignored him. "The names, including yours, had special meaning to Maynard."

He snorted. "Why shouldn't they? I happen to be on this list, if you can call it that, because I'm his executor. The others can be explained as simply."

"Even Dr. Nordstrom?"

"Why not?"

"The night Maynard molded these slugs, he put one of them in his pocket, the one with Doctor Nordstrom's name. It ended up in Rose's sugar bowl. She gave it to me this morning. Why didn't Maynard give that one to me along with the others?"

Al shrugged. "Who knows?"

"On the farm Dr. Nordstrom just happens to own I found a hundred thousand dollars in cash hidden there."

Al began to laugh. I must have hit the top of his laugh meter with that one. He was so convulsed I thought he would slide off his chair.

"Does that amuse you?"

He removed his handkerchief and wiped his eyes. "And how do you know that? Did you go to the farm and count it?"

"That's exactly what I did."

Al began snuffling as he tried to compose himself.

"Bill, you deserve an Oscar for that performance."

He was really getting to me. "Damn it!" I shouted. "The money was hidden under the stairs in a safe deposit box. The bills were neatly wrapped in bundles of tens, twenties and fifties, and I'm not the only one who saw it!"

Al put his handkerchief back in his pocket.

"You weren't alone?" he asked, looking at me warily. "Who, might I ask, was with you?"

I could have bitten my tongue. I was trying to goad Al into saying something incriminating but I was the one who got trapped.

The interview was over. The last thing I wanted to do was involve Bev. How could I have been so careless!

I stood up. "It's been nice entertaining you."

Al sat forward in his chair, and his feet actually reached the carpet. "You don't have to hurry," he said anxiously. "You haven't eaten lunch have you? I'll send Marilyn to the Cozy Corner for sandwiches. How does corned beef sound?"

He was edgy now, the humor that jollied his countenance had disappeared and his eyes narrowed with...with what? Fear? Just because I was leaving? He had me perplexed. What was bothering him?

"Some other time, Al."

I walked to the door and put my hand on the knob. Behind me I heard sounds of desperation, the chair tipping over, a desk drawer being yanked open, papers and files being clawed through. And then there was an ominous silence accentuated by heavy, adrenaline-charged breathing.

I looked back. Al was standing behind his desk holding a blunt-nose revolver. I could see bullets waiting in the cylinders. Al's eyes, only seconds ago watery with hilarity, were now as cold and as blue and as steely as the muzzle pointing nervously at my chest.

In my entire life I never had a gun pointed at me, not

even a gun that wavered in sync with the agitation of the aimer.

"What in hell are you doing, Al? Put that thing away."

"It's not a thing, Bill, it's a Colt Cobra .38 Special. I've never had to use it, but that doesn't mean I don't know how. I have a Marksman's Medal from the NRA. I keep my gun in the bottom drawer just in case. A lawyer can't be too careful. You never know when some crazy nut might come into my office."

"I'm not a crazy nut, so point that thing, that .38 Special or whatever you call it, somewhere else."

He stood with his legs spread apart, and waved the muzzle in the general direction of the chair I had just vacated.

"Sit down."

I shrugged and returned to the chair. I'd better humor him. I seemed to be getting awfully good at it.

"Is it too much to ask why you pulled a gun on me?"

"Making sure you don't leave."

"Why can't I leave?" I asked.

"Don't you know?"

"Should I?"

"I'll let Sheriff Amundson answer that question. He should be here any minute."

When he said that, my mind replayed the moment Al scratched a message and gave it to his receptionist. *Call the Sheriff* he probably wrote. I wondered why. Hitting Jensen? But how would Al know about that?

I crossed my legs and tried to maintain a casual demeanor. I didn't want Al to do anything rash, like pulling the trigger.

"I thought lawyers kept a bottle of scotch in their desks, not a gun."

"I have a permit for this."

"Does it give you the right to hold someone against his will?"

"It gives me the right to make a citizen's arrest."

"Arrest? For what?" I leaned forward and Al tensed.

"Don't try anything!"

"Ok, ok," I said leaning back. "Speaking of booze you wouldn't happen to have some scotch, would you? I sure could use a shot…I mean a drink."

My humor did not sit well with Al. "You just made your last joke, funny guy. You won't be laughing much longer."

I put my hands on the arms of the chair, my fingers kneading the wood, and stared out the window behind Al's desk. The sky was blue and cloudless. Out there, as cold as it was, was where I wanted to be, walking to my car, and driving back to Minneapolis in time for the Pop Goes the Easel show at Walker Art Center.

A buzz on the intercom interrupted my reverie. Al crabbed sideways to his desk and felt for the on-button, all the time keeping careful watch on me. His eyes did not blink once.

"Is the Sheriff here?" he asked, bending slightly toward the speaker.

The secretary's voice came through with metallic efficiency. "Yes, he is, Mr. Lewis."

"Have him come in right away."

The door opened in less time than it took me to exhale. Amundsen entered wearing a sheepskin car coat over his uniform.

He trained a disdainful look at me. "I've been looking all over town for you. I didn't expect to find you in Al's office. "

He looked at the Colt .38, steady in Al's hand now that the Sheriff had showed up.

"You can put the gun away now, Al."

Al laid the gun on his desk, as would a child who wanted to keep playing with his toys.

Amundson unbuttoned his coat and sat on the edge of

Al's desk, his leg dangling in front of me. He sighed expansively.

"Bill, I sure judged you wrong."

"I didn't know I was being judged."

"Until this morning you weren't, and that was my mistake, the biggest one I've made in more than twenty-five years in law enforcement."

"What are you talking about, Sheriff?"

A funereal sadness crimped the corners of his eyes.

"Don Jensen is dead."

25

Thoughts inside my head tumbled like clothes in a dryer as I tried to make sense of this new, unexpected assault on my senses. I couldn't assimilate Amundson's lugubrious statement that Jensen was dead. Reject it. It's not true. You're being baited, lied to.

I stared dumbly at his big, silver belt-buckle that was shinier than his badge.

"Dead?" I said softly as though talking to myself. "I just hit him. I hit him with the desk lamp. I only knocked him out. He was snoring when I left."

"That may be all well and good, Bill, but when I found him this morning he had a bullet hole in the middle of his forehead."

I lifted my gaze to meet the Sheriff eye-to-eye. Everything was so surreal I felt like I was trying to hide inside a de Chirico landscape.

"I didn't shoot him, Sheriff, if that's what you are implying. I told you, when I left him he was lying on the floor snoring. So charge me with assault and battery, or whatever the charge is, and let me out of this insane asylum."

"Insane asylum?" Amundson snapped back. "If anyone

is crazy around here it's you, Bill." He leaned toward me. "Let me explain something. Don's gun was not in its holster. I found it on the bed in the cell you occupied. It had been fired. You had to be the only one with him until I showed up this morning. There was no sign of forced entry. I want you to come quietly with me to the office so I can take your prints. If they match those on the gun, you better retain a lawyer." He looked at Al with a half smile. "In fact you got one right here."

"No, no," I stammered, "You've got it wrong. I didn't shoot Jensen."

"Then how did his gun end up in the cell?"

"I pulled it out his holster."

"Why would you take his gun unless you meant to shoot him?"

"I was afraid he would wake up and use it on me. So I put it out of reach in the cell." This sounded so weak and made-up, that it almost made me laugh, even if it was true.

"I wish I could believe you, Bill, but in addition to opportunity you had motive. You told me on the phone that you wanted to kill Don for what he did to you and Beverly."

"Sheriff," I pleaded, "Maybe I threatened to kill Jensen, but *actually* do it? I'm not a murderer!"

"No one is until he kills someone. I have a warrant for your arrest. Let's go."

Al had been staring in awed wonder but he found his voice when the Sheriff took me by the elbow to usher me out of the office.

"Looks like you've written your last article about Clear Lake," he said, nearly giddy from resurging self-confidence.

Even though I was in a state of shock, I managed a parting shot. "Don't bank on it, you might not get five per cent."

Stares followed us to the elevator and out to the patrol

car parked at the curb with its rack lights flashing. If Amundson had wanted to draw attention to me he couldn't have done a better job. I was exhibit A.

Once again I had to suffer the indignity of an officer of the law putting his hand on my head to keep it from hitting the doorframe as I crawled into the caged back seat of a squad car.

"How come you didn't handcuff me?" I asked before he shut the door in my face.

""I don't think you'll try anything foolish."

"How do you know?" I asked as he climbed into the front seat, and we continued our conversation through the steel-mesh cage separating us.

"You're not the type," he replied over his shoulder.

"You said I killed Jensen."

"I'm not saying you killed him, Bill, I'm saying you had plenty of motive because of the way Don treated you and Beverly. I'm sure a jury would be sympathetic."

"You're already talking about a jury?"

"I'd testify as a defense witness that Don had a hot temper. Manslaughter, three years with good behavior. "

"Gee, thanks."

Amundson looked at me briefly in the rearview mirror as he navigated the squad car toward the courthouse. "Don and I were not close friends."

"I wonder if he even had any," I mused as I looked out the window at Clear Lake's nearly empty main street. "Someone out there finished him off after I left."

"That is a pretty weak defense, Bill. You admit that you struck him with the desk lamp and knocked him out. So your fingerprints will be on the lamp. And you admit you handled his gun, the gun that was used to kill him, so your prints will be on that, too. The way I see it, you were so incensed with the way Don humiliated you and Beverly that you went berserk and after you knocked him down you pulled the gun and finished him off. You don't remember any of this because it is not uncommon where there are crimes of violence by normally law abiding persons, they are committed during moments of such intense passion that the killer can't remember what happened."

I looked up at the roof of the squad car. There were scratches on the fabric as if someone had clawed it in a desperate effort to escape. Welcome to my world.

"Do you really believe I was like that last night?"

He nodded.

"You already have me convicted!"

"It's not up to me, its up to a jury." Amundson laughed wryly. "I wanted you to get out of Dodge, as you said, but now it looks like you'll be here for awhile."

"According to Al, I won't be writing any more articles."

"Nope.

"So what are you going to do to me?"

"First you will be booked…"

"Meaning?"

"I will take your fingerprints."

That didn't sound so bad. "Then what?"

"Arraignment. You will go before the judge and plead not guilty."

"Because I am."

"Everybody pleads not guilty, that's the only charge a defendant is allowed to make."

"Great."

'Then the judge will set bail."

"How much will that be?"

The Sheriff shrugged under his sheepskin coat. "That's up to the judge, but you shouldn't have anything to worry about. I'm sure your rich boss will take care of that."

"He'd better." I thought of Brewster wearing his shiny wingtips and rep silk tie raising bail for his reporter.

The Sheriff pulled into the parking lot, nudging the

nose of his car close to the quarried stone wall. He got out and opened the back door for me.

"Ok, here we are."

'When do I see the judge?" I asked, as he led me down the steps to the jail.

He indulged me with a smile. "You have become a celebrity around these parts so I'm sure the judge will want to proceed as quickly as possible, but not till Monday at the earliest."

A white chalk mark on the concrete floor outlined the shape of Jensen's body. The round area for the head was stained dark with his blood. "My god, do I have to look at this until Monday?"

"At the earliest."

When I left, Jensen was lying inside that chalk mark snoring. He wasn't dead until someone came in, took his gun and shot him with it.

"Give me your hat and coat, and take off your overshoes."

Amundson collected them and placed them in a closet on the far wall.

He reached under the counter for an ink pad and a sheet of paper with ten squares imprinted on it, one for each finger.

"Roll up your sleeves."

The procedure took less than a minute.

"That's it?"

Amundson gave me a Kleenex soaked in alcohol to clean my blackened fingertips.

"That's it."

He opened the cell door, the hinges squeaking admission.

I hesitated, trying to buy time. "How about lunch?"

"I'll have it sent around."

I stared at the steel bars, at what amounted to the end of my life as I knew it. Three days ago I was an art critic for the Minneapolis Citizen Ledger, a respectable writer making a respectable living, and now I was being incarcerated for murder.

No, I thought. I can't go in there again. I can't sit in that trap while some prick is out there free to keep doing what he's been doing: killing people, first Schultzman, next Maynard and now Jensen.

Amundson felt my resistance. "Bill, don't make this any harder on yourself."

"I can't," I heard myself say, "I can't."

His features thickened with concern. "Don't give me any trouble." Instinctively, his right hand dangled by to his holster. "Get in there."

An uncontrollable fury began to shake my body, reacting to the Sheriff as I had reacted to Jensen.

Amundson had positioned himself between the door and the cell to make room for me to move inside. For a second he was vulnerable, trapped in a triangle made up of the door, the cell and me. Without warning or even giving a second's thought to what I was doing, I turned and pushed hard against him, slamming him into the wedge of steel, and then I put my weight against the door,

His face got trapped between bars, narrowing his lips into a forced kiss.

"What the hell..." the words squeezed out of his mouth as if he had been eating alum.

I could see that he was trying for his gun. As long as I pushed he was crunched too tightly to allow his elbow to bend. Still putting on the pressure, I reached around the door and pulled the gun from its holster. The Sheriff watched bug-eyed with anger and impotence. I put the muzzle between the bars and poked his sixty-year-old gut with it.

"Can you feel this, Sheriff?"

He tried to nod.

"If you believe that I killed Jensen, then you better

228

believe that I will use this gun if you try anything."

I stood away and the door swung away from him, his body acting like a spongy spring. Red marks creased both sides of his face, giving him the look of an Indian brave in war paint. He stepped into the open, rubbing his cheeks.

I wiggled the gun. "Get in there," I ordered, using the same words he used on me.

Amundson glared at me. "You're locking me up, and then what? Play the hero and find the 'real' killer? You have shit in your brains."

That was the second time I heard him swear.

"And a gun in my hand. Sheriff, if you please."

"You won't get away with this."

"You are charging me with murder. What have I got to lose?"

"If you're innocent, everything."

"Spencer Tracy had better odds in Black Rock than I have in Clear Lake."

He didn't know what I was talking about.

"If you do this, Bill, you are guilty for sure."

"If I have any chance of clearing my name it's better on the outside than sitting in a cell."

The Sheriff walked into the cell and turned to face me as I slammed the door. Still pointing the gun at him I went to his desk and searched the drawers till I found the ring of keys Jensen used on me.

I dangled them in the air. "Which one?"

He didn't answer nor did I expect him to. After the third try I found the right key and turned the lock. I tossed the ring on his desk, making a clattering noise that was deafening in its import: I had put away the Sheriff of Clear Lake County.

I grabbed my belongings from the closet and left him stewing.

26

The police garage was on Third Street North, a block from the courthouse. I entered the front office, where a mechanic in blue work clothes sat behind a grease-smudged desk. A glass partition separated the office from the garage itself—four service bays with hoists and tool chests. Two squad cars were in the bays awaiting service. My Pontiac was parked facing the big garage door, waiting for me.

"I'm Kouros, here to pick up my car." I motioned with my head at it.

The mechanic was not happy. "You're late."

"What time is it?"

"Almost twelve-thirty, otherwise I'd be home eating lunch. The Sheriff told me to wait till you came. By the way where is he?"

"He dropped me off at his office. I walked from there."

"Sign here, both copies. Keys are in the ignition."

"You got her going ok?"

"I suctioned out the tank, flushed it and cleaned the carburetor. I put in enough gas to make sure it's running. You better fill up right away."

I did, stopping at the Sinclair station on my way to the hotel. Waiting for the attendant to fill the tank, I checked myself in the rearview mirror. My eyes reflected the anger that was making my hands tremble. I had to calm down and think clearly. The attendant wanted to check the oil and I lowered my window a notch to tell him everything was fine, everything, that is, except me.

I found Claire and Don sitting in the empty lobby. Claire's crossed leg was waving little circles in the air.

"You said twelve. It's nearly one."

"Something came up."

They looked at me, reading the concern on my face.

"Trouble?" Don asked.

"Real, and I haven't got time to explain right now. We have to check out."

I went to the front desk. Tina was working. No school on Saturday.

"Any messages?"

"Not unless you count Sheriff Amundson coming in this morning looking for you. He had his siren going."

So that was the siren I heard. Do not ask for whom it wails, I said to myself, it wails for thee.

"My boss is going to hate to see you go, Mr. Kouros. You brought in a lot of business. I never saw so many people having breakfast. I had to run over to Brozik's yesterday because we ran out of English muffins."

"Is that a compliment?"

"Absolutely."

I leaned over the counter and gave her a farewell hug.

"If you ever need a referral for a job, for college, whatever, call me at the Citizen Ledger."

And then a thought sucked my confidence like quicksand. What if she does call and the switchboard operator says, "Bill Kouros is no longer at the Citizen Ledger. He's in the Stillwater Penitentiary."

"What's the matter?" Don asked when I rejoined them.

"You look like you lost your best friend."

"In a way I have. Get your coats."

"Are we going to lunch?" Don said.

"No."

"I heard the pecan pie at the Cozy Corner is very special," he said, picking up his bag.

"I'll take you to the Lincoln Del when we get home and you can eat a whole pie all by yourself."

Claire made fun of my new hat when I put it on outside.

"Don't laugh," I said. "It keeps my ears warm," but when we got to the car I tossed it into the back seat next to Don.

I handed the keys to Claire. "You drive."

"Where do you want me to go?"

"Around the lake. I need to tell you how my morning went."

As we drove, the only sound other than my voice was the heater blowing hot air, better than I was doing.

Don began squirming in the back seat. "This is getting too hot, Bill. Why don't you drop me off at my car? I shot everyone you asked for except Jensen and he's dead."

"You got a photo of Amundson?"

"In the hotel when he came looking for you, but I didn't know it at the time. He was really steaming."

"And Lewis?"

"I took a walk down Main Street for the hell of it and he was coming out of his office. I don't know where he was heading but he was moving pretty fast for a fat guy."

"Fantastic. You're worth your weight in Ektachrome."

"Forget the flattery. I want to go back to Minneapolis and develop my film."

"Nothing will happen while the Sheriff is in that cell."

"But I don't want to be dragged into this mess." He shook his head numbly. "If you're wanted for murder…"

"I didn't kill Jensen."

"I didn't say you did but you are in big trouble. Locking that Sheriff away isn't helping your case any."

"That's why I have to prove my innocence."

"And how do you plan do to that?"

"Find the killer."

Don laughed nervously. "I have a better idea. Find a lawyer."

We were driving past the all-too-familiar sights along Clear Lake Drive: Maplewood Park, Rose's house, the golf course…

"Why the hell are we driving around this frozen landscape?" Claire asked.

The imperativeness of her words brought me back to the present tense.

"To collect my thoughts."

"What thoughts? I wasn't sure you had any."

She was in a testy mood, all right.

"I need time to sort things out. And don't drive too fast. I don't want to attract unwanted attention."

As if on cue, we all stopped talking. To focus my mind I reached into my pocket and fingered the slugs of lead like a Greek with his worry beads.

What was the common denominator that connected three murders and a farmhouse with a hundred thousand dollars hidden under a stair?

Drugs.

And drugs brought me to Bruno. How did he get his hands on it? As I told Al in his office, Bruno is the key. I had to talk to him.

I turned in my seat. "Don," I said, looking at him over my shoulder, "do you have a small camera?"

"Smaller than my One-O-One?" He patted the camera case on his lap. "I got an Olympus A11."

"Can you use it to take close-ups without being detected?"

Don smiled confidently as the pro he was. "Like

234

Walker Evans? In the thirties, he concealed a small camera in his coat and shot people on a New York subway without them knowing it."

"No flash though."

"I can push that high-speed Ektachrome you just complimented me with." He pulled out the small camera about the length of his palm with a slide over the lens. It was neat and compact. "Who do you want a candid of?"

"Bruno."

"The Schultzman kid?"

I nodded.

If I have to go down I might as well go down swinging. I'll write a final piece, a Sunday spread with photos of the principal characters.

"You just said he was in an isolation ward. How do you propose to get to him?"

"Dr. Nordstrom."

27

Claire pulled into the Clinic parking lot. I told her to park in the furthest slot because across the street, looking like a picture on a Christmas card, was the Nordstrom house. I didn't want to risk the possibility of Bev looking out the window and spotting my car.

But I gave myself the brief luxury of wondering what she was doing behind those windows, reflecting sunlight in the harsh cold. Eating lunch? Giving Tod his nap? Thinking of me?

Huh, fat chance on the last one.

"What do you want me to do?" Claire asked, interrupting my reverie.

"Stay in the car. There's plenty of gas to keep you warm."

"I hope you know what you're doing!" she yelled after I slammed the door.

Don slipped his small Olympus in his overcoat pocket and walked with me to the emergency entrance at the side of the building. We entered a whisper-quiet lobby.

An admitting nurse sitting behind an elbow-high counter looked up at us. On her pristine desk sat a gray Royal typewriter and a white telephone with illuminated buttons.

She looked at us quizzically, wondering no doubt what the emergency was.

"It's so cold, we decided to come to the ER rather than the front entrance."

She smiled understandingly. "Are you here to see a patient?"

She was correct but I didn't tell her that. "Doctor Nordstrom."

She came to attention and studied my face, no doubt asking herself who is this stranger asking for the man in charge, and then I detected an expanding hint of recognition in her eyes.

"I'll see if he's in."

She picked up her phone and pushed a button, and the soft gong of an automatic call transmitted the doctor's code through the building. Presently one of the lights on her phone flashed.

"Dr. Nordstrom? Someone to see you."

She said to me, "Name?" pretending that she didn't know who I was.

"Bill Kouros."

She repeated my name into the phone, listened and cupped the palm of her hand over the mouthpiece.

"Would you pick up the phone on the table over there," she said, pointing to a waiting area that looked like someone's living room. "I'll connect you."

I walked over and picked up the phone, glancing down at a month-old National Geographic and a day-old Morning Citizen Ledger.

"Bill," the Doctor said expansively, "what brings you to the Clinic?"

I had my back to the nurse and spoke softly. "Bruno Schultzman."

He hesitated before replying. "How did you know he is here?"

"Al Lewis told me."

"When did you see him?"

"This morning."

"Did he give you permission?"

"No."

"Well, if he didn't I can't take the responsibility."

"Why not?"

"Al is Bruno's guardian. No one is to see Bruno without his explicit permission."

I had the sense that the Doctor was putting the phone, as well as me, down.

"Wait a minute, Doctor"

"Bill, I'm busy."

"Too busy to be curious about a hundred thousand dollars squirreled away on the Schultzman farm? A farm, by the way, that you happen to own?"

I could hear cloth rubbing against the mouthpiece as if the phone had left his ear and slipped to his shoulder. His voice came through hollow and distant. "Stay where you are," he said, anger scraping his voice like a rake on gravel. "I'll be right down."

I hung up and waved Don over.

I spoke quietly in his ear so the receptionist couldn't hear me. She was certainly trying to.

"Nordstrom is coming to meet me. Start walking down the hall and when you see him, take his picture."

"How will I know it's him?"

"Are you kidding? He's upset."

"Like everyone else you know around here?"

"Yeah," I said. "Get going."

"What about the kid?"

"We'll have to improvise. I don't know where he's being kept but I'm pretty sure the Doc will take me there. Try to follow us. Pretend like you're lost. You're good at that."

"Thanks," he said. He really thought I meant that as a compliment.

I checked my watch, thinking about Amundson stewing in the cell. How long before someone finds him? I didn't now how much time I had and it unnerved me.

Speaking of time it didn't take long for Doctor Nordstrom to show up. He came into the lobby full-steam-ahead and the nurse behind the admitting desk actually drew back.

"We can't talk here, follow me to my office," he said sternly. He was wearing the uniform of his trade—a white jacket so well starched the lapels and pockets seemed glued down.

I walked behind him toward the front of the Clinic and we passed Don who gave me a surreptitious nod. He got his picture.

Nordstrom's office was up a flight which he took two steps at a time, pretty good for a man his age. I guess he didn't want to wait for the elevator or run into someone on his staff.

Walking into his office, I was surprised at its modernity. Instead of a conventional desk he had an elevated Herman Miller table and a chair known in the trade as a Perch.

Four Prague chairs, their original caning burnished to a berry-brown, were grouped around a Mies coffee table of thick glass, and opposite sat a pristinely elegant George Nelson sofa of creamy leather you'd rather look at than sit on.

The Doctor's taste was eclectically modern and very much like Brewster's except for one thing: no art. The only adornment on the walls was a group of three, vertically stacked medical certificates from the University of Minnesota Medical School.

He shut the door behind us and motioned me to sit on the sofa. I unbuttoned my coat and sat down. Again I was reminded of Brewster: sitting in his office on that fateful day when he told me to go to Clear Lake and cover a murder.

Will Nordstrom be as smooth as Brewster? Will he patty-cake my questions the way everyone else has done so far? Or will he let me talk to Bruno to clear up the mysteries shrouding this ill-fated town?

"Now," he said, sitting next to me, "tell me about this money you say is hidden away on the Schultzman farm."

"I can't tell you exactly how much there is because I didn't take the time to count it all. But there must be close to a hundred thousand dollars in tens, twenties and fifties neatly stacked in a strong box."

"When did you find this cache?"

"Last night."

"When you and Bev were supposed to be out dancing?"

"I didn't intend to involve her," I said. "I didn't know the way to the farm and she offered to show me."

"Sounds like my daughter, always helping someone out. But why did you go out there in the first place?"

"A reporter's instinct I suppose—trying to get to the heart of the story. Maybe that's hard for you to understand, Doctor, but I wanted to visit the scene of the crime. Sheriff Amundson wouldn't let me go there and so I took matters into my own hands. Right or wrong that's what I did."

"And by doing so you came across this large amount of money. Where did you find it?"

"Under one of the steps leading to the second floor."

"When I bought that farm little did I know there was a fortune hidden on it."

"The money hasn't been there that long."

"How can you tell?"

"The strong box was clean, and the step appeared to have been jimmied recently."

"But where would Alfred Schultzman get that kind of money?"

"He didn't. Someone else put it there."

"Someone else?"

I stared at the doctor trying to decipher the expression on his face, trying to interpret the tone of his words. Was he pretending he didn't know?

"That's what I'd like to find out," I said.

"Have you told the Sheriff about this?"

I couldn't tell him that Amundson was cooling it in one of his own coolers.

"He and I are not exactly on speaking terms."

"I am not surprised after reading the article you wrote about him. But you need to go to him with your information, not me."

"I'd rather talk to you first."

"Do you think I'm involved in this mess in some way?"

"You own the Schultzman farm."

"I bought the farm as in investment," the Doctor said defensively. "The last time I saw it was when Alfred Schultzman moved in. I drove out to sign the lease."

"Why did you rent it to him?"

"Good lord, why not? He was a farmer looking for a place to live on and operate, and I had a farm that needed renting. He was a reliable tenant, always paid his rent on time. I had no reason to be concerned, no reason to think that anything other than farming was going on out there. In any case," he said dismissively, "the murder has nothing to do with my ownership."

"What about the fact that you were nearly run down night before last? Does that have anything to do with your ownership?"

A shot before the bow to get his reaction. But all he did was run his arm along the back of the sofa, his hand near my shoulder, as if he were going to tell me something confidential. The smell of antiseptic soap grazed my nostrils.

"How did you find that out? Who told you?"

"Your daughter."

"That little informer. I told her not to worry."

"She was worried enough to call me."

He pondered that for a moment, then said, "It was accidental. I don't even know who it was."

"Well I do."

He lifted his eyebrows. I finally got a reaction from his otherwise stoic manner.

"You are a fountain of information."

"I try to be." My smile was nerveless, like that of a stroke victim.

"Well, Bill, we shouldn't keep the mystery name a secret any longer, should we?"

"Rose Sorenson."

The Doctor laughed mirthlessly. "I should have said *mis*information."

"It was Rose, all right."

"How do you know?"

"She told me this morning, not more than three hours ago."

"Rose is a terrible driver," Nordstrom scoffed. "She's legendary around here. Ask anyone."

"That's the excuse she used, too. She told me she lost control of the car and nearly hit you. But that still doesn't explain why she was there in the first place. I think she deliberately and with premeditation tried to run you down. I'd like to know why."

"You weren't able to worm that out of her as well?"

"She gave me an explanation but I didn't buy it."

I reached into my coat pocket, getting ragged now from the sharp corners, and pulled out the slugs of lead. I laid them on the coffee table, making clanking sounds on the glass.

"What are these?" the Doctor asked, leaning forward cautiously as though peering over a cliff.

"Slugs of type Maynard set on his linotype machine."

The Doctor moved them around with an index finger.

"The letters are backwards."

"That's the way type is set. When you print them, the words become readable."

"Of course, mirror image."

I nodded. "Maynard gave four of them to me. He kept one." I separated the four.

The Doctor held them up one at a time, reading the names out loud: "Amundson, Sorenson, Schultzman, Lewis."

"Why did he give these to you?"

"Each is a piece of a puzzle and Maynard expected me to put them together to form a picture, like clues in solving a crime."

"Why didn't he just tell you what he thought instead playing this game?"

"The editor in him. He wanted me to get the story by interviewing these people and from the information gleaned put the puzzle together. Which, by the way, is I what I've been trying to do."

"But Alfred Schultzman is dead. You couldn't have interviewed him."

"Not Alfred. Bruno."

Nordstrom stared at me. "So when Maynard set his own name in type he meant Rose?"

"Yes."

"And the fifth slug?"

"I remember him looking at it, still hot, moving it back and forth in his hands as though he was deliberating something, trying to make a decision, and finally putting it in his pocket after it cooled off. Rose went to the shop the night of the murder. She found the slug in his pocket."

I slid it over.

He held it as delicately as he would a scalpel.

"Nordstrom," he said softly.

"She thinks you killed Maynard."

Nordstrom stared in shock. "Rose is mistaken."

"She doesn't think so. But why did Maynard keep the fifth slug and not hand it over? Was he protecting you?"

Nordstrom shook his head "From what?"

I shrugged. "Maybe he was concerned that I might uncover something that would compromise you."

The Doctor seemed offended. "The only thing that could compromise me is owning that farm and that is hardly unique. Lots of professionals invest in real estate. Maynard happened to know that I bought it."

"He did?" I asked. "How?"

"I ran a blind ad in his paper inquiring about farms for sale in the county. Only he and Rose were aware that it was my ad."

"Why a blind ad?"

"Professional anonymity. I didn't want my investments to be public knowledge. Maynard processed the replies to my ad, and he knew I finally settled on the Schultzman farm...the Fischer farm as it was known then. So I can only guess that, because of this, Maynard suspected some further connection between Schultzman and me. As you said yourself, Maynard was an oddball. How else can you explain those ridiculous slugs of lead?"

"I can explain them another way."

"The floor is yours," he said, standing. "But before you begin, let's have a drink. I certainly could use one."

"So could I," I said between parched lips.

"If I remember from the other night when you came to my house, it's Scotch with a splash of water."

The Doctor went to a cabinet door I hadn't noticed before because it was set flush to the wall and painted the same light gray color. He inserted a small key into a slot, releasing a spring lock, and the door swung open. Behind the disguise was a well-stocked bar: bottles of liquor and mix on shelves, a small counter, a compact refrigerator-freezer.

He busied himself making drinks, leaving the secret cabinet open, I was pleased to see, for seconds. I noticed he was pouring Glenfiddich. I didn't know about his nerves, but mine needed all the soothing they could get. Here I was, having a drink with Doctor Nordstrom while Sheriff Amundson was locked in his cell. I still had to figure out a way to let him out without being his replacement.

Nordstrom returned to the sofa with the drinks.

"All right," he said sitting back down, "start explaining."

I took a long swallow of Scotch. It stung my throat but I was in a stinging frame of mind.

"Those names represent a drug ring," I said.

Nordstrom held his glass steadily but I could tell that it required effort for him to remain calm.

"Well, well, well, you certainly start out strong. I thought an art critic believed in a slow dramatic build-up."

"I believe in fast resolutions."

"But a drug ring," Nordstrom said, as though chastising me. "That's a serious charge."

"Murder is a serious charge, too."

He sipped, his eyes peering over the glass rim. "All right, then, I'm listening."

I leaned against the cushion. "Let me begin with my arrival in Clear Lake on Wednesday. My first stop was to see Maynard. I was on a tight deadline and I wanted to talk to the person who knew the most about a community: its newspaperman.

"Even though I hadn't seen him in nearly twenty years, I was still surprised to find that he'd changed so much. He had been my close friend, my mentor, a warm, courageous, good man. And these qualities were not simply the opinion of an unseasoned kid. He was all of these. But when I saw him Wednesday he was…how can I put it…dispirited, soulless. He was a sad person."

"I agree Maynard has changed in recent years," the doctor said, but I took it as a part of the aging process. You will realize yourself someday, Bill, what getting old does to a person. You should read Simone de Beauvoir on the subject."

"It was more than aging, Doctor. Like Faust, Maynard sold his soul for a soft bed and security. Look at his lifestyle—a new retail store, expensive house, the big Toronado that nearly speared you the other night. You don't buy these on the revenue of a weekly newssheet with an audited circulation of twenty-seven hundred.

"It wasn't until I conned my way into Al Lewis's house and saw puncture marks on Bruno's arm that I began to suspect a pattern, a pattern by the way which was confirmed when I found the money hidden on the farm."

I stopped long enough for a taste of Nordstrom's splendid Scotch. "In addition to all of this, I found the murder weapon, a crow bar…"

"Wait a minute stop right there!" The Doctor jumped up. "Let's refresh our drinks," He went back to his little bar and this time brought the bottle.

"All right," he said, swallowing Scotch as if to fortify himself. "The murder weapon, a crow bar you said. Where did you find it?"

"In the trunk of Maynard's car wrapped in a pair of coveralls probably belonging to Schultzman. I got into Rose's garage last night and found it under the spare."

"My God, you've been busy. But how can you be so certain it was the murder weapon?"

"There was encrusted blood on the end."

"Do you know that it *is* blood?" Nordstrom demanded. "The murder happened on a farm, after all. Maybe it's animal blood. It has to be analyzed. Where is this so-called murder weapon?"

I cleared my throat, getting a little nervous now that Nordstrom was beginning to sound skeptical. "I looked for it this morning to show it to Rose and it was gone."

"Gone?"

"Rose must have removed it. She'd seen me sneak into her garage the night before but didn't do anything about it. Which would suggest that she knew it was there and removed it after I left."

"Why? To protect Maynard?"

"Or herself."

"This is all circumstantial, Bill. I don't see how you can make a case for a drug ring."

"Can you think of a better motive to explain three murders?"

"*Three?*"

"You haven't heard about Jensen?"

"The Deputy? My God has he been killed, too?"

"I thought you would have known about it."

"I was in surgery all morning." He rubbed his squeaky-clean hands together. "When did this happen?"

"Sometime after two last night." I went on to explain what happened in the jail.

A smirk separated his lips. "You're on top of everything else that happens around here, so why should it surprise me that you were the last person to see Jensen alive?"

"If you don't count the murderer, that is."

He shook his head in dismay. "I just wonder how much of this happened because you turned up and began nosing around."

"Don't you want to get to the bottom of this?"

"Of course I do but your behavior isn't helping. You are really worrying me. You keep throwing yourself into the eye of Clear Lake's terrible hurricane with this misplaced need to solve a crime."

"I have good reason."

"I can't imagine what that would be."

"I have to clear myself of a murder charge. The

Sheriff thinks I killed Jensen."

Nordstrom's face turned to the color of his jacket. He drained his glass and glared at me. "Let me speak frankly to you, Bill. I know you and Beverly have made up a great deal of ground since you returned to Clear Lake. I could see it in the way she reacted to your presence. She's like a flower that has reopened its petals after a rain storm, like a woman who's found love again."

I was both thrilled and numbed by his words, my pulse leaping high hurdles when he described Bev as a flower opening. Yet I also knew I would never be able to get close enough again to breathe in her fragrance.

"I have admiration for you, Bill, please understand that. You have become very successful and I want Beverly to marry again someday not only for her sake but for Tod's as well. I've always thought you two would make a fine match. That's why I welcomed your return to Clear Lake. Any father is sad to see his daughter languish her life away. But you are no longer an asset to her. In fact you've become the opposite—a liability, a dangerous liability.

"Your life is your own, Bill, I don't have any business preaching to you about that, but Beverly is my daughter, my concern and, as long as she remains in my home, my responsibility as well."

I sighed with resignation. "You don't have to worry. I'll never see Bev again."

"I'm relieved to hear you say that. But I'd like you to go one step further."

"What's that?"

"Get out of town. Now."

God almighty, I thought to myself, another precinct heard from.

"I'll leave, Doctor, when I'm ready but I'm not ready yet."

Nordstrom bristled. "You are being foolish and stubborn. You'll do nothing but provoke further pain and suffering upon Beverly if you don't clear out."

"I appreciate your fatherly concern, Doctor, but I don't think that's really why you want me to leave Clear Lake."

His eyes narrowed in growing anger. "Who are you to question my motives—an interloper, an outsider stirring up a devil's brew with your meddling!"

"And what are you?" I shot back. "An innocent bystander?"

"If I am not an innocent bystander, as you so delicately put it, what am I then?"

"You are the fifth slug in a drug ring."

The Doctor was too stunned to say anything and so I kept talking. And why not? All that ever mattered to me in Clear Lake was Bev and she was lost to me. So why should I care about anybody else, including you, noble Doctor?

"The Clinic provided the perfect cover for a drug ring," I continued, "making it easy to procure large quantities of drugs without casting suspicion. The Schultzman farm was the transfer point and that's how Bruno got onto drugs."

Nordstrom finally found his voice. "A single teenager on drugs doesn't prove your wild theory."

"I think Bruno came across the stuff during one of the transfers and began experimenting. "

"You're wrong," he replied wearily. There was no energy or anger left in him.

"Let's find out if I'm right or not."

"How do you expect to do that?"

"Give me ten minutes with Bruno."

28

We came out of the Doctor's office into the hallway, and near the elevator door stood Don. In the intensity of my conversation with Dr. Nordstrom, I had forgotten about Don waiting in the hall and Claire waiting in my car. How long had I been in the office? I looked at my watch. Half an hour.

Don would have been more obvious but for a woman standing beside him waiting at the elevator. He had taken off his overcoat and slung if over his shoulder. When the doors opened, he politely waited for the woman to enter and then made as if to join her, but at the last moment he snapped his fingers as though he had forgotten something and stepped back as the doors closed.

Don is great at improvising, I thought admiringly.

I said loud enough for him to hear me, "Where are we going, Doctor?"

"Down the hall. Bruno is in a private room."

We walked past a call station with a nurse sitting behind the counter. Next to her was a metal file cabinet on rollers. She nodded respectfully at the Doctor, which gave me an opportunity to glance back. Don was walking behind us and he stopped at the station and began a conversation with the nurse who appeared, it now occurred to me, quite interesting in her formless starched whites. I reminded myself to ask Don later what he was saying to her.

At the end of the hall, the Doctor stopped at a door with a small narrow window. He peeked in and then opened the door.

"Bruno," he said almost deferentially, "there is someone here to see you. We'd like to come in."

Nordstrom walked into the room but I hung back, lingering in the hallway.

Behind me Don came by and asked, "This way out?"

I turned, flattening myself against the door, pointed and said, "The other way."

Don thanked me and turned. His swagger as he walked away telling me that he got his photo.

Mission accomplished.

I entered the room. Bruno, sitting up in his bed, flinched when he saw me. On the opposite wall a black and white television screen flickered Days of Our Lives.

He was wearing a hospital gown of faint blue pinstripes and his hairy legs extended beyond the hem. His sallow face looked me over suspiciously.

The Doctor said, "How are you feeling today?"

"Better. They put me on that methadone stuff. When can I see my sister?"

"Tomorrow."

"How is she?" I asked Nordstrom.

"Her condition has not changed."

I wondered if Sarah could identify Maynard as her assailant. I wished she were able to talk. I was becoming exhausted by the sheer lack of proof, like an engine, nearly out of gas, burning fumes.

"Bruno," the Doctor said, "Bill wants to ask you a few questions. Are you up to it?"

His attention kept flitting back and forth between me and the television screen, as though he was worried he might lose the thread of the soap opera plot.

"Ok," he said with resignation, and shut off the set with a hand control lying on the mattress next to him.

Nordstrom sat on the edge of the bed as if to provide moral support. Bruno grudgingly shifted his bare feet. His toe nails needed trimming.

I stepped around to the other side of the bed, taking a position next to the darkened TV set which sat on a metal stand with casters. It seemed to bother Bruno that I would have the gall to lean on his electronic soporific whose still-hot tubes inside the plastic case warmed the bottom of my arm.

"Bruno," the Doctor said soothingly, "you don't have to answer any question you don't feel like answering."

Now why did Nordstrom say that? The hayseed was as good as warned to take the fifth on just about anything I might ask.

"Bruno," I said, "I want to apologize for the way I treated you at Al Lewis's house, but maybe it was for the best because it forced Al's hand to get you medical attention."

He nodded wearily. "I never wanted to get hooked. I was just fooling around sniffing but then I started using a needle because snorting it didn't give me a high any longer." He looked at the Doctor. "I hope I can get through the treatment. "

Nordstrom smiled encouragement. "You will, others have."

"Where did you get it?" I asked Bruno.

"I found it," he replied and looked at Nordstrom with an expression of did-I-say-too-much?

"Where?" I pushed on.

He was still looking at Nordstrom for guidance.

The Doctor nodded. "It's all right, Bruno."

"In the house."

"Where in the house?"

"Under a step."

"How did you find it?"

"I was in the cellar. I have some…well, some stuff hidden down there and I was looking at it."

It was not hard to imagine this sad, socially inept kid hiding behind the water heater with a girlie magazine in one hand and his penis in the other.

"I was home alone. I thought it was Dad at first because the back door opened. There was no knock or anything, just the door opening."

"So someone came in like he owned the place."

The Doctor gave me a sharp look, but I ignored him.

"There were footsteps across the floor and going up the stairs about halfway. I heard this yanking noise like nails coming loose. Then I knew it wasn't Dad so I was careful not to make any noise of my own."

"Did you stay in the cellar?"

He nodded. "But when he left I looked out the cellar window to I see who it was."

"Did you recognize him?"

He shook his head.

"Does that mean you don't know or you're not telling?"

Bruno stared down at his feet.

"Was it your father?"

"Dad?" Bruno laughed. "He didn't know what was going on."

"Was it Dr. Nordstrom?"

Nordstrom had had enough. He stood. "Bill, I think you'd better stop this line of questioning. We're not in a courtroom and he is not under oath."

"All right, Doctor, all right. Bruno, did this person know you were there?"

"No,"

"So then what did you do?"

"I snooped around and found that step. I took it apart

and found a cardboard box full of small packages of white powder."

"You knew what it was?"

Bruno smiled knowingly. "Sure, coke."

"Did you find anything else?"

"Like what?"

"A strongbox filled with money?"

He looked at me in surprise. "Money? No just the cocaine."

So that was how it worked—the money was payment for a shipment—drop off the drugs and pick up the cash.

"What did you do when you found the cocaine?"

"What do you think I did," he asked as though he was talking to dummy, "leave it alone?"

"So you decided to experiment."

"It wasn't new to me. I mean, I've popped pills and smoked marijuana."

"Where did you get marijuana?"

He snorted, a young-old man. "It's anywhere you want to look. If you want it you can get it."

"Even in Clear Lake?"

"Sure. Piece of cake. Or maybe I should say piece of coke." Bruno laughed at his cleverness.

Nordstrom was shaking his head, a pained expression on his face.

"But snorting coke is a lot worse than smoking marijuana."

Bruno smiled ruefully. "I wished you told me that before I helped myself to the stuff. I was king of the hill for a while. I never saw so much. I sold a lot of it, which was a mistake."

"So you ran out."

He nodded. "I nearly went crazy."

"What did you do?"

"Looked for more."

"Find any?"

"No." The forlorn look in his eyes said it all.

"Where did you search?"

"I hoped more would show up under the step but nothing happened. Maybe I scared him away."

"Him? Who is him?"

He looked away.

I bent close to his face. His breath was foul.

"Since you didn't find anymore under the step where else did you look?"

Bruno pressed his face against the pillow and pulled his legs up. "Leave me alone."

Nordstrom reached across the bed and gripped my arm. "That's enough, Bill. I think you've asked enough questions."

"But this is the same question," I persisted. "Where did you go looking for it, Bruno?"

Bruno covered his face and then heavy tears forced their way between his fingers.

"You went to Maynard's office, didn't you?"

"No!" Bruno cried out his voice muffled by his fingers pressing all the harder on his face.

"Bill!" Nordstrom said sharply. "This is a hospital, not a court of inquisition."

I straightened, ignoring the Doctor. "You thought you would find cocaine in Maynard's print shop, didn't you, Bruno? You were so driven by your need for the drug that you would kill to get more, isn't that right, Bruno? Even kill Maynard Sorenson!"

Bruno cried like an infant for his two a.m. feeding while Nordstrom tugged on my arm shouting at me to stop.

A nurse came through the door, her face a mixture of anger and surprise. She was ready to bawl us out for making so much noise when she saw that one of us was the head of the Clinic she worked for.

"Dr. Nordstrom," she said with the same surprised look she might have had if she caught him with a candy striper.

"Get a hypo for Bruno, Mrs. Dawly," the Doctor said. "The boy is having a difficult time."

"Right away, Doctor."

"And keep an eye on him."

"Restraints?" she asked, almost in a whisper.

The Doctor watched Bruno, his body shaking with sobs. "I don't think that will be necessary."

We left Bruno lying on the hospital bed and my question lying with him unanswered.

29

Claire and Don were waiting in my car, the engine idling, Hot fumes from the exhaust collided with the bitter cold air, enveloping the rear deck in a thick white vapor. The temperature was hovering around zero even though it was the middle of the afternoon.

I told Claire to drive and I got into the rider's side of the front seat.

"Let's get some carry-out hamburgers." I said.

Claire made a face. "I could use a hot toddy."

"Can't risk it. Besides, we don't have the time. There's a McDonald's on Highway Thirteen. Let's swing by there."

Claire turned left and headed north on the County Road that would take us to Minneapolis if we had the time to drive through the main streets of Montgomery, New Prague and Prior Lake.

"What did you find out?" Don asked from the back seat. He was slouching sideways, his long legs having trouble finding enough space to stretch out with his camera bag in the way.

"Bruno broke down when I accused him of killing Maynard Sorenson."

Don whistled. "Holy shit, you think the kid did it?"

"Bruno was desperate for a fix because he ran out of cocaine. He thought Maynard had some hidden in his print shop. Only someone who was really desperate, like an addict looking for drugs, would resort to such a brutal killing."

"Did the kid admit it?"

"No, but he came apart. An innocent person would not act like that."

I looked out the window. "There it is," I said, pointing to the golden arches.

Claire pulled into the lot, nearly empty now in the mid-afternoon. I gave her money and she went inside.

"You got your photos?" I asked Don when we were alone.

Don patted his camera case. "I'm going to hit Bailey for a raise."

"You did your job," I said. "Now I have to do mine."

Claire returned with three white bags of hamburgers, fries and hot apple pie, and a pressed cardboard tray of steaming coffee.

We ate like there was no tomorrow, or the day after for that matter. None of us had eaten much breakfast and it was nearly three.

"Don?" I asked.

"Yeah?" he replied, his mouth attacking a Big Mac.

"I want to borrow your camera, tripod, strobe and a roll of film."

"What for? Going to enter an amateur contest?"

"I want to set a trap."

His thin eyebrows crested, communicating on behalf of his full mouth.

"There's nearly a hundred thousand dollars hidden in that farmhouse waiting to be picked up. And I want to be there when it happens."

Don put down his hamburger and drank some coffee. "Let me get this straight. You think you can set up my camera, wait for someone to show up and then record the moment forever on celluloid?"

"Yep. If I can get a photo, then I'll have my proof."

"People get killed for less, or haven't you noticed? You're not dealing with Sunday school teachers you know."

Claire was anxiously following our conversation, looking back and forth between Don and me.

"Darling," she said, "you can't be serious."

"Someone is going to come for that money, and soon. It's no secret any longer. There are at least three people who know that I know there's money on the farm."

"Who?"

"Al Lewis, Rose Sorenson and Robert Nordstrom."

"The Doctor? Beverly Nordstrom's father?" Claire asked, her interest snagging on the name.

"Yes."

"Do you think *he* could be mixed up in this?"

"I hope not. I told him I thought so, though."

"What did he say?"

"He denied it, but that doesn't rule him out."

Claire stared dolefully through the windshield at the snow plowed into dirty banks along the walls of the drive-in.

"I think you have gone absolutely crazy."

Don began fidgeting in the back seat. He did not enjoy witnessing our personal conflicts.

"Maybe I have," I said, and let it go at that.

But Claire wouldn't. "I can't let you do this! I don't want to claim a corpse, how many would that make, four? If you really love me, you'll come back to Minneapolis with me right now."

I read the inscription on the cardboard casing holding the apple pie, warning me that the contents were hot. Well, I thought, they can't be any hotter than Claire is right now.

"You know I can't leave. I'm in this too far to back out now."

"So that's it, then," she said, "If I go back alone, it's over between us because I can't take it any longer."

Don leaned forward, his arms folded on the back of the seat, a sharp elbow pointing at each of us.

"This is none of my business but since you've aired your grievances in front of me I'd like to tell you, Bill, that I agree with Claire, although I don't agree with her approach."

"You're right," Claire said, turning to face Don.

"Really?" he said, his voice rejoicing.

"It *is* none of your business."

Don fell back as if her words had pushed him. "I give up."

I glanced over my shoulder. "Sorry, Don, but I have to go through with it."

Don sighed. "We have to go back to my car because I don't have everything you need in my case."

"Ok, let's go."

Claire squeezed the steering wheel for a few recalcitrant seconds and then threw the transmission into reverse so hard I was afraid the gearshift lever would break in the steering column.

She pulled onto the highway squealing rubber.

"Keep this up and you'll draw attention that I don't need."

The rest of the drive was in angry silence but I was confident this would pass like all of her tantrums. I'd grown accustomed to her moody swings. Like everything else about her, she was easy to predict, easy to read, easy to lay—maybe too easy.

I looked at Claire, her profile sharply defined, her high cheekbones and her intense dark eyebrows. Inevitably I compared her to Bev, whose features were softer, lighter, buoyant.

I looked back at the road, feeling guilty for even letting Bev slide into my thoughts. We were finished. I needed to make my peace and tell Claire that she was the woman for me. And yet I had misgivings. I couldn't help it. I was infatuated with Claire but I was in love with Bev.

Claire pulled up alongside Don's car parked diagonally across the street from the hotel, bumping the curb in one final act of petulance.

Don jumped out, rummaged through his trunk and returned with the equipment I requested.

"This stuff is bone cold but I didn't want to leave it in the hotel room. You have to give it time to warm up."

"I'll have time."

"Know how to work a Minolta?"

"Show me."

From the back seat Don proceeded to give me a lesson in camera technique on the SRT 101. "With the strobe, you use fast speed, two-hundred-fiftieth of a second, f-stop at eight, and ASA at four hundred. I'll load the camera with Tri-X film and set it for you. Its fast, and excellent for taking indoor shots."

Don opened the back of the camera, inserted a little metal film canister and fed the leader into a sprocket wheel. Then he closed the back and advanced the film until the indicator was on number one.

"Set your focus with this outer ring. Got it?"

"I think so."

"Try it."

I looked through the viewfinder and turned the ring till my image came into focus: Claire's profile.

"What are you doing?" she asked, turning her head self-consciously.

"Practicing."

"You need a lot of it," she said, still sulking.

"Oh," I said, remembering the photo of Maynard that Rose had given to me. I pulled it out of my overcoat pocket. "This is Maynard Sorenson. Can you make something of it?"

Don studied it. "No worse than the Schultzman family pic. I'll see what I can do." He slid it into his camera case.

I looked at Claire one more time, sullen and silent behind the wheel.

"Don, you drive."

Claire's head swiveled and her eyes burned me down. "Don't you trust me?"

"You've been driving like a maniac."

"Why should you care? You're going to get killed anyway."

"You want to take care of it first?"

Don was shaking his head as the two changed places.

"I've seen less hitting in a Vikings game."

Don remembered the way to the Schultzman farm very well. I had to correct him only once.

"Let me off here by the gate."

"You won't have any wheels."

"I can't give myself away with a car parked out here. I'll stay through the night. If no one shows, I'll take the money and turn it over to the St. Paul Crime Bureau."

"What do you want me to do with your car?'

"Don't park it by the hotel. I'm not supposed to be in town. Leave it on a residential street."

"Which one?"

I thought a moment. "I know…park it in front of the house I grew up in, across from Trowbridge Park, 404 Second Street Northeast."

"You are too clever for words." Claire said from behind the wheel.

"The farm has a phone. I'll call you at the hotel in the morning."

I opened the door and got out with the equipment Don gave me, and the extra McDonalds' bag. I held it up. "Dinner."

"Can you carry all that?" Don asked.

I nodded. "I'll take good care of your camera."

"I'm not worried. It belongs to the Minneapolis

Citizen Ledger." Don made a smile but it was etched with worry lines. "What if we don't hear from you?"

"You better drive out and see if I'm ok."

With everything in my arms I leaned in again and kissed Claire on the cheek. A tear fell and moistened her lips.

"I'll never see you again," she prophesied.

"Of course you will," I said, but in spite of my effort to treat the matter lightly I felt I was saying goodbye to her for the last time, and an undercurrent of sadness coursed through me.

Claire felt it, too, and slid across the seat and threw her arms around my shoulders. Her mouth reached for mine, and she lavished a long, pained kiss on it.

I straightened slowly, her gloved hands sliding down the front of my overcoat. I got out and shut the door.

Don put the car in gear and backed out of the drive. I stood watching.

He was heading up the road when suddenly I shouted, "Hey! Don! Wait!"

The Pontiac's tires ground to a stop on the frozen gravel. Don backed up. Claire was staring at me through the window, her eyes filled with vindication, her face flushed with relief. She thought I had changed my mind.

I opened the door on her side.

"Darling!" she shouted, "I knew you'd come to your senses!" She slid over. "Get in."

"No, I'm not leaving."

Her face fell.

"I nearly forgot about the Sheriff. Call the fire department as soon as you get back and tell them that Amundson is locked up in one of his cells. Don't say anything else, just hang up."

Don shook his head. "I can't wait to get out of this fucking crazy town."

"Tomorrow, I promise."

30

The farm was only one percent less foreboding by daylight. The gray clapboard siding of the house blended unpleasantly with the leaden afternoon sky, and the gnarled oak trees with their black spidery limbs seemed like skeletal sentinels guarding the building's gloomy contents.

I inspected the rear door and discovered that Jensen had simply tied the inside knob to the screen door latched with a piece of rope. Quality police work.

I set my load down on the stoop and removed my gloves to untie the rope. It was more difficult than I realized. The rope was stiff from the cold and soon my fingers were the same. I didn't want to cut the fiber. The door had to keep its un-tampered look.

Eventually I loosened it but not without cracking the nail of my right thumb below the quick. It stung like hell.

The door came open accompanied by the sound of more wood from the jamb cracking and falling to the floor. I looked down. Nothing had been swept up, so the additional bits of wood appeared normal.

Once inside, I put the camera equipment and my

bag of food on the kitchen table. Then I opened the window, unhooked the storm and crawled outside again. I retied the rope the way I'd found it and climbed inside.

Home.

I peeled off my coat and hung it in the closet along with my scarf and winter cap, and tossed my overshoes into a corner. They got lost with the other winter clothing in there. The furnace was running. I could hear air coming out of the floor registers. Dr. Nordstrom wasn't going to let the pipes freeze on his rental investment.

I walked around, getting the feel of the place again and trying to work off my anxieties. The icy fingers of fatigue and fear were touching the back of my neck.

Was this a good idea? The question kept nagging on my brain. Well, if it isn't it's too late to recast the die. You'll have to follow through, Kouros, I told myself. And needing relief from my anxiety, I began wishing no one would show up.

The sink rate for the sun is more rapid in winter and now, at four o'clock, natural light was at a premium. I could not risk turning on a lamp and so I needed to get my work done right away.

I walked up the stairwell to the second floor, shadows looming like vampires. First I removed the step to make sure the money was still there. No sense setting a booby-trap if there was no booby to trap. I did not remove the strong box, just felt under its lid. The bills where still there, crisp and fresh.

I replaced the step and set up the camera on the tripod at the top of stairs, pointing it down at a point just above the step. I figured this would be the best vantage to snap a picture of a surprised person as he pried his way to a hundred thousand dollars.

But what if he turned out to be a she?

I looked through the Minolta's viewfinder and focused on a spot on the handrail above the step. I moved the lens ring back and forth until the handrail became clear. That done, I locked the small strobe unit atop the camera.

Now for a test. I pressed the button and the strobe flashed as the shutter opened and closed with a quick click. I advanced the film and then leaned against the wall; for some inexplicable reason I was out of breath.

I remained like this in the upstairs hallway until my rapid breathing subsided. The setting sun was trapped behind a layer of clouds and the light inside the house was growing dim. This will be a very creepy night, indeed, waiting here all by myself, I thought, as I made my way down to the kitchen and opened the bag with the hamburger and fries. It was for the want of something to do, I wasn't hungry. I checked the cupboard for a glass, found a mason jar, and poured myself water from the old-fashioned pump. Then I checked the refrigerator. Not much: eggs, butter, bacon and a half a loaf of Wonder Bread. Well, at least I can make breakfast in the morning, however unappetizing the idea seemed right now.

Feeling discouraged, I sat at the table, covered with the patterned oilcloth, and munched on my dried-out Big Mac. My eyes were adjusting to the dimness. They'd better, there won't be any lights on tonight. I looked at my watch. Just four-forty-five. I'd been here less than an hour and already it seemed as if the sun should be coming up, not going down.

Will I be able to stand the wait? I'd never before had to contend with this kind of forced inactivity. Maybe I misjudged my ability to stick it out. And to think there are people who spend their lives unable to do anything— paraplegics, shut-ins, sick people waiting to die, like my mother...

I slammed the hamburger down on the oilcloth and stood up, stretching. I've got to force myself out of this funk. Why didn't I remember to buy a transistor radio? At least I could catch up on the news of the outside world.

Or a newspaper.

Any newspaper, no matter how old. I walked into the parlor and looked around wondering if Schultzman subscribed to one, maybe the Independent, but found nothing, not even a farm journal. I opened the front door and checked the stoop in case someone had dropped off a handbill or a throwaway. Then it occurred to me that there is only rural delivery here. I was sorely tempted to walk down the drive and check the mailbox by the road when a sound broke through my consciousness. I stood still and listened. In the distance an engine of some kind, not very well muffled. What was it? Then it came to me, a tractor. A farmer was coming down the road. The sound got louder, stayed even for several seconds, then grew in intensity again.

Jesus! He's coming up the drive! How did he open the gate? Did he see me get dropped off? Did he know I was hiding in the house?

I shut the door quickly, went to the parlor and pressed myself beside the window to the back yard. I lifted the edge of the curtain and peeked out.

The farmer was riding a Minneapolis Moline that was so dirt encrusted you couldn't tell the color; its huge, cleated tires turned hypnotically, pulling a wagon-load of what appeared to be slop in a large galvanized metal tub. He passed close to the house. Sitting up high on the tractor seat, his head was level with mine, his face easy to read. He was old with a grizzled weeklong growth of beard. He was wearing a fur-lined trapper's hat with ear and forehead flaps pulled down. His upper lip was encrusted with frozen mucus.

He stopped in front of the barn and climbed down to pull open the double doors. I couldn't see inside the barn, but I could hear the delighted oinking of the pigs that were anticipating dinner. So Dr. Nordstrom followed through again, making sure the Schultzman's livestock did not go hungry.

The farmer backed his load into the barn and took his time feeding the pigs. He probably enjoyed the camaraderie. If I lived on a farm I'd be talking to the animals, too.

I stood by the window, in a state of tension until he came out again, closed the barn doors and drove past my window.

The intensity of the tractor's diesel reversed itself now, getting fainter as he moved down the lane, but stayed at an even level as the farmer stopped to lock the gate (of course, Nordstrom must have provided a key to the neighboring farmer so that the pigs got fed), and then grew more distant until I could hear it no more.

It was not till then that I moved away from the window, breathing a big sigh of relief. My leg muscles ached angrily as I walked around the small parlor working blood back into them.

I should not complain though. Nearly forty-five minutes had passed from the time I heard the tractor till it became a memory, and I was barely conscious of the minutes ticking by.

I returned to the kitchen and finished my cold burger, my stomach complaining occasionally from the assault on it. I found a tin of instant coffee in the cupboard and boiled a cup; drank that and tidied up the kitchen so it didn't appear used.

I returned to the parlor and sat on the sofa to begin my long night's vigil. Outside, falling darkness erased detail, and it seemed to slither through the weather stripping to coil itself around my body like a ghostly snake. Within minutes I could see only flat silhouettes of what had been three-dimensional trees, fences and outbuildings, and when I stared out the window, I was met by my distorted reflection in the panes of wavy old glass.

As the brittle cold of night settled on the roof, the house came alive with sounds of joists snapping and floor boards creaking, a macabre composition being played for a captive audience of one, and as I listened my imagination soared uncontrollably. Everything I looked at danced to the sounds. The old mashed-down leather rocker that Schultzman himself must have dozed in on similar winter nights waltzed back and forth. The faces in the wedding pictures hanging in an oval frame sang in cunning accompaniment, while hissing blue flames pirouetted behind the metal grid of the propane-fed space heater.

My head began to ache; the dry musty air had evaporated the moisture in my sinuses. I fought a growing drowsiness, my body yearning for sleep to escape the pain. I fought both, but the dull throbbing persisted, weakening my resolve and pushing my eyelids down...

A noise outside the house interrupted my uneasy slumber. "What's that?" I said aloud, opening my eyes.

I looked around having forgotten for an instant where I was. During my nap the moon had risen, casting enough light through the windows so that I could see reasonably well. One by one, I took in the pieces of furniture and, like parts of a jigsaw puzzle, they fell into place and I saw the full picture: I was in the Schultzman farmhouse waiting for a killer to pay a visit.

I breathed a sigh of relief. At least my headache had cleared up.

Suddenly I heard another noise. Was it a hand scraping the siding? I couldn't be sure. I listened intently as I sat rigidly on the sofa. Then I heard the rear screen door being tested. I jumped from the sofa and quickly ran up the stairs to my camera. The moment had arrived!

I waited for the sound of the door opening, footsteps coming down the hall below me.

Who will it be? I wondered, my heart thumping.

Who will it be?

The tension was broken by the slamming of a fist on the wood frame of the screen door. This was followed by rapping on the kitchen window and a feminine voice shouting my name.

What in hell…?

I trotted down the stairs, anger mounting as I walked to the kitchen window. Claire hadn't given up after all. That stubborn broad had returned to foul up my plans. I raised the bottom sash of the window, unhooked the storm and shouted through the cold air rushing in around me.

"Goddamnit, Claire, why did you come back?"

"It's not Claire, Bill. It's me, Bev."

Bev? I pushed the storm and stuck my head out. She was looking up at me, her figure huddled against the cold, making her seem smaller than she really was.

I was in shock. Seeing her made no more sense than seeing a ghost and, for a second, that's what I thought she was.

"What are you doing here?" I asked.

"Waiting to be let in."

"Walk around to the front. I'll let you in through the front door."

I drew the storm closed and shut the window, wondering what was going on. I walked through the house and let her in.

She entered the house shivering. Hanging from her arm was a grocery shopping bag. She set it on the floor and then shed her heavy jacket, pulling off her knit cap and shaking her head until her brown hair fell into place.

I hung her things in the hall closet.

"I brought some food. You must be starving."

"How did you find out I was here?"

"Your friend Claire called me. I was surprised to hear from her, my competition I guess you could say."

"So she put you up to this."

"No, it was my decision after she told me what you were doing, setting up a camera hoping the killer will come so you can take his picture. That sounds completely crazy, Bill."

"She should not have told you."

"Well she did. You have two women who care about what happens to you. How often does that happen?"

"I haven't been keeping track."

"She thought that if she couldn't talk you out of it, maybe I could. So I told her I'd give it a try."

"Where is she? Waiting outside?"

"No, she drove back to town and is expecting a call to pick us up."

"Us?"

"You and I."

"If you think you can talk me out of doing this you're wrong."

"I told her I'd give it a try. We both know how stubborn you are, but Claire is very concerned. She loves you, in case you haven't noticed."

"No, I haven't noticed," I replied, frustrated that Bev was here and yet incredibly happy to see her again.

"Damn it, Bill!" Her eyes flashed in the dark. "Do you have to be so indifferent toward other people's feelings?"

"I'm sorry," I said defensively. "It's just that Claire should not have involved you." I led Bev into the kitchen. "Did she tell you that I'm wanted for murder?"

"Everything, including locking the Sheriff in a cell."

"That's why I have to prove my innocence. I'm in so deep the only way out is to find the killer."

"And you think you can do that with a camera?"

"And a flash."

"I hope you know what you're doing." Bev spotted my half-eaten hamburger. "Doesn't look like you're eating very well." She dropped the cold remnant of my dinner in the wastebasket beside the sink as though it were a dead mouse. "It's a good thing I brought fried chicken."

"I don't believe it," I said.

"It's true. It really *is* fried chicken."

"I mean seeing you again."

"You can thank Claire for that."

"Here's to Claire," I said, lifting my hand in an imaginary toast.

"I can do better than that." Bev pulled out a bottle of wine from the bag. "Chardonnay half finished from dinner with dad, but I was in a hurry."

"All we need are glasses." I went to the cupboard and brought two mason jars. "These will have to do."

"Appropriate for the occasion," she said as she poured.

We toasted Claire with a solid clank. The thick rim of the jars made for awkward sipping but they served as a fitting metaphor for our ad hoc meal together, bit players in a Theatre of the Absurd—our stage props fried chicken, wine in mason jars, and a fortune hidden in a stairwell—expecting a murderer to show up in act II.

"Did you tell your father where you were going?"

"No, and I had to lie to him again. I told him Tod and I were spending the night at my cousin's. I left Tod with her. It's something I don't like to do…"

"Lie to your father?"

She nodded.

"Did he tell you what happened at the Clinic today?"

"That you accused Bruno of killing Maynard Sorenson? Yes, that was quite a scene." Bev picked up a chicken leg and took a bite. "If you think Bruno did it," she added, chewing between words, "then why bother to lay a trap? He's in the Clinic under 24-hour surveillance. He won't be coming here."

"Bruno did not kill his father. Someone else did, and not for drugs which would be Bruno's motive, but for the money that's hidden here. I'm sure of that."

"Ok, if you say so."

"Did your Dad tell you anything else?" I asked.

"Like what?" she asked, nibbling away.

Her innocent reply told me Dr. Nordstrom did not tell her.

"He owns this farm."

"My father owns this farm?" she said, clearly taken by surprise.

"So you didn't know?"

"No, he never told me." She shook her head. "How did you find out?"

"Some fast work by the Citizen Ledger lawyers in Minneapolis. He bought the farm about a year ago just before leasing it to Schultzman."

"I wonder why he never told me."

"Maybe he has something to hide."

"Like what?"

"I don't know, but Rose Sorenson tried to run him down in her car. Why would she do that unless your dad knew something?"

I could read her mind—the misgivings, the doubt, shock even. "Are you suggesting," she asked in measured tones, "that dad is somehow involved in this mess?"

"I can't rule it out."

Shadows played strange tricks on her face and the anguish written there reminded me of the mask of tragedy. "Do you think he might come here?"

"He has plenty of reason. Drug money is hidden on his property. Your dad has a reputation to protect, not only his own but the Clinic, even Clear Lake itself. In any case I don't think you should stick around. It could be dangerous." I got up from the table. "I'll call Claire at the hotel and tell her to pick you up."

Bev grabbed my arm. "You can't ask me to leave, not after the things you said about Dad."

"You shouldn't be here."

"Now that I am, I have to know if he comes. I have a right to be here and see for myself."

"And if it is your father, what will you do, what will you say to him?"

She straightened, exuding renewed confidence. "It won't be Dad, I just know it won't."

"Are you willing to take that chance?"

"Yes."

We left the kitchen and sat on the sofa in the parlor, immersed in our own thoughts, mine full of concern for Bev, hers being here in what could become a dangerous showdown. And, if her father shows up, if anyone shows up at all, what then? I had no answer and neither did she.

It was nearing midnight when suddenly I stiffened.

"What is it?"

"Shhh. Hear that?"

We froze, straining to hear. Footsteps on the frozen ground were crunching their way up the drive toward the house.

"Someone is coming," I whispered. "I'm going to take a look."

I tiptoed to the kitchen window and pressed my cheek against the cold frame, giving my vision the best possible angle. I could just make out the corner of the back stoop. Part of a figure came into view, a shoulder, then an arm, and finally I saw someone dressed in a long, dark coat and it wasn't the meter reader. I stepped back and rejoined Bev, frozen in place like Lot's wife.

"He's here."

"Can you tell who it is?" Bev asked anxiously.

"No, it's too dark. I couldn't see his face…quick, upstairs."

I led the way to the second floor. The stairway and the upper hall came together in a T and the camera was set up in the junction. We hid around the corner.

"What are you going to do?" Bev whispered.

"When he pries the tread up and has the strong box in his hands, I will take his picture."

"Can't we just confront him?" She was obviously thinking of her father.

"No, a picture is incontrovertible proof. That's what I need."

I could feel Bev shivering against me. "What if he has a gun?"

"The flash will blind him. The element of surprise is on our side."

Bev suddenly gripped my arm. "Oh my god, Bill!"

"Keep your voice down."

"The food!"

What was she talking about? "What food?"

"The chicken, the wine. We left everything on the kitchen table."

"Shit!" I started to run down the stairs but I bumped one of the legs of the tripod and the camera nearly came with me. Bev rushed to help and we grappled with the thin legs, our nervous hands getting mixed up together in our haste to right the camera. In the meantime, I heard the back door open and close.

Too late! He was in the house.

I wanted to make sure the camera was aimed and focused properly but I didn't have time. And the remnants of our dinner still on the table! Everything was going wrong.

All we could do was hold our breaths and wait. Below us was an awful stillness. No sound of footsteps, nobody moving...

What in hell are you waiting for?

Seconds passed grudgingly; as if they did not wish

to lose their brief hold on the present, and the longer we waited in this interminable silence the more difficult it was to suppress a compulsion to scream for relief.

Doubt began to seep through the chinks in my self-confidence, exposing my shell for what it was—sheer bravado. Was this what had carried me through the last few days, recklessly following a path that could easily end in disaster?

What stupidity! Why had I gone this far? Was my ego so inextricably tied to Clear Lake? Did I need this crowning test of my masculinity, which placed me in conflict with the whole town?

Could be. Could very well be.

The realization of my incredible folly, the end product of my stubborn pride, sent shivers through me. I no longer wanted to go through with it. I no longer wanted to find out who would be coming up the steps to claim the money. I no longer cared.

Bev sensed my growing doubt. She dared not speak but her eyes widened in fear.

Below us, there was finally movement. The person was walking slowly through the house toward the stairway. Only the old pine boards we were standing on separated us.

Hearing footsteps, my mind snapped back to the present and the present danger. No time to second guess motives, the moment had arrived.

I shifted my weight so that I could peek around the corner and a board creaked. I froze. I nearly died from self-induced suffocation, fearful of even breathing. The footsteps stopped for a moment. Had they heard the sound? Had their eyes adjusted to the dark enough to see the bones of a half-eaten chicken on the kitchen table, the two mason jars, the empty bottle of wine?

I forced myself to peek, exposing just enough of my face until my left eye could detect a shadowy figure.

He was at the bottom, a figure in black. I could see no face, just the silhouette of a person in a wide brimmed hat. Could he see the camera setup? Were the shiny metal legs of the tripod visible from down there? From here they were as bright as the chrome on a Cadillac.

But the man kept his head down, looking only at the treads. He seemed to be counting them in his head.

It's the fifth one up, I thought, knowing exactly where the money was hidden. Did he know this or was he guessing?

Move, will you? Climb the stairs and start looking!

After what seemed like an interminable moment he placed his left hand on the newel post and climbed the steps one at a time with deliberate slowness. Then he stopped, his head bent down, his shoulders stooped. No more than six feet of electrically charged air separated us. I could clearly hear his breathing, coarse and nervous, so nervous I could even smell it.

Then I saw the crow bar in his right hand. I could barely make it out but I swear it was the same one I found in the trunk of the Toronado. He bent over and worked the curved end of the bar under the step. He pried and grunted and the tread came loose, the nails complaining as they got separated from their holes. He pulled the step free and it fell behind him, clattering down to the bottom of the stairs with such shocking unexpected noise Bev and I both jumped.

His hat completely covering his head, the brim pulled low over his eyes, he reached into the hole and removed the strongbox. Then he turned away from me to go back down the stairs. I wasn't going to get a good look at him! His back was to my camera, and I couldn't get a clear picture of his face!

Turn around, damnit, turn around!

Would my nerves hold up? Would my guts stay together? Another second and it will be too late!

I stood in full view and shouted, "Hey, you! Where are you going?"

My voice spun him around just as surely as if I'd grabbed him by the collar. He stumbled and nearly lost his footing. He fell against the wall to regain his balance, his hands gripping the strongbox, his face raised toward me.

I snapped the shutter and the strobe flashed, flooding him like a bomber caught in the crossbeams of enemy searchlights. In the instant of illumination, before it went dark again, much darker this time, black, inky and dense, he was looking up at me, his face startled, twisted and cruel like a wild animal lured into a trap.

In that millisecond of flashing light I saw the face of John Amundson, Sheriff of Clear Lake County.

31

There was no time to reflect on this totally unexpected revelation, since the Sheriff hurled both an epithet and the crow bar at me. I heard the swear words but didn't see the crow bar because it was pitch black, but he knew where the voice and the sudden flash of light that blinded us had come from, and so the odds were in his favor that he might hit something, either me or the camera.

It was me. I heard something crack before I felt the pain in my rib cage. It worked its way up my arm, through my shoulder and into my head where it exploded into a million blinking dots.

I was stunned into a kind of paralysis, I did not jump, dodge, duck—I just stood there. Then a flash not unlike the camera's strobe suddenly lighted up the staircase, and a deafening, echoing report blasted my eardrums. Behind me, over my shoulder, over the pain in my ears, I heard the soft sound of a bullet plunking into the plaster.

The bastard was shooting at me! Of all the people I guessed who might come here, the last one I expected was the Sheriff, the only one who would logically have a gun.

I ducked behind the wall. I could hear Bev's anxious breathing behind me.

"Go into the bedroom and lock the door," I whispered.

Then I reached for the camera, gripping it at its base, where the three legs of the tripod came together, to get it out of the way. It contained my precious evidence. As I grabbed for it two quick shots rang out and the camera disintegrated, the film ripped to shreds.

Jesus, does he have x-ray vision?

My hand snapped back from the force of the bullets, and my fingers grew numb as though they had been injected with Novocain.

My best laid plans—the film that captured the startled expression of the Sheriff, dressed in an overcoat to conceal his identity, the strong box under his arm—all of it destroyed.

In impotent fury, my fingers till tingling, I flung the shattered camera still attached to the tripod down the stairs. Another pair of shots rang out as the tripod met Amundson charging up the steps. There was cursing and furious body movements in the dark as he disentangled his legs from those of the tripod's.

Five rounds spent. If he's using the same revolver he arrested me with, he had one bullet left. As I stepped back my heel stepped on the crow bar resting on the floor. I leaned down and groped for it—the murder weapon was now going to be my weapon of self-defense. I grasped the flat end, the weight of the bar pulling on my aching chest muscles as I waited for Amundson to reach the second floor.

"Don't be a fool, Sheriff!" I yelled at him from around the corner. "You can't get away with killing me."

The Sheriff did not know that I was not alone and I wanted to keep it that way.

His sentences came like labored hisses between clenched teeth: "I was dumb enough to think that you hightailed it to Minneapolis after locking me up, but I was wrong—dead wrong, because the next one dead will be you."

"Don't be even dumber, Sheriff."

"It's just you and me, Bill, no one will ever know."

"I called Minneapolis," I lied, hoping to throw him off balance. "Federal narcotics agents are on their way down. They'll be here before dawn. They know about the drugs."

"You're lying, you bastard!"

"They know you killed Jensen."

I sensed a miniscule hesitation, a tiny crack. He had been prepared to rush me but now he held his ground, only the corner separating us.

"Why would I kill my own deputy?"

Amundson hadn't changed his mind about finishing me off, he just wanted to find out how much I suspected. So I had to keep talking—keep on talking, I thought, and keep on living. I must create doubt, break down his confidence and his terrible advantage. I hadn't planned on Amundson, but now that he was here, I saw the rest of the pieces fall into place in my gory jigsaw puzzle, a grizzly expressionistic painting of a true-to-life death scene.

"Your precious money-making scheme was getting the glare of too many headlines courtesy of yours truly. You wanted me out of the way. What better method than to finish off Jensen and put the blame on me?"

"Far-fetched, Bill, nobody would believe you."

"Maybe not, but I think you decided to come to the jail after Jensen called you, and you found him lying unconscious on the floor. It was a double-dip opportunity for you. By getting rid of Jensen, you not only put me out of circulation, you also reduced the number of cuts of pie. Right, Sheriff?"

He laughed, a maniacal wrenching of the vocal chords.

"What of it?" he cried. "You won't live to tell anyone so you might as well know. Sure, Jensen was a problem. He had a hair trigger temper and you couldn't trust him to keep his mouth shut. I'll give you this much, Bill—you did me a big favor providing me with both an alibi and a suspect."

"Jensen was in on it then?"

"He came in late, by accident, caught me dealing. I had a nice recipe and he was one cook too many. Jensen did serve a useful purpose though."

I could guess. "Some dirty work, right?"

"Cleaning up, you might say. He took care of Schultzman."

I thought so.

"Good old Alfred was going to blow the whistle on the operation. He told me I could no longer use his house."

"Why not?"

"His son, Bruno, got hooked but it was his old man who got the fuzzy stomach. You need guts for this Bill, lots of it. Schultzman couldn't take it after he saw what it was doing to Bruno."

"And Jensen was the assassin."

"Go ahead, use your fancy word. But he became a liability after killing Schultzman. Once a man like him sees blood you can't trust him, you know what I mean?"

I knew what he meant but I didn't reply.

"He was a braggart. He had to go. As you put it, Bill, a double-dip opportunity. Jensen dead, and you charged with murder. Everything would have been perfect if you hadn't locked me up, leaving you to roam around and get into more trouble. No percentage in that. All you will accomplish is to get yourself killed. I should have remembered my flashlight and I would have got you by now. But all I need is one bullet, which I have. There is nowhere to go, Bill, you are trapped. Where will you hide? In a closet?" He laughed again. "Doesn't matter. I'll find you."

The latch on the bedroom door clicked behind me. It was Bev opening the door.

Even Amundson heard it. "What was that? Goddamnit is someone up there with you?"

Bev came out and stood next to me. She squeezed my arm in sheer fright.

I tried to keep my voice calm. "I opened the door to the bedroom, that's all."

"You expect me to believe that? You aren't alone after all. You had it all figured out. A witness. Well, that witness won't help you, Bill, because you'll both die!"

Suddenly Bev pushed me aside. "It's me, Bev Nordstrom," she called out.

There was a moment of silence punctuated by agitated breathing as Amundson took this in.

"The Doc's daughter trying to save her boyfriend, is that it?"

"I'm trying to save us all, Sheriff. "

"Go back," I pleaded to Bev in a whisper, "he won't hurt you. It's me he's after. He has to get even. He's not looking to hide his crimes, not any more. Please, save yourself…"

"No," she whispered back, "I'm not leaving you. He won't try anything with me here."

"We can't be sure," I whispered back, and then said out loud: "Think about it, Sheriff, you know you can't get away with murdering both of us."

His breathing was getting more labored. "What have I got to lose? It's all over one way or the other."

I nudged Bev with my elbow. "Go back in the room. Lock the door."

"I won't leave you, Bill." Then before I knew what she was doing, she pushed passed me. "Sheriff, I heard everything you said. You destroyed all that you stood for. Once you represented law and order in Clear Lake. What changed you? Don't you have a shred of decency left?"

"Shut up, Beverly, just shut up!"

"You've known me since I was a child. Do you really want to harm me?"

"It's not you I'm after. I want Bill Kouros, the one who

ruined everything. Everything that was going just great till that nosy newspaperman came to town." Amundson raised his voice to a shrill. "Can you imagine? Brought down by a pansy art critic?"

I heard his coat sliding against the wall as he moved up. "I'm going to get you, Kouros. Tell your girlfriend to get out of the way. I won't hurt her. It's you I want."

"Then come and get me!"

I hefted the crow bar, waiting for him to reach the landing. Inexplicably I felt calm, as if I were standing in the eye of a hurricane. Surrounding me was wind and fury but in the center of my being there was an aura of peace and serenity.

He was getting close, very close. In a second or two he would appear on the landing, a shadowy figure, the emissary of death. Will he rush me? Will I have time to swing the crow bar and knock the gun from his hand? There was still an altruistic part of me that said don't hit him on the head; you might kill him the way Jensen killed Schultzman. A gale of doubt began blowing away the shingles roofing my confidence. I was getting buffeted, rattled by the approaching storm.

I trembled for myself, for Bev, regretting my mistakes, my failures—certain now that I won't have any future to atone for them as death inched closer. I tasted his hot bitterness deep in my throat as if he had forced my jaws open and was urinating into the cavity, choking me and gagging my resolve.

32

Amundson entered the shadowy confines of the second floor, a thicker shadow that loomed larger than he actually was. He was moving stealthily because he could not see any better than I could—at least we had that in common—but he still had his gun with a bullet in the chamber and I had only the crow bar.

I could not allow fear to paralyze me. I had to be the aggressor. I had to force his hand, not the other way around. The element of surprise had to be mine if I expected to survive.

I leaped from behind the wall and crashed into him. He instinctively brought his gun up and it went off like a thunderclap, the noise echoing and re-echoing in the narrow hallway. I felt a searing, boiling pain tear through my side.

I heard Bev scream and call my name but in that instant my mind recalled a vivid scene in a Civil War novel I had read. Battle-seasoned soldiers familiar with wounds tore at their uniforms as soon as they were hit to see if the bullet hole would be fatal. They were expert in the art of dying.

But I wasn't. I didn't have time search where the bullet

hit me. All I knew was that my entire body was aflame as I went pinwheeling down the steps with Amundson in my arms, our heads, shoulders, hips, knees taking the brunt of our crashing fall to the bottom of the stairwell.

We ended up with the Sheriff on top, a terrific weight keeping air out of my lungs and preventing me from answering Bev's distraught cries from the top of the stairs, "Bill, are you all right? Answer me, answer me!"

With great effort, and while excruciating pain racked my body, I managed to roll him off. Panting, I raised myself and looked at his face. I could see well enough now to tell that he was unconscious, his eyes were vacant and his mouth sloughed open. His chest was heaving. I put my hand on his heart. It was pulsating wildly.

"Bev!" I shouted, thinking she was still at the top of the stairs. As I turned I saw a figure standing over me. I recoiled instinctively.

"Bill, it's me!" Bev cried. She pulled me to my feet and held me as my body shook from the strain.

"You're hurt!"

"I'm ok," I lied, "but Amundson isn't. I think he's having a heart attack."

Bev suddenly stepped away and I almost lost my balance. She had brought her hand close to her face and was studying a stain on her palm. It was my blood but in the dark it looked like ink.

"Oh my god! You've been hit!"

"It's nothing serious," I said without knowing for sure. I could see tears glistening in her eyes. Her head began to quiver from bottled-up hysteria.

"It's awful. I can't stand it…"

"Hang on, Bev! Don't break down on me now."

"Tell me it's over," she asked meekly.

"It's over."

"We're safe now?"

I took her in my arms but she held me more than I held

her. "We're safe."

"Thank God."

We separated and I looked down at Amundson. "We have to get him out of here."

I bent over and with a grunt rolled Amundson on his side. The key ring I was looking for was attached to his wide black leather belt that held his now-empty gun holster and handcuffs. I pulled the prowler keys free and handed them to Bev. "The car is probably parked on the road. We can't carry him down there. It looks as though you'll have it bring his car to the house."

"But the gate is locked."

"Crash through it."

She hesitated.

"Think you can do it?"

She walked to the closet and grabbed her overcoat and hat. "I can do it," she shot back at me as she went out the front door buttoning up.

I sat on the bottom step next to Amundson. His breathing was getting shallower. He probably would die.

I found the strong box with the money intact and placed it next to him, a symbolic epitaph of a miserable end.

I touched my side with my fingertips. The bullet had torn through my belt, slowing it down before hitting my body. Had I been that Civil War soldier I would be smiling. Worse were the aches in my joints from rolling down the stairs in a death lock with Amundson. I will probably have lots of bruises. But, all in all, I was lucky to be alive.

Outside I heard Bev rev the squad car. Then there was a grinding crash of metal on metal as she tore through the chain-link gate in the flat-out roar of an engine at top RPMs.

She opened the front door and helped me pull Amundson across the stoop and down and the steps, his heels bouncing. Dragging him across the snow was easy but getting him into the back of the squad car required all of my remaining energy.

"Don't forget the strongbox," I said, almost too weak to be heard.

Bev drove at breakneck speeds, careening around corners on squealing tires. If she knew how to operate the siren she would have used that too.

"It's you I'm worried about," she said at one point.

She caromed into town, turned a corner and ground to a stop by the emergency entrance to the Clinic. I thought that Amundson had a better chance of surviving his heart attack than this ride, but I was proud of Bev's take-charge attitude. She was the hero of this scenario, not me. She ran inside for help. Two attendants came with a rolling stretcher and Amundson was taken through the automatic doors to an emergency room.

Bev helped me out of the car and into the waiting room. We were alone except for the startled duty nurse behind her glass partition.

I sat down in a chair breathing heavily.

"You better have that wound looked at."

"And you better go home."

"Are you trying to get rid of me?"

"There is no need to stick around here while I'm being treated."

"I'll stay with you until I know you are all right."

Behind her the outside door swung open and Dr. Nordstrom strode in, having hurriedly dressed, a brown wool overcoat over his shoulders, not through his arms.

Bev turned and jumped to her feet.

"Dad!"

The two embraced and exchanged a few words. I could not hear what they said but it was clear Nordstrom was hugely relieved to see his daughter safe and sound.

"I got called. Amundson is in surgery. I have to hurry."

He gave me a quick, disapproving glance. "You don't look so great yourself."

"Nothing serious."

Nordstrom called to the nurse. "Check this man in, have Dr. Pierce look him over. I have to go."

I joined the nurse at her desk. Now cool and professional, she looked me over. "This has been a rather unusual night, first the Sheriff and now you."

I nodded. "Two casualties."

She rolled a form into her typewriter and asked what seemed to me an interminable number of questions but I answered them all: name, address, occupation, marital status (which I hoped to change soon), next of kin (a dying mother), BlueCross/MII Group number, age, sex (she managed that all by herself) and, finally, the nature of my injuries.

"I have a tear in my side, maybe a cracked rib, some bruises, that's all."

"That's all?"

"Maybe a couple of sprains."

She shook her head as she typed away. "Car accident?"

She had no idea. "Well," I explained, "The tear in my side is from a bullet."

She stared at me as she would a rare specimen, and then added two and two together.

"You and the sheriff…." She pulled the form from her typewriter and placed it in a folder.

"Follow me." She got up and led me to a narrow examination room with a curtain.

"Strip down and put on this gown," she said. As she drew the curtain, I quickly waved to Bev.

Bev waved back. I knew she was tired, really tired, more likely exhausted, but she was not going home.

Presently the curtain parted and a young doctor walked in.

"Dr. Pierce," he said to me.

Like all young doctors, Pierce was no exception, doing his internship in the ER, working long nights and long hours.

He placed his stethoscope on my bare skin and pressed here and there.

"Ow!"

"You'll need stitches for that wound. All I can do is tape your ribs but I'll need x-rays which we can't do till morning."

I lifted myself from the narrow examination table by my elbows and winced. "I can't hang around that long," I said.

"I'm the doctor."

"It's important. Give me an hour and I'll be back."

"You'll be back with a collapsed lung." He prepared a hypo. "This will ease the pain."

"Will it put me out?"

"Just drowsy." He dabbed my arm with alcohol and plunged the needle so deep I thought it would come out the other side.

"Rest now. I'll be back in a few minutes to stitch you up. Then we'll put you in a room for the night."

After he left I pulled myself to a sitting position and remained like that until the sharp stab of pain accompanying my movement subsided.

Come on hypo, I said to myself, work, work, kill the pain.

I got down on my knees and pawed through the drawer under the table until I found surgical tape and gauze. I made a makeshift bandage for my side where blood continued to ooze. Then I dressed, having to take more time than I wanted to give it. Now fully clothed, including my overcoat, I peeked around the curtain.

Bev was in her chair, an open magazine on her lap. Her head was hanging over her chest. She was fast asleep. The night nurse was at her desk, her back to me. All quiet on the western front.

I had to work fast. I tiptoed around the corner of the hallway. I walked quickly and with each step felt better. The hypo was easing the pain.

I climbed the stairway to the second floor, room 215. The door was ajar. I slipped inside and closed it. A night-light over the bed provided soft illumination. On the bed a lumpy form lay on its side, its hands stuffed into its crotch.

I shook its shoulder. It stopped snoring and began grumbling gutturally.

"Wake up, Bruno," I said.

He turned over on his back, his eyes slow to open. He didn't want to be awakened.

"Come o-n-n-n," I persisted, shaking him again. "I haven't got all night."

He stared at me for several seconds, his dull, sleep-laden mind cutting through the cheese.

"What are you doing here?" he asked, reaching for the call button by his pillow.

I slapped the button out of reach. The hard rubber handgrip bounced to the floor and dangled from its cord.

"Once more with feeling, Bruno," I said. "Who did you see parking the coke under the step?"

He shook his head, panic beginning to tighten his nostrils. "I'm not talking. You heard what Dr. Nordstrom said."

"Nordstrom isn't here to protect you now."

"You'd...you'd better leave or I'll holler for help."

"Take one peep and I'll slug your teeth down your throat." I meant it and he knew it.

"Please...leave me alone. I don't have to tell you anything."

"It's over Bruno. Sheriff Amundson came to your house tonight to take the money. I was waiting for him. He shot at me, one bullet got me in the side. I tackled him and we both rolled down the stairs. I got bruised but he got it

295

worse: a heart attack. He's in intensive care right now. I don't think he'll live."

Bruno's eyes widened as he gathered in the information.

"The Sheriff admitted that Jensen killed your father."

"Jensen killed dad?"

I nodded. "And Amundson put him up to it."

Bruno began blubbering; tears washed the acne on his cheeks. He was a corrupted kid who wanted to recapture the innocent adolescence he put down as collateral for cocaine. But it was too late.

"I'm scared, Mr. Kouros." He shook like a puppy left in the rain. "I haven't got anybody now. Dad is dead and they told me today that Sarah died. Did Jensen do that, too?"

So Sarah is dead. Number four, and a fifth near death, the sum total of viciousness and greed.

"Yes," I said wearily, "Jensen did that, too."

"What will happen to me?"

"That depends. Did you kill Maynard?"

It was an almost imperceptible nod. "I didn't mean to hurt Mr. Sorenson."

The confirmation came as no surprise, yet I still felt emptied of spirit, as depleted as a reservoir in a drought.

"Did you find anything when you tore his shop apart?"

He shook his head, tears staining the bleached white pillow.

"I have to know this, Bruno. I have to know for Maynard's sake. Was he mixed up in this?"

"I don't think so."

"Then why did you go to his print shop?"

"I was looking for coke."

"But why *there*?"

He turned his head sideways, his cheek pressing the pillow, and stared at the wall beyond his bed. "Because

Rose Sorenson said I'd find it there."

I slouched on the edge of Bruno's bed. The air in my lungs grew stagnant.

"She was the one you saw hiding dope under the steps in your house?"

He nodded, his adolescent whiskers making faint scratching sounds on the pillow.

"You went to her house first?"

"I was sure she had some, or at least knew where I could get more. I was really desperate, torn up by dad's murder. I needed a fix bad. She told me she didn't have any in the house but there was some hidden in the shop."

"Did she tell you where?"

"In the case where they keep the typefaces. I went to the shop and told Mr. Sorenson what Rose told me. He just laughed and I got angry and started throwing type on the floor, looking for the stuff. When he saw what I was doing he went nuts and jumped me."

Rose, Rose...you knew you were sending a crazed kid to see Maynard. You knew how he would react to someone ripping up his job case, destroying the work he loved so much. Was your life so barren you wanted to see Maynard die? Wanted him out of the way?

You killed Maynard, Rose. Bruno was merely the executioner.

I sighed, a sorrowful sound that filled the still air of Bruno's room. When did Rose decide you were a liability, Maynard? When did she decide it was a good idea to have you out of the way? Maybe from the day she placed her soul on the trading block.

"Thanks, Bruno," I said. "You've been very helpful."

"What are you going to do now, Mr. Kouros?"

"Leave so you can get some sleep."

"I feel bad it came out this way. I didn't want it to happen." He began crying in earnest now, the agony inside him spilling out in heavy, choking sobs.

Little boy lost.

I stepped quietly across the linoleum floor, opened the door and slipped out, leaving him to struggle alone with his private misery.

33

I left by the Clinic's rear delivery door, circled to the front of the building where the black and white prowler still sat. I noticed for the first time that the vehicle's push bumper had protected the grille from damage when Bev rammed through the gate.

The keys were in the ignition. I got in and drove the empty, cold streets of sleeping Clear Lake. You can rest without fear now, aiming my thoughts at those sleeping behind the darkened bedroom windows, the plague that afflicted your town is all but snuffed out.

I parked in front of Rose's house and got out, the spread-out ranch shrouded in darkness. Halfway up the sidewalk I was surprised to see the front door open and Rose stick her head out. She evidently had seen the squad car pull up and someone get out, someone she expected...

"John!" she called and then a small shriek escaped her lips. She jumped back and slammed the door.

She was expecting the Sheriff. Instead she got me. I leaped the steps and tried the knob but it was too late. She had locked me out.

My unexpected appearance must have made her truly desperate, no telling what she will do now, something foolish, perhaps try to kill herself. I had to stop her. I ran around to the rear of the house, beating on windows, shouting her name. A light came on in a neighbor house across the yard. I was attracting attention I didn't need but I had to get to Rose. I came to the back door and pounded on it.

As I worked on the door, I heard a sudden shriek of tires being punished on the driveway. The angry echoes came up over the roof and fell on me like shock waves.

I ran to the front again, in time to see Rose shift the lurching Toronado into forward gear and head up the street, the front wheels spinning beyond their ability to grip pavement. She left a trail of black smoldering rubber burning through the impacted snow.

I jumped into Amundson's prowler and U-turned as quickly as I could. The car had power, probably souped-up for police pursuit—pound-foot of torque versus front-wheel drive. Was it a standoff? We'd soon see. I chased the Toronado's taillights, a pair on the bumper and a pair under the rear window, stylistically questionable yet distinctive. They were not hard to follow.

Rose was a bad driver. Dr. Nordstrom was not kidding. She had trouble controlling a car whose power was in the front wheels. She lurched around corners, the rear of the car sagging behind the front, and she plowed into snow banks, churning up bushels of crusted snow as she fought to free herself. This recklessness inevitably shrank her lead and within a few blocks I was able to catch up to her.

Under the glare of my headlights I saw the damaged trunk lid straining against the length of clothesline Rose had used to tie it down.

At one intersection I nearly slammed into her when she failed to negotiate a left turn and spun completely around. I hit the brake pedal and as I skidded helplessly past her I saw her face illuminated for an instant by the overhead light of a lamppost. Stark terror had contorted her bland features, turning her into someone I did not recognize.

The nose of the squad car came to rest on snow piled along the curb. In the meantime, Rose had straightened out and was heading down the street she had intended to turn into before her skid.

It took several precious seconds to pull the car free, and when I got back on the road, she'd disappeared. I slowed down at each intersection I passed, checking both to my right and left. After several blocks I saw evidence of her passage. A broken fire hydrant was spewing a geyser of water, which was freezing quickly on the street. I drove over it slowly, slipping and slithering. By the time I was through the mess, the car was drenched in cascading water that turned into glistening ice as it fell.

I groped for the windshield wiper control on the unfamiliar dashboard and pushed the fan to high defrost. The glaze on the windshield refracted the streetlights, distorting everything in front of me. Damn it, Rose, you did it this time!

I rolled down the window and stuck my head into the intensely cold wind. My eyes watered and my cheeks got so cold it felt as if my skin were burning. I could not do this forever without getting frostbite. Work, defrosters, work! Slowly the hot air melted two holes at the base of the glass and I crouched down to see through the one ahead of me, and it was ok to roll up the window. Through this hole, getting larger as the defroster and windshield wipers cooperated, I was able to pick up speed and as I passed an intersection I saw red lights flash in the distance. It was Rose, braking for another turn.

I slammed my brakes and skidded twenty feet before coming to a stop. I backed up and sped down the street in full pursuit. Ahead, Rose was going through the futile motions of escaping another snow bank. I was nearly upon her and, as I tried to block her, she freed the Toronado and the tightly turned wheels sent chunks of hardened snow spattering my grill. I heard a popping noise and glass shattering and one of my headlights went out. She is determined, I have to say that for her.

Coming out of her trap digging for traction, she fishtailed her way down a new street. This one was narrow, and now parked cars proved a threat. She caromed off one of them pushing it forward several feet. This impact sent her to the other side, where two more cars were parked. She creased the sides of each one, metal thumping on metal, strips of chrome ripping off and clattering along the pavement. Rose had quickly used up her Allstate deductible.

Then another even more surreal scene unfolded in front of me. The rope securing the trunk lid snapped from the strain and the lid swung open, revealing a pile of suitcases. So she and the Sheriff were planning to split with the money.

With the trunk lid bouncing up and down, a new hazard presented itself. Suitcases no longer secure began to jostle and bump against each other inside the trunk. Presently one fell out and I ran over it, ripping it to shreds, the prowler bouncing like a clown car. I damned near lost control as articles of clothing went flying helter-skelter behind me.

What a mess. Our trail littered with a broken hydrant, damaged cars, bent chrome and torn clothing. What next, I wondered? Could I stop Rose before anything more happened? Unfortunately I could not.

We were closing in on Highway 13 heading south, a two-lane road that leads to Interstate 90 and, presumably, freedom. The residential street we were on ended at 13 and I could see a red and white stop sign shining from the glare of Rose's headlights. Across the highway was a grove of large trees. She wasn't slowing. She was bearing down on the intersection at breakneck speed. She'd never be able to make the turn. I watched in horror as she steered the Toronado to the right, hugging the curb to widen her turning radius. But it was not enough, not at that speed, not in this weather. She then yanked her wheels to the left and the car screamed onto the high way on ripping rubber, hung on for an instant, then careened sideways into the trees.

There was a shattering bang as the middle of the car collapsed into a tree trunk. The front and back of the dying Toronado twisted around the tree as if they wanted to meet behind it.

Stillness fell on the gruesome scene. I parked on the shoulder of the highway, ahead of the Toronado, and turned on the emergency flashers.

A flashlight was clamped horizontally under the dash. I grabbed it and ran to the car. Hot anti-freeze was hissing out of the radiator and oil was spilling onto the frozen ground. The driver's door had sprung open. I looked in using the flashlight beam to guide me. Rose was lying across the bench seat, her legs under the crushed dashboard. She had hung on to the steering wheel and bent the rim into an oblong while the rest to her body hurtled toward the impact.

I stared at her upside down face, at her eyes, flashing with fear like a trapped fox.

"Rose," I implored, "why didn't you stop?"

"It doesn't matter," she said and coughed.

I checked her legs. One was bleeding badly. I pulled off my scarf and twisted it into a rope, then looped it above her knee and made a knot.

I used my pen to tighten my makeshift tourniquet to stem the flow of blood, which quickly congealed in the cold air.

"Hang in there, Rose, help will come."

"Where is John?" she asked, her voice scraped raw from pain.

"At the Clinic."

"Clinic? He's hurt?"

"He came to the farm for the money. We fought and he had a heart attack."

"You were waiting for him?"

"I didn't know who might show up. I didn't think it would be Sheriff Amundson."

"Who then?"

"You."

She sighed deeply struggling with her breath, which was coming from her mouth in long sheets of frosted air. "I told John to forget the money. I had a premonition something would go wrong."

"You both were planning to run away?"

"Everything was closing in." Almost as an afterthought she added: "Because of you."

I heard footsteps crunching on the snow behind me. I turned to see a man trotting across the road, an overcoat hastily thrown over his pajamas.

"I heard a crash," he said, approaching cautiously, the carnage of a badly hurt woman and a wrecked car an image almost too awful to take in.

"Who is it?"

"Rose Sorenson."

"Oh my god, Maynard's wife?"

"Get help. She's bleeding badly"

He turned and ran back to his house.

Rose looked at me pleadingly. "If you have any feelings left for me, Bill, just let me be. There is nothing to live for…"

She was right, but I could not be responsible for making her death wish come true. "I can't walk away and let you die."

"You'd be doing me a favor, saving me from prison. It was my fault Maynard died."

"I know," I said. "I talked to Bruno."

She managed a wry smile. "You were the thorn in our side, Bill. You made us panic, do foolish things. If you hadn't come to Clear Lake, John and I would have succeeded."

"But why you and John?"

"How do you suppose I kept my sanity all these years? I told you how drab my life was. John was the man I should have married. Instead, he and I were secret lovers."

"When did drugs come into it?"

"About a year ago. It was insane. But it was exciting. We had enough money to run away, leave this boring town, start a new life. It would have given us freedom."

I didn't say anything about the misery it gave others. "Was Maynard mixed up in this?"

"No. We led separate lives. If he guessed anything he said nothing."

"But the way you were living…"

"He liked it well enough to keep his mouth shut."

"You said he kept track of your income."

"I lied to throw you off. Maynard was only interested in that miserable newspaper. He only cared about words, not deeds."

Maynard, Maynard, I thought. You purposely saw no evil so you could lull yourself into thinking there was none. You were guilty, too, because you looked the other way.

Her chest heaved suddenly. I felt her pulse. It was racing. "Rose!"

She gasped for air. "My leg, it hurts. Very bad…"

I removed my gloves and gripped her cheeks with my hands to keep her face warm.

"Stay quiet."

She shook her head inside my hands. "I want to talk, I need to talk, get it out. I have to tell someone. I should hate you, Bill, but you did what was right. I deserve this. I'm going to hell."

"We don't know about those things."

"John told me everything would be fine, not to worry. But I knew…deep inside…I knew we'd never be able to get away with it. Too many people were involved. Someone, something, was liable to slip."

"What about Dr. Nordstrom?"

"He wasn't part of it."

"But you tried to run him down."

"I thought he knew about us."

"How could he have found out?"

"I was afraid that Maynard had told him. They were good friends, always had been. And after I learned it was the doctor's name Maynard had set in type and then hid in his pocket, I was convinced he did this to keep *me* from seeing it, not you.'"

My mind brought back that day in the print shop. Maynard may have been worried about the Doctor's safety. After all, Schultzman was murdered the night before, and Maynard may have begun to sense Rose's cohabitation with evil.

"What about the other names?" I asked. "Why did he include his own name if he wasn't involved?"

"He meant me, Bill. I was frightened because I thought he wanted to expose me. That's why I sent Bruno to see him. I knew how desperate the boy was, and with things closing in on me I even hoped he might kill Maynard. That's why I tried to run down Dr. Nordstrom. With my husband and the Doctor out of the way, I felt John and I would be safe."

"And the farm? Was Nordstrom's ownership a coincidence?"

"Yes. And when you told me yesterday morning that he owned it I was terror stricken. I was sure then that Dr. Nordstrom knew all about us."

I remembered how nervous Rose became when I told her that Nordstrom owned the farm.

"Why did you use it as a hiding place?"

"Alfred Schultzman helped us. It was a remote place. No one would suspect the farm."

"How did Schultzman get mixed up in this?"

"He's related to John."

"Amundson and Schultzman are related?" I asked in surprise.

"Through marriage. Alfred's wife and John were cousins. She was from Rhinelander. That's where John grew up."

"And the last person on Maynard's leaden list... Al Lewis. Is he part of it, too?"

Rose moved her head up and down within the frame of my hands. I thought so. Al Lewis. The clever little lawyer who married the richest girl in town. His greed was insatiable. He was rich, and he wanted more.

"How did your scheme work?"

"Once the cocaine came in we hid it on the farm. Then, when John had the opportunity, he would drive to the Twin Cities on police business and sell it to a contact there. Who would suspect a small town cop? Then John would bring back the money and we'd hide that on the farm until the payoffs were made. What was left we divvied up, and it was a lot."

"Did you go out to the farm?"

"Once. I didn't know it then, but Bruno saw me. It was a careless thing to do. Usually Alfred hid the money and the drugs but he was away that time, he'd gone to Rhinelander, and John didn't want the cocaine sitting around. He was worried about Bruno getting into it."

"How did you get the drugs in the first place?"

"Al brought it back from Mexico in that airplane he keeps in Mankato."

I had wondered where Al parked his twin-engine Beechcraft. It was too large a plane to land on Clear Lake's grass airport, hardly long enough for a Piper Cub.

Mankato was a convenient drive from Clear Lake.

"Two years ago," Rose continued, "Al brought some property in Mexico for a winter vacation place for his family. It wasn't long before he came up with the smuggling idea. Who would question a respected attorney? It was child's play to get cocaine in Mexico and hide it in his airplane. He had a dozen different places worked out, under the cabin floor, inside the wings. Even inside the tires. He was sharp, very sharp."

"It was Al's idea in the first place?"

She nodded between my hands. "But he wanted only the clean part. He didn't want to worry about distribution and sales. That's where John came in. He recruited Alfred and arranged to have him move from Rhinelander and lease the Nordstrom farm."

"He also recruited you."

Tears made little pools in the corners of her eyes. "I was his lover, Bill. I wanted what he wanted."

"What about Jensen?"

"Jensen became nosy and found out what was going on. Naturally, he wanted to be cut in."

"And he murdered Schultzman."

"You know that, too?"

"How did the crow bar end up in your car?"

Her tears spilled over and ran down my hands. "The three of us, John, Jensen and myself, went out to the farm that evening. Maynard was working late as he always did and I had the car. John wanted to talk to Alfred, talk some sense into him, as John put it, because Alfred was getting to be a problem. He was getting worried about Bruno and wanted out. I was in the car waiting. I didn't want to know what was going on.

"Did you see Jensen chasing Schultzman into the orchard?"

Her tears turned to sobs. "Oh, God..." she wailed. "Yes, and he attacked poor Clara in the house. Don't remind me, Bill, please don't remind me!"

I inhaled, trying to keep my voice from shaking. "And when it was all over, Jensen brought the bar with him, wrapped in a pair of Schultzman's overalls?"

"Yes," she replied faintly.

"He put it in the trunk, under the spare tire?"

She nodded this time.

"He was careless, Rose. He lost the wing nut that secured the wheel cover. It made me suspicious, and that's how I discovered the crow bar."

In the distance I heard an ambulance siren. There was an air of finality about its persistent, high-pitched whine. Rose sensed it, too.

"That's it, isn't it, Bill?" Rose said to me.

"Afraid, so, Rose."

"I feel better having told you. I never learned how to unburden myself. It's a saving grace."

I didn't say anything. How could I tell her she had no grace left to save?

The ambulance pulled up alongside the bent Toronado its siren slowly dying. The man who jumped out of the passenger side was wearing a shiny red jacket and white pants, and he was carrying a black case. It was Doctor Pierce.

"We meet again," I said to him.

"Well if it isn't the missing Mr. Kouros. I should have known I'd find you where the action is."

I didn't tell him I was the one who caused it. I slid out of the car to let him work on Rose.

"Hold your flashlight so I can see what I'm doing."

He injected a hypo into Rose's arm right through her jacket. Then he studied her legs.

"Did you tie this tourniquet?"

"I did."

"Not bad for an amateur."

Rose was getting groggy from the morphine. Pierce

must have given her a substantial dose.

"Thanks."

"Good thing you did. She would be gone by now."

The ambulance driver came over and looked in.

"What do you think?" he asked.

Pierce gave him a negative look but spoke positively. "We may have a bit of a problem getting you out of the car, Rose. You did a good job wedging yourself under the dash."

"I don't do anything by halves, Doctor," she replied groggily, nearly unconscious, but she had enough left over to open her eyes wide and cry out, "Bill, stay with me!"

"I will Rose."

They covered her with a blanket and worked together for several minutes to extract her. By that time a small knot of onlookers had gathered around the car, braving the cold to satisfy their morbid curiosity. Just as well, there is no Clear Lake Independent to read about it. Finally an unconscious Rose was placed on a stretcher and carried to the ambulance.

"Kouros," Dr. Pierce said, "ride along. You need some repair work, too."

"I'll bring the squad car back."

"Ok, but you better come straight in. I'm amazed you haven't collapsed by now. Maybe you will when you see my bill." Laughing, he got into the rear with Rose, shut the big door, and the ambulance sped off, the twin red roof lights turning like bloodied airplane beacons.

The sound of the wailing siren reminded me of the ambulance's forlorn cargo long after I could no longer see it.

I didn't need to hurry now. I drove slowly, relief washing my body and soul clean. I took a detour past Al Lewis's house, staring at the expensive colonial. There was no need to take Al on. Let the law deal with Mr.

Lewis, the law he practiced and, finally, violated. The sick bastard. The little, fat figure with the big, fat ego.

I reached the clinic several minutes after the ambulance. It was parked in the reserved spot. I parked in the adjacent visitors' lot: opened Amundson's trunk, put the strongbox away, locked the Charger and went inside.

The duty nurse looked up, her manner critical because of my unauthorized absence. I was probably the first patient she had who skipped out on her. But her RN pin was holding her together. A nurse rarely loses her cool or her starch.

"I'm back," I said.

"So I see."

"I have a reservation, I believe."

"Room three-seven-five. An orderly will take you up."

"Thanks. By the way, how is Rose Sorenson?"

"You'll have to ask the doctor."

As I waited for the orderly, Pierce came down the hall toward me.

"How's Rose?"

"On the operating table. She may lose a leg. Broken pelvis, smashed hip. She'll never walk again."

"She'll live?"

"Oh, yes. We never lose a patient."

"What about Amundson?"

"Well … almost never."

"He's dead?"

"His heart gave out. I don't know what he was doing tonight, but the shock of it was too much."

Perhaps, I thought grimly, it was not only the shock of what he was doing tonight, but what he was doing to his soul as well.

34

I woke up slowly, testing one muscle at a time. I was a well-wrapped package underneath my ridiculous hospital gown, open in the back for practical but not very modest reasons. It seemed as if half the hospital's supply of bandages was tied around my chest. Princess Ananka would jealously return to her mummy wrapper for a refitting if she could see me.

I reached for my watch on the table next to my bed. I felt a slight tug at the stitches in my side. More carefully now, I extended my fingers the last five inches and caught the strap. I held the dangling watch in front of my face and looked at it.

Twenty minutes past eleven. This information did not compute. Why did they let me sleep so late? I asked myself, strapping my watch on. I thought hospitals were as tough as the army for waking you up in the morning.

Someone must have left word to let me sleep. Probably Nordstrom.

I yawned and pressed the call button clamped to the open end of my pillow cover.

A candy striper opened my closed door. "Good morning, Mr. Kouros."

She was cute. "Don't tell me you're on the work study program, too."

She acted surprised. "How did you know?"

"Doesn't anyone get an education around here?"

She laughed. "Schools don't educate."

Wise kid. "Well, as long as you're not in school, how about some breakfast?"

"Breakfast? It's lunchtime."

"Maybe for you it is. For me it's bacon, eggs, toast and coffee–lots of coffee."

"Coffee, yes." She consulted a menu she unfolded from her uniform pocket. "Today you're having meat loaf, wax beans, mashed potatoes and gravy, roll and butter, and cherry cobbler."

"Oh, God."

"I'll be right back with your tray."

"Hand me the telephone before you go. I may smuggle in some food."

She gave me a naughty-naughty look, but placed the phone on the bed by my side.

"One more thing."

She waited by the door expectantly.

"Bring me the morning paper."

I asked the operator for the Clear Lake Hotel.

"Clear Lake Hotel … good morning."

"Hi, young lady. This is Kouros."

"Mr. Kouros! Where have you been?"

"For the last ten hours in the hospital."

"I've heard all kinds of terrible rumors. Are they true?"

A town without a newspaper becomes victimized by rumors. What will happen to Clear Lake if no one publishes the Independent "I don't know what you've heard, but you can be certain that the murdering is over."

"Are you all right?"

"Cracked rib. I'll be here just a couple of days. I wonder if you would check me out of my room and have my clothing sent here?"

"It's already been taken care of."

"Really?" Sounds as if Claire is still good-deeding. Why didn't she go home? "Is Miss Quinn around?"

"Miss Quinn? Oh, no, she left last night with Mr. Wright."

I'll be damned. "Then who checked me out?"

"Mrs. Holmquist."

"Mrs. *Who*?" I had visions of a matronly hospital auxiliary lady packing my skivvies in my bag. Then it came to me. "You mean *Beverly* Holmquist?"

"Yes."

"Well, that's different."

"Different?"

"It doesn't matter. Any messages?"

"Mrs. Holmquist took them. There was a note from Miss Quinn and about ten calls from Mr. Bailey."

"Only ten?"

"That was yesterday. There were five more this morning. I didn't know where you were, and Mrs. Holmquist didn't say. So all I could tell him was that you'd call back."

"You've been great," I said.

"So have you."

I hung up and looked out the window. Droplets of moisture clung to the sun-drenched pane. The frost was melting. Must be warming up outside. Maybe the cold snap was over and we were getting a January thaw. About time.

There was a tap on my door. "Bring it on," I said, bracing myself for lunch.

I was expecting the candy striper with the meat loaf, but I was happily surprised on two counts: it was Bev instead of the kid, and she was presenting me with a breakfast tray!

"Good morning, Mr. Kouros," she said as if she had been taking lessons in hospital etiquette. She set the tray on the rolling table and cranked me up to a sitting position.

There were eggs scrambled lightly, several strips of bacon, toast with squares of butter melting on the slices, a carafe of coffee, and the morning Citizen Ledger folded on top of the napkin.

"How did you arrange it?"

"My Dad runs this place, if you recall." She kissed me on my stubbled cheek. "I heard about your desire for breakfast, and called the kitchen. Simple as that."

I ate without ceremony. Everything was delicious. As I ate, I told Bev of the events following my hospital escape. She listened intently, patiently, but there was a look of chastisement in her eyes.

"You did this with a cracked rib and a bullet wound?"

"If I hadn't, Rose might have gotten away. Everyone is accounted for but Al Lewis. And he won't wriggle out of this. I'll call the federal narcotics agents in Minneapolis. They can arrest Al."

"Are you satisfied now?"

"Aren't you?"

"Relieved is a better word. Relieved for us…for Dad."

"Your Dad had nothing to do with it. I was mistaken."

"Thank God." She reached into her handbag and removed an envelope. Hotel stationery, and my name was printed on it in Claire's bold, distinctive hand.

I slit open the envelope with the handle of my spoon and read the note:

Darling Bill:

In a few minutes, I'll be gone. Don is warming up the car. It's late and I still haven't heard from you.

I hope everything will work out all right, and you will be alive to read this. I decided to leave because I thought it would be better not to confuse the issue with me hanging around. Besides, I'd rather not see you two together.

I'm not writing this in bitterness or jealousy. I'm

truly happy for you. It would just be too painful to see two people in love, like a hungry person pressing her nose against a restaurant window. Maybe someday I'll find out what it's like.

All Best,
              Claire

I handed the note to Bev.

"It's addressed to you."

"She'd want you to read it."

Bev read quietly. Her eyes misted over. "I hope she does," she said.

"Does...?"

"Find out what it's like."

I nodded. All best to you, Claire, I thought. All best.

I unrolled the newspaper. "I don't have a story this morning."

"You didn't have much time to do any writing."

I smiled. "It was a busy day." I opened the newspaper and found a full-page photo essay on the Clear Lake murders. Beneath each photograph Don had taken there was a short caption I had supplied. No big story, no late developments. Bailey must be seething.

I turned to the Arts Page, such as it was, looking for Bailey's review of Pop Goes the Easel. It was not a page, but rather a half-page, next to the TV/Radio log. Apparently, without me around, the Citizen Ledger was no longer as committed to art reviews as it was to crime reporting.

I folded the paper down to a more convenient size, expecting to be burning with jealous anger as I read Bailey's pre-emption of what should have been my review. But after the first paragraph I relaxed and tried to keep from laughing. It was terrible.

I handed the folded section to Bev. "Read this, too."

"What is it?"

"Bailey, my editor, wrote this. It's a review of the new exhibition at Walker Art Center. I was supposed to have covered it, but I got delayed by other matters."

I picked up the telephone again and called long distance. When Bailey answered—attacked is a more apt description—I said, "Guess who?"

He blew up. A day, a night of strangled frustration splattered the airwaves with the shrapnel of his exploding anger.

"Guess who? He thundered. "Guess *who*?"

"Bailey, you're repeating yourself."

"You rotten lousy sonovabitching bastard! Where the hell have you been?"

I began to tell him.

"Don't bother, I know! Wright came back last night and told me you were holed up in that goddamned farmhouse waiting to snooker someone. What kind of Dick Tracy shit is this?"

I began to tell him.

"Shut up! Wright also told me there was another murder...the deputy you loved so much...the Sheriff arrested you for it...and you broke jail to try to trap the lunatic who killed him."

"I did."

"Who was it?"

"Sheriff Amundson. He, Rose Sorenson, Al Lewis and Alfred Schultzman had a drug smuggling operation. Jensen was ordered by Amundson to kill Schultzman because the old man got cold feet over his son's addiction, and they were afraid he would talk. After I knocked Jensen out in the jail, Amundson showed up and finished him, his theory being that he could arrest me for the crime and have both me and Jensen effectively, if not altogether permanently, out of the way. Bruno killed Sorenson because he thought Maynard had cocaine hidden in the print shop. Rose is really responsible because she sent Bruno to see Maynard knowing the kid needed a fix. Rose also tried to run down Dr. Nordstrom because she was afraid he suspected what was going on. Last night I chased Rose when she tried to escape in her Toronado and she piled it into a tree. She's critically injured but she'll live. Amundson died of a heart attack following my fight with him and I ended up in the hospital from injuries he inflicted on me ... are you writing this down?"

Bailey continued screaming, punishing my ear. Had he heard what I was saying? I could see the newsroom shocked into silence by his unseemly conduct; probably the first time in the Citizen Ledger's history that everyone stopped working during the busiest part of the day.

"Bailey," I said, trying to still the cacophony, "settle down."

"Settle down?" he screamed, ignoring my advice.

"There's another matter," I said. "It's Don Wright's camera. Amundson tore a bullet through it. I hope the Citizen Ledger has insurance ..."

"After I get through with you, Kouros, *you'll* be needing insurance! Brewster is boiling and I nearly lost my job because of you. We got killed! Do you hear me? Killed! The biggest story of the year and we don't have anything but lousy pictures from Wright. We held the deadline forty-five minutes waiting for you to call, and then end up with a page spread of pictures because that's all we had!

"I waited for you all afternoon and half the night. Nothing. Not even a call back on my messages, and you're trying to tell me to settle down? Kouros, I'll have your ass served on the same platter John's head was served on..."

After what I told him, he knew I was too busy to call, but Bailey wouldn't listen until he vented his anger. Finally he shouted, "I'm turning you over to rewrite, and you're going to extemporize. Give him everything! It better be good and it better be fast!"

"Before you transfer me, there's something you should know…"

"Save your breath for rewrite."

"Bailey, I'm quitting."

"Hold on, I'll get you transferred…" Bailey's words trailed off, a vocal castration of fury. "You… what?"

"Quitting, as in terminating my employment." I watched Bev's reaction. A huge smile spread over her face.

"This has been a bad couple of days, Bill. Don't play games with me."

"No games, Bailey. The Clear Lake Independent is out of business unless someone takes over. I've always wanted to be a publisher, like Brewster, except that I'd be a big guy in a small town."

Bailey moaned. Maybe it was a death rattle, I couldn't be sure. "You haven't got the money. I never paid you enough to buy a newspaper."

"You never paid me enough to buy a new car, but I have an idea."

I could practically hear Bailey's brain beginning to focus. "What idea?"

"I'm going to serialize my articles and sell them to the New Yorker, just like Truman Capote did when he wrote *In Cold Blood*. "

Bailey began to sputter.

"And then I'll publish it as a book. Bet I could interest Random House."

"That won't even cover the down payment for a newspaper, not even a weekly," Bailey recovered long enough to blurt out.

"I'll line up investors. How about you, Howard, are you interested?"

It was the first time I called Bailey by his first name.

On Saturday, May 18, 1929, a farmer and his two children were bludgeoned to death in rural Waseca, Minnesota. The murders were never solved. Still considered an open case by the St. Paul Bureau of Criminal Apprehension, the crime served as the inspiration for this fictional story.

Made in the USA
Monee, IL
22 April 2024

57326509R00194